CREOLE
CONJURE

maudlinhouse.net
twitter.com/maudlinhouse

Creole Conjure
Copyright © 2021 by Christina Rosso

CREOLE CONJURE

a short story collection

by Christina Rosso

For New Orleans.
This is a love letter to you.

Table of Contents

Prologue

You are a tourist walking through the very heart of the Crescent City, Jackson Square Park. You have just waited in line for an hour for beignets from Cafe Du Monde. Even though you wiped your hands with the pile of napkins presented to you, your fingers are filmy, powdered sugar embedded in the grooves of your skin. You rub your fingers together as you walk. Hoping to get some shopping done and to escape the circus with its collection of freaks—psychics; men and women frozen in various positions, their bodies coated in metallic paint; or the stilted, hunched over creature with large diamond-shaped purple eyes that can only be described as the cat-spider of your nightmares—you exit the crowded area of the park.

As you head down Chartres, you find an old woman sitting in a forest green lawn chair, the type with cupholders on each armrest. Her seat is pulled up to a small faux wood table that folds at the knees. A white cloth yellowed at its edges covers the table's chipped and scratched surface. There is a cloudy crystal ball on top. The woman wears a purple and gold turban, large gold hoop earrings, and a floral caftan with rainbow-colored tassels down the bell sleeves, like any other psychic. White curly q's hang by her ears, showing her endurance.

She squints when she sees you—her eyes aren't quite what they used to be—and once she decides she can shake you down, she waves you over with wrinkled hands covered in sunspots. "Don't be shy, honey. I don't bite," the old woman says. "Hard." Then her face cracks open as she erupts in laughter, cackling in the cliché way we have come to expect of witches and wicked women. Her face is tanned to a dark roast and deeply lined. It appears soft to you, not rubbery. She motions to the chair across from her. This one is foldable and made of faux wood like the table.

Once you sit down, as you inevitably do, as the ones she picks always do, she introduces herself as Madame Bashiri. She then says, "I can tell you your fortune for just $5.00." She makes it sound like a deal. Tells you she's the real thing. "Not like those phonies in Jackson Square." She leans forward, tongues her dry, split upper lip, and says, "For an additional five, I can tell you when and how you will die." Madame Bashiri smiles wide then, revealing several gaps in her teeth. "I don't usually offer this, but you, you seem special. Like you can handle this kind of truth. Can you? Can you handle the truth?" she says. You nod emphatically, whether out of fear, politeness, or confusion, it doesn't matter. She continues, "For another five, I can tell you who or what you are going to be in your next life. Special deal. Just for you today, honey."

After she tells you you're going to fall in love in New Orleans, die in your bed when you're seventy-five next to the love of your life who you met during your trip to the Crescent City, and be a beignet in your next life, Madame Bashiri puts out her hand to collect her fee. "A beignet?" you say. She shrugs. "I said who or what. Fried dough's a what."

You accept her answer as every other tourist does and go to pay her with a twenty, asking for change. The crone grips the money in her palm, making a fist, and shakes her head, pressing her empty hand to her chest. "Sorry, honey. Don't got any change." She lowers her hand to the table, and clasps it with the other, the money hidden from view. You are confused, maybe even angry, but she doesn't give you the chance to think about it. She keeps talking, her speech quickening. You can't get a word in. "Thanks for coming. Tell your friends. I'm here every day at 9:35. I'm never late." The old woman says this with pride, the skin around her mouth and lips twisted in a sinister knot. She then tells you she has to go. It's 3:25. She never stays past. She doesn't offer an explanation.

But before Madame Bashiri allows you to leave her table, she slips you her card. Gold, decorative letters spell out her name on thin, white cardstock. Below, in small font, it says, *Mistress of Fortunes*. She smiles, and says, "I'm available for parties. Birthdays, weddings, wakes. No booking necessary; I know when you want me, where you want me."

She narrows her eyes, waiting for the hint of a grin or the lift of an eyebrow, before she says, "Just kidding. Please call the number on the back of the card. I'm not a mind reader." She winks at you before she tells you to get out of her freaking chair. It's time for her to pack up and go home. She grabs the chair and folds it as soon as you rise and waves you away with her hand.

Welcome to New Orleans, my dear tourist friend. You're in for a ride. Warning: keep your arms and legs inside the boat at all times. The gators have developed a taste for fingers and toes. Then there are the witches and the Honey Island Swamp Monster. Proceed with caution.

And, as always, laissez le bon temps rouler.

Alligator Blues

A young maiden, two months shy of her eighteenth birthday, sat on the steps of the St. Louis Cathedral. She had just graduated from high school the night before and was starting her summer at her favorite spot in the French Quarter. She glanced up from her book, *The Bloody Chamber*, to study the various street performers surrounding Jackson Square Park. Bourbon Cowboy, a homeless and beloved drunk, had stolen the microphone from a local jazz band and howled Elvis songs from the depths of his gut. The band was kind and humored the man by playing alongside his bellowing. To the right of the concert, black and white charcoal sketches hung from the midnight slats of the iron gate enclosing the park. When the artist saw Rosaline, he always shouted: "My love! My beauty!" The girl didn't know his name, yet she always smiled and said bonjour.

The perimeter of the park served as a market for a variety of artists. Rosaline dog-eared the page she was on and stood, slipping the book into her backpack. She wandered Jackson Square, pausing atpieces she liked. Bell-shaped breasts, fleshy hips, and dimpled buttocks lined a section of the gate. The oil paintings resembled the style and vibrancy of graffiti. Rosaline stepped closer, reading the artist's statement. Two years ago, the woman had been diagnosed with breast cancer and her artwork reflected living beyond it. One piece said *Fuck Cancer* in sprawling flamingo pink letters, and it made Rosaline shudder. Exactly, she thought. A man, or creature, in a black bodysuit with neon lights and a nightmarish cat-like face, crouched past her on stilts. The girl shivered, then laughed at herself. Growing up in New Orleans was like riding the carousel at the carnival; no matter how many times you went around and around, there was always a new attraction waiting for you.

Rosaline's phone rang. *Maman* flashed across the screen. "Bonjour Maman. What's up?"

"You in town?"

"Yeah. Do you need me to get anything on my way home?"

"No, thank you." She paused. "I just got a call."

Rosaline knew her mother struggled with sharing the brutality of work with her daughter.

"They found a body at Honey Island."

"Is Poppop okay?" Dr. Albert sighed. Rosaline pictured the vertical ridge between her mother's fair eyebrows deepening as it always did when she was upset. "Mom?" Rosaline pressed. "Is Poppop okay?"

"He's fine. I already spoke to him. He said Julia found the body and came over to use his phone. I don't know much more than that."

Rosaline scoffed. "When was the last time those two talked?" The only thing neighborly between Poppop and Julia Baudin was their proximity to one another.

"Probably five, maybe ten years. Look, Rose, I have to go. The autopsy might be late, okay? Order in pizza or chinese."

"Sure, Mom. I'll order extra spring rolls and leave them for when you get home."

"Thanks, honey. And one more thing."

"Yeah?"

"Hold off on visiting your grandfather, will you? I know you were planning to go today, but with all of this...I just want to make sure the swamp is safe."

Her throat tightened. "Yeah. Of course." A beat. "I love you, Mom."

"Love you too, babe." The call ended.

Rosaline continued walking the square. Sweat dripped down her arms at the thought of a dead body surfacing at Honey Island. She imagined her grandfather's neighbor, Julia Baudin, the type of old woman who had always looked to be a hundred years old, hobbling over to the shoreline to inspect the bloated, blue mass. As the child of a coroner in the city with the nation's highest homicide rate, Rosaline had what she thought to be a normal interest in morbidity and anatomy. Between the warm water and air temperatures, it was likely the body was a week or so old. And given the fact that only two people resided at Honey Island year round, the cause of death was likely an accident. Or homicide.

Murder was a part of life in the city, but in the swamp? It didn't seem possible that Rosaline's favorite place could be just as dangerous.

There was nothing more beautiful than the swamps outside of the Crescent City. Clear yet dark water—not quite brown or green in color—stretched on for miles as it kissed the equally clear but blue sky. If Rosaline ever married, she wanted to exchange vows on Poppop's boat; she pictured them floating down the river with the line of trees cloaking them from the rest of the world. Spanish moss blowing in the breeze would be all the decoration needed. Whenever Poppop took his granddaughter out on the boat, it was as if time stood still, even if just for a moment. The swamp was another world, totally different from topsy turvy New Orleans.

"Can I help you?" a middle-aged woman behind the window said.

Rosaline shook her head, realizing she had walked over to Cafe Du Monde. "Three beignets, please," she stammered.

The woman handed her the greasy bag as Rosaline gave her cash. Then muttered have a nice day after Rosaline thanked her.

The girl went back to Jackson Square Park and sat in the grass to eat the pillowy fried dough that was famous in her city. Rosaline stuffed one doughnut after the next into her mouth, barely chewing. Fried food always soothed her. Her mother had tried to break Rosaline of the habit many times, but as she liked to remind her mother, smoking cigarettes wasn't the healthiest of coping mechanisms either. Rosaline made a point to tack on, "And you're a doctor, Mom. You know better."

Powdered sugar coated her fingertips. Rosaline licked the sweet substance from her digits before throwing out the white paper bag. A body found in Honey Island Swamp. It sounded like the premise of a small town mystery. Rosaline wondered what her grandfather made of the whole thing. She would ask him when she visited next, which hopefully would be in the next day or two. Rosaline held out for the possibility her mother would come home that night having ruled the death an accident. Perhaps a boating accident of some kind. Rosaline nodded. Yes, a boating accident sounded more plausible.

If she were able to visit Poppop that week, she had to make one more stop before heading home. Rosaline dashed across Decatur Street, weaving through tourists, metallic-painted people posed like statues, vendors selling art, and fortune tellers, through the center of Jackson Square. St. Louis Cathedral loomed majestic and haunting ahead of her, its spires piercing the cloudless sky. She passed it, her sneakers padding on the cobblestone street known as Pirate's Alley. Rosaline's destination: Faulkner House, her favorite bookstore. She wasn't sure why Pirate's Alley was given such a name as it was a narrow, cobblestone street that housed nothing more than a few apartments and this bookstore. Nevertheless, the girl liked the name and the sense of adventure stepping onto that street gave her.

New Orleans had many wonderfully quaint bookshops, yet this one Rosaline thought to be a treasure trove. First editions and beautiful hardbacks of hundreds of authors lined the tiny shop's walls. She loved its variety, as well as its history. William Faulkner wrote his first novel *Soldier's Pay* at that house in 1925. Poppop had always been fond of the writer, saying Faulkner was *the* novelist of the South. When Rosaline was four, her grandfather started reading Faulkner's novels to her at bedtime. *As I Lay Dying*, *Absalom, Absalom!*, even *The Sound and the Fury*. She ran around the house yelling, "My mother is a fish!" for a year, driving her mother to hysterics more than once. Rosaline laughed at the memory, her mother taking Rosaline's little hands as the girl squirmed, balancing on one foot, then the other. "Rosaline, please," she begged the five-year-old.

Rosaline stopped in front of the bookstore's collection of William Faulkner. Running her finger along a spine with the writer's name always made the bookworm smile. Coming back to Faulkner's novels felt like a homecoming. Her finger paused on several books before finding a first edition hardback copy of *As I Lay Dying*. "My mother is a fish," she murmured, her face stretching into a grin. Poppop, she knew, would be pleased. And she hoped she could use it to bargain with him. Even after the diagnosis, her grandfather refused to limit his beer intake. She was already practicing in her head how to con her grandfather into limiting himself to one beer every other day. I'll find every first edition copy of Faulkner's work if I have to, she told herself.

Rosaline walked to Louise, the older woman who worked at Faulkner House.

"Just this today, Rose?"

"Yes, it's for my grandfather."

"You two have similar tastes in books?"

"I guess we do." She grinned, handing Louise payment.

The first edition tucked safely in her backpack, Rosaline stepped onto the street. Her body collided with a woman, nearly toppling on the uneven pavers.

"I'm so sorry." Rosaline regained her balance, her hand gripping the woman's arm. The woman was already erect, standing several inches above the girl, as thought nothing had happened. Embarrassed, Rosaline pulled her hand away.

"It's quite alright," the woman replied in a deep, buttery voice. Rosaline tracked the tip of the woman's pink tongue peeking from bone-white teeth.

The woman's dark eyes glittered, reminding Rosaline of coffee beans, a dark roast. She wore linen pants and a tank top, the fabrics pale against her copper skin. Even in casual attire, this woman's beauty was striking.

"I wasn't looking where I was going," the woman stated, no hint of embarrassment evident on her unlined face. She flipped her long ebony braids behind her shoulder.

"Neither was I." Rosaline's face burned.

"No harm, no foul."

The girl swallowed. A chill creeped down her spine. There was something familiar about this woman.

The woman smiled at her, and Rosaline felt her cheeks rise to match the woman.

"Who's the book for?"

"My grandfather." The woman asked how long he'd been sick. Rosaline's forehead wrinkled. "About a year."

"What kind of cancer?"

"Lung." Rosaline wasn't sure how this woman knew such things— maybe she was one of those ladies who claimed to be a psychic in Jackson Square, who in reality was just good at reading people and making guesses, offering to read your palms for $5.99—but she felt herself opening to this woman, spilling her secrets and deepest wishes as though they were old friends instead of strangers.

"I'm very sorry to hear that. You look after him?"

"My mom, too. When she isn't working."

"She's a coroner?"

"Yes," Rosaline said, her voice rising.

"And your grandfather lives on Honey Island?"

She frowned. "Yes. But how did you—?"

"Call it intuition. My apologies, but I have to get going—" The woman waited for Rosaline to fill in her name.

"Rosaline."

"Beautiful name for a beautiful girl," she replied.

Rosaline's cheeks pinkened. She always blushed when someone complimented her. "Thank you. I don't think I caught your name." She hoped to deflect attention away from her.

"Zelima Delacroix."

She offered her hand. "It's nice to meet you."

Zelima took it, giving a firm shake. "You as well. As I said, I must be going, but it was lovely meeting you, Rosaline. Come by my shop sometime. Lavender's. Off Bourbon."

"I've heard of it. Isn't it on St. Anne's?"

"Yes."

"Awesome. I'll stop by sometime."

"Lovely. You take care of yourself and your grandfather, too. I'll keep him in my prayers."

"That's very kind of you. Thank you."

"One last thing," Zelima said. She raised her pointer finger as though she were about to teach a lesson.

The girl raised her eyebrow in response.

"Be wary of swamp creatures when you visit Poppop. I've heard they've been acting strange lately. The swamp can be a dangerous place for a young girl like you."

"What do you mean by that?" she said, but Zelima just nodded and turned to walk away, her braids bouncing as she went down Pirate's Alley toward Jackson Square.

Rosaline stood there in a daze, unsure of what had just happened. Zelima seemed to know things—like that Poppop was Rosaline's nickname for her grandfather and that he had cancer. The woman's warning about the swamp stuck rattled Rosaline. Did she know about the body found in the swamp? And if so, how? The police hadn't released the information yet, waiting for her mother to determine the cause of death. So, who was Zelima Delacroix and what did she want?

Rosaline rode her bike onto the grass outside of her house. It was only about a ten-minute bike ride from the French Quarter in the Bywater District; Rosaline had always been glad they didn't live downtown. It was peaceful and open in their neighborhood, just like at Honey Island Swamp. She parked it against the wood side. The house was painted forest green with black shutters and a black door. A narrow porch ran along the front of the house. Rosaline unlocked the door and headed inside, making sure to slide the deadbolt into place.

The girl spent the next few hours slumped on the couch with her cat, Jinxy, one police procedural melting into the next until night had swallowed the day. As promised, when Rosaline ordered chinese, she got extra spring rolls for her mom. No amount of food or T.V., however, could distract her from the fact that a body was found in the swamp.

When her mother came in a little after 10 PM, Rosaline sat up straight. "Hi, Maman."

"Hi, Rose." Her mother's hair was slicked back in a wet ponytail; she must have showered after the autopsy. She wore a simple shift dress and black flats.

Rosaline waited until her mother had changed into her pajamas and filled a plate with spring rolls and lo mein. "Was it murder?"

"My day was fine, thanks for asking." Her mom took a bite of spring roll and eyed Rosaline while she chewed. She sucked on her teeth. "Rosaline Grace, I spent the day dissecting a man who looked more monster than human."

Rosaline kneaded her lips with her teeth before giving her mother a wry smile.

Her mother twisted her neck to one side and then the other. "I know you're just going to google it in the morning if I don't tell you. Parts of a man's body were found at Honey Island this morning."

Her eyebrows lifted. "Parts?"

"We've identified the remains as belonging to Caleb Knight, an art curator at a local gallery. Based on the condition of the remains, I've ruled the death a homicide." She held up her hand to keep her daughter from interjecting. "I believe he was murdered before being brought to the swamp. But I want you to hold off seeing your grandfather until at least next week."

Rosaline protested. "Please, Rose," her mother said. She noticed the deep half moons under her mother's eyes. "I have to meet with his wife in the morning and then the police chief. You can see your grandfather next week."

She offered a noncommittal groan.

"Promise me you'll stay away from the swamp. I mean it. Promise me."

Rosaline raised her hand as though she were about to recite a pledge. "Okay, Mom. I promise."

"Thank you." She gestured to the T.V. "Do you mind if we watch something else? It's a little too close to home after the day I've had."

"Of course," Rosaline said and changed the channel to a renovation show. Mother and daughter sat and watched T.V. until their heads drifted together, the soft sound of their breathing mingling with the chipper sound of the television show host.

Rosaline spent the morning clicking from one tab to the next, looking for news about the murder of Caleb Knight while reading about Lavender's, the shop owned by the mysterious woman she'd met the day before. An article popped up about Zelima Delacroix and Priestess Miriam Chamani of the Voodoo Spiritual Temple partnering after Katrina. In New Orleans, the word *Voodoo* was tossed around like creole seasoning. The girl knew the salacious, bloody depiction of Voodoo as black magic was just part of the serpentine lore that floated from one tourist's mouth to the next. To the locals, Voodoo was a religion, not witchcraft.

Rosaline had been raised in a no nonsense kind of family, a group devout in its disbelief of such unexplainable things. Sometimes she thought belonging to such a family meant being an outsider in the vibrant, superstitious city they called home. Sometimes the girl wished magic would find her.

Earlier that morning, Rosaline's mom had asked her to grab some things from the market before starting looking for a summer job. Really, Dr. Albert wanted to keep her daughter busy so she wouldn't be tempted to drive out to the swamp to see Poppop. Rosaline made a plan for the day: hit the French Market first, where the best produce was. Call Poppop. Check out Lavender's. Look for a job.

She scrolled through Lavender's website, a seemingly endless supply of magical materials available. Unlucky in love? Zelima had a potion that would make you irresistible. A cheating spouse? There was a potion for that, too. A sick loved one? There was a powder for that. Crystals, amulets, and charms were also featured on the website. Even if this kind of stuff wasn't in her DNA, as her mother had always insisted, Rosaline was intrigued by the woman she'd run into outside of Faulkner House Books and wanted to speak with her again. Maybe it could even lead to a job, which would check off two things from her list.

Cantaloupe. Check. Lettuce. Check. Red peppers. Check. White onion. Check. Cucumber. Check. Rosaline went through the grocery list in her head. Satisfied with her produce, she wandered through the rest of the French Market, eyeing vintage-looking rings, handmade clothing, kitschy trinkets, and New Orleans merchandise. She popped in headphones to call her grandfather. Ring. Ring. Ring. She nodded her head along to the shrill sound. Ring. Ring. Ring. Her forehead wrinkled as the ringing droned on until the call disconnected. Ed Albert only installed his landline at the insistence of his daughter and granddaughter. Setting up a message for the answering machine was too much for him. "What's to keep someone from recording my voice and using it to steal my identity?" he had said to them.

Rosaline figured her grandfather was fishing or making lunch. She would try him again in a bit. Having secured her bag of produce on her shoulder, Rosaline headed toward Magazine Street, the local's version of Bourbon Street. She slipped from one side of the street to the other, seeking shelter under the awnings from the boiling sun. The sounds of brass and percussion leaked from open windows and doorways into the street. She often thought about jazz as being the perfect storm. Some brass instruments were light and striking like lightning, while others were thunderous. And drums always made her think of the pitter patter of rain hitting pavement.

She called Poppop again. The line rang until it went dead. Fear slithered up her spine, wrapped itself around her throat. What if the person who had killed Caleb Knight had Poppop? What if Poppop's body was being offered to the Honey Island alligators as a buffet? Alligators use their jaws to crush the bones of animals before swallowing them whole. Rosaline had seen it once, when an alligator caught a deer. Its massive jaw slammed down on the animal; loud snaps echoing before it gulped the deer into oblivion. Rosaline remembered wanting to cover her eyes with her hands, to duck down into the safety of her grandfather's boat, but she knew it would disappoint Poppop. It was the first Father's Day without her dad, since he had started a second family with his new wife, Michelle, and Rosaline worried if she didn't make her grandfather proud, he would leave too. So, she crossed her arms to hide her trembling fists and watched the survival of the fittest. Poppop glanced at her sideways and nodded. She had made him proud.

Yes, Rosaline had promised her mother she wouldn't go to the swamp. And, yes, there was a high probability that her grandfather had ripped the phone from the wall jack after Julia had used his phone to call the police; he didn't trust the police or his neighbor. Poppop was probably napping on the couch. Yet Rosaline couldn't shake the feeling writhing around in her veins that her grandfather was in trouble. She turned on her heels and ran back the way she had come.

The drive to her grandfather's cabin took about forty minutes. She parked on the gravel driveway, and on foot, jogged the long and windy dirt path to Poppop's house, finding it empty.

"Poppop?" she said, announcing her presence.

No answer. Rosaline walked through the small cabin. The front door opened onto two of the four rooms of the house—the kitchen and the den. The front door of the cabin to the back was all of ten steps. Rosaline walked past Poppop's hunting souvenirs along the wall—deer, wild hogs, and alligator heads—as she went out the back door.

"Poppop, where are you?"

Again, no response.

Rosaline made her way to the swamp. He wasn't there either. "Poppop," she yelled.

The swamp was pristine in its silence. Heat crawled from the water as the temperature continued to climb in the afternoon sun; it looked almost like tiny spirits floating from the surface of the swamp. Poppop's boat bobbed in the reeds, tied to the small wooden dock by braided rope that resembled golden locks of hair.

Rosaline ran back into the house to see if there were any hints to where he may have gone. Or what might have happened to him. Her grandfather's rusted pickup was out front, its weathered key chain was on the counter. His hunting rifles were in the cabinet in the den; even his walking stick was against the kitchen counter. His only modes of transportation were the truck, the boat, and his own two feet; it didn't matter if he were going to the dock or on a hike, Poppop never left the house without his trusty walking stick.

Rosaline scoured her mind's catalogue of police procedurals, ticking through the checklist her favorite primetime partners, Benson and Stabler, would go through. Nothing was out of place. There was no ransom note. No blood. She closed her eyes and breathed deeply, slowing her inhalations and exhalations. No blood was very good.

It was in the doorway when Rosaline opened her eyes. From its size, she concluded the reptilian creature was male. He looked to be about ten feet long, nearly full grown, and was navy in color instead of the usual ebony or dark gray. The alligator's slitted yellow eyes tracked her. Rosaline screamed and grabbed her grandfather's walking stick, as it was the closest weapon. She held it high.

"Don't come any closer," she shouted. "I mean it."

Rosaline immediately regretted the words, how they made her sound like a damsel in a bad thriller. Everytime she went to open her mouth she closed it, her tongue pulsing with other overused adages. She puffed up her chest and held the stick higher, hoping the beast didn't notice her hand shaking or the sweat building at her temples and under her arms.

The alligator's massive jaw cranked open like the mouth of a nut-cracker, revealing rows of jagged, pointed teeth speckled in black. They reminded Rosaline of the dinosaur eggs in *Jurassic Park*. She expected him to advance, ready to devour her. He spoke instead.

"What do you think that stick is going to do? Honestly, you'd be better off running and grabbing one of Poppop's hunting rifles." His voice was throaty and his tone mocking, especially when he said her grandfather's name. Rosaline felt like a schoolgirl being picked on during recess. "Gator got your tongue?" he taunted.

Rosaline was sure she was imagining this, but it looked like the alligator was grinning. He reminded her of one of the colorful paintings exhibited in front of Jackson Square Park, more caricature than living reptile. Your anxiety is getting to you, she told herself. It's all in your head.

"It was a shock to me too."

"What?" Rosaline felt the weight of the question and its answer raw in the seat of her throat, dry and hot as a desert.

"Seeing myself like this. Covered in scales, having claws, webbed feet. The diet isn't so bad though. I eat most of the same things I did before." The beast paused before saying, "Just fresher."

Again, Rosaline was sure she was seeing things; had the alligator just winked at her? "Before?" was all she could manage to say.

"Before the curse."

Now she knew this was all in her head. She sighed. "Look, Mr. Alligator, if you aren't going to make me your next meal, I'm going to go. I need to find—"

"Your beloved Poppop."

"How do you know that?" she stammered.

"Let's just say his presence was required by a certain reptile."

"*You* took him? Where is he?" Her grip slid a little from perspiration as she squeezed the walking stick. The girl had forgotten she was still holding it over her head.

"He's in an old cabin on the other side of the swamp. I can take you to him." A beat. "On one condition."

"What do you want?" This past school year Rosaline had learned about psychotic breaks in psychology class and was starting to wonder if she were experiencing one. After all, she was negotiating with a talking blue alligator.

"You have to stay with me until the curse is broken."

Rosaline lowered the walking stick. She crossed her arms. "You're serious about this curse, huh? Next you're going to tell me that magic is real and that a kiss will break the spell."

The alligator's tail thumped on the thin, brittle grass. "Something like that."

Rosaline considered her options. She could go with the alligator's earlier suggestion: run, grab one of her grandfather's guns, and try to shoot the beast before it locked onto her with its razor-sharp teeth. She could forget the gun and run to her car, drive home, and get the police. Or she could take this talking alligator at his word. The whole thing seemed antiquated to Rosaline, belonging in another realm, one of knights and dragons and maidens locked in towers. It reminded her of a bedtime story her father had told before he left. Her mind felt dense, full of fog and uncertainty, however, Rosaline knew her grandfather wasn't at the cabin and she needed to find him. Zelima's words came back to her. *Be wary of swamp creatures when you visit Poppop. I've heard they've been acting strange lately.* "Fine. We have a deal," she said. "One thing before we go. What's your name?"

"Charlie."

She nodded, not knowing what to say. The girl didn't know what kind of journey she was embarking on, but Poppop was worth the risk. "I have a few conditions of my own." Not giving Charlie the chance to respond, she continued, "We're taking the boat and I'm bringing one of Poppop's rifles, as well as this walking stick."

"Alright. Let's get a move on it."

"I'll be right out."

Rosaline watched as her grandfather's kidnapper tried and failed to move backward out of the doorway. Poppop had explained to her once that alligators move on land by crawling on their bellies. They aren't able to crawl backward, but they can move backward if they do what is called a *high walk*, where they lift their massive bodies and tails off the ground. Whatever Charlie was, he definitely hadn't been an alligator for very long.

She thought about offering to help him. Instead Rosaline took advantage of Charlie being distracted. She propped the walking stick into the crook of her arm and grabbed her phone to type a quick message to her mother. "Going to find Poppop. Will explain later. Love you."

She slipped the phone into the back pocket of her shorts. Then she went into the den to get a hunting rifle.

The girl chose a .22-250 Remington Weatherly Vanguard and loaded it, stuffing extra ammunition into her shorts. The gun in one hand and the stick in the other, Rosaline slid the king ring for the boat onto her finger. Then she followed Charlie, who had finally managed to rotate himself, to the boat.

That boat was the nicest thing Poppop owned. It was a sixteen-foot aluminum fishing boat, painted a deep cherry red. He had bought it a few years ago and doted on it like a new parent does a newborn. He washed it every week, made sure it was covered during every storm, and never drove it over 13.03 knots even though it could clear twenty-six. He kept the three storage spaces—one in the bow and one on each side of the hull—completely empty. The beverages allowed onboard were beer and water. Food was banned as, according to Poppop, food left crumbs and attracted critters. Rosaline had laughed at this. "Isn't the point of fishing or hunting to attract critters?" she asked.

His face set like stone, her grandfather replied, "A true forager only needs his mind, his eyes, and his weapon to catch his prey."

"If you say so, Poppop," she said, to which he replied, "Damn straight I do."

Rosaline smiled at memories like these; she had been on Poppop's boat countless times, it was their thing. This, however, was the first time she was out on it without him. It was unnerving to be there; she imagined this is what it felt like to play hooky from school and steal your parent's car to go hang out with friends. Rosaline had never done anything like that—she liked school and following the rules—nor had she ever been offered to join such shenanigans. Being a coroner's daughter provided more ridicule than friends. Kids at school referred to her as Wednesday Addams. On Halloween one year, a classmate asked where her costume was, sniggering that he was surprised she didn't dress in all black. Rosaline replied, "This is my costume. I'm a homicidal maniac. They look just like everybody else," repeating a line from the 1991 *The Addams Family*. Color bled from the boy's face. She delighted in his fear.

Her classmates' bullying didn't bother Rosaline; she had always been more interested in hanging out with her mom and Poppop or escaping into the pages of a novel than going to sports games or parties. She was a self-described loner and she wore that label proudly. Now Rosaline wondered if another label fit her better. Magic had always been something that existed in books or in the city's lore. Yet here she was on her grandfather's boat with a talking blue alligator, who was busy sunning himself on the bow as she stood at the console, driving. Maybe she wasn't just a loner who followed the rules. Maybe there were parts of herself to be discovered.

Charlie dictated directions. He did so every few minutes. In between, the only sound was the boat gliding along the water with a low hum, the dull disturbance echoing against the thick trees that wore Spanish moss like tapestries. Rosaline usually liked the silence on the water; as you gazed at the world reflected in its murky surface, it seemed as though you had slipped into an entirely new, serene world. Sometimes she imagined this was what Heaven was like. Today, however, the quiet creeped along her skin, causing goose pimples to run up and down her limbs. The swamp was the one place her mind relaxed, but today it buzzed. She cleared her throat. "So, tell me about this curse."

It was quite simple, he said. Simply stupid. Unfair. Charlie had stolen something; theft was his bread and butter. Maybe, just maybe, he hadn't thought it through though. You don't steal from the likes of her, oh no. But he had. He had been peddling the tourists of New Orleans since he'd left Baton Rouge, his hometown, at age sixteen. For the past three years, he sold artwork, t-shirts, rosaries, and even tickets to fake tours. That ruse lasted nearly a year. Charlie set up an a-frame in Washington Artillery Park that overlooked Jackson Square, providing a picturesque view of the statue of President Andrew Jackson set between two bouquets of palm trees with St. Louis Cathedral right behind, looming haunting and majestic. The sign read: "Authentic Ghost Tour. Best in the Quarter! Special Rate Today Only: 2 Tickets for $22." Most tours around the city ranged from $20-30 per person, so this seemed like a great deal.

It would have been if there were any such tour. Many guided tours collected payment hours or even days beforehand. Charlie stood and collected a thick wad of Jeffersons, Lincolns, and Washingtons, standing beside the cannon monument in the park. In exchange, the patrons received a lime green wristband stamped with "Authentic Ghost Tours: Prepare to Scream!" The con artist had thought of everything. The patrons were told to return to that same spot fifteen minutes before their chosen tour time. He said, "I look forward to sharing the authentic tales of horror and hauntings with you." The customers chuckled and thanked him, saying how excited they were. Of course, there was no tour and Charlie never showed, pilfering thousands of dollars from unsuspecting visitors.

Eventually, the cops caught on and arrested him. Charlie spent a fair share of his saved cash on bail. Broke and out of a scheme, he needed money and fast. So, he moved his charade to Bourbon Street, browsing shops and tourists for anything he could pickpocket. This street was like the Las Vegas Strip, or how he imagined it; overflowing with people, who were usually inebriated, at all hours. It was the perfect spot for thievery, and there was a high probability he wouldn't get caught. Charlie wandered into Lavender's after snatching several gold NOLA necklaces, four crawfish-shaped bottle openers, a handful of NOLA magnets, and two Bourbon Street shot glasses.

"Lavender's," Rosaline interrupted. Was Charlie talking about Zelima's shop?

"That's what I said." Charlie continued telling his story.

A circular, pale purple sign hung outside of the three-story building just below the balcony of the second floor. White cursive letters spelled out *Lavender's*. The brick building was painted light gray and the wooden storm doors were a deep shade of eggplant. These were drawn open like curtains, inviting customers to enter the store through the single glass door with a chalkboard hanging from it. The word *open* was etched in the same cursive as the store's sign. A piece of white chalk dangled from the board by a string.

The con artist knew Lavender's was like many other voodoo shops in town—carrying incense and candles, good luck charms, and potions. The store was one long, narrow room filled with promises of magic.

Charlie's fingers slid over items like rabbit's feet and incantations as he went through the shop. A woman approached him, braids dancing like dozens of tiny snakes.

"How can I help you?" The snakes idled by her sides.

Charlie couldn't guess the woman's age; she had strong body language, shoulders and breasts back, chin held high, yet her skin was unlined, without blemishes. She was exquisite, as was the necklace resting just above her breasts.

Made from clay, the circular necklace was about two feet tall and wide with an intricate symbol carved into its face. It dangled from leather cording around the woman's neck. At its center was a small circle. Horizontal lines extended from the middle and curved into open hearts. Triangles were etched above and below the lines. Small x's and + signs floated around the symbol.

Fixated on the amulet, Charlie mumbled, "I was looking at some of these potions you have. I'm afraid I don't know much about this stuff." He smiled in an attempt to come off as sweet.

"What are you looking for? A love potion?" The woman paused, looking him over. "Or maybe your interests are darker." Her eyebrows, painted into thick, straight lines, lifted. "A negative energy surrounds you."

Charlie tongued his incisors. He wanted the amulet around her neck—he had seen enough African Creole jewelry from years of conning to know this was authentic, possibly even one of a kind, and therefore, expensive—and he would need to use all his tricks to get it. This woman wasn't the type to let her guard down easily, especially around a white boy. Charlie's tongue was his greatest tool for deception and illusion; it spun tales without hesitation. He looked around the store; it was mostly empty. Two young women, probably on spring break, pointed and giggled at every item they came across. Go time, he told himself, before letting his tongue loose. "You see, ma'am, I have a bit of a problem. It's my old man. He has a temper and drinks too much whiskey. And he, well he…" Charlie let the words trail off for dramatic effect. "He gets rough with my mom."

"He hits her."

He swallowed, flexing his Adam's apple. "He does, ma'am."

"And he's threatened to hit you."

It wasn't phrased as a question. Charlie stopped himself from grinning. This was going to be a breeze. He pushed his lips down into an exaggerated pout and nodded. "I was hoping to find something to give him, to slip into his drink. Maybe make him more gentle."

"Or stop him for good," she replied, her expression unchanged. "I have just the thing for you. I'll have to mix it up now though, there are a few special ingredients I want to add for your specific situation, if you have a few minutes."

Charlie thanked the shopkeeper and said he would wait while she went into the back to gather her secret supplies and mix the potion. The conman had stolen his fair share of jewelry, but never from a woman like her. Charlie had learned over the years how to spot a fellow phony—it was to protect himself and whatever scam he was working—and he could tell this lady was the real deal. "Let her vengeance be delayed," he prayed under his breath.

His hands started shaking. Weird, he thought; he hadn't felt like this since he'd left home. To make a lie appear as a truth, one should ground the story in sincerity, which is exactly what he had done. His father was a drunk who beat on his mom and threatened to go after him too. Charlie took matters into his literal hands, pummeling his father into a hospital bed, the old man in need of reconstruction after his nose split. That's why Charlie had left Baton Rouge. And this truth made the woman believe his tale.

But that alone wouldn't get Charlie the necklace. He sauntered over to the two girls and said in a voice just above a whisper, "If you want the real stuff, go over to Marie Laveau's House of Voodoo."

One of the girls, whose brown hair stopped at her waist, brushing her spray tanned abs, said, "What kind of stuff?"

Charlie glanced around the shop before answering. "I'm sure you know a rabbit's foot"—he slipped one into his hand and rubbed the light brown fur—"doesn't do anything. Neither do these charms. But voodoo dolls—"

"Oh, c'mon," the other girl said. She had blond hair, obviously artificial, pulled into a nest on the top of her head, her dark brown roots yanked by the tight updo. Like her friend, she sported a spray tan that made her look like a carrot. "That's not real. None of this stuff is."

He leaned in toward them. "Of course not all of it is. But voodoo dolls are very real. And everyone knows Marie Laveau was the Queen of Voodoo."

The girls looked at each other and shrugged. "Why not?" the brunette said.

"Let's go," said the blond.

Charlie grinned.

Once they had left, he wiped off the word *open* with his palm, and scribbled *closed* with the piece of chalk. He didn't want anyone getting in his way of escaping.

It happened quickly. The shopkeeper returned a minute later with a small glass vial filled with a sapphire blue liquid. She smiled and held the bottle out for Charlie to take. He closed his hands around it and then let go, the vial propelling to the ground with a shatter, the vibrant liquid exploding on the floor. "Shit. I'm sorry." He dropped to a squat as if he were going to clean it up.

She pulled the skirt of her dress up and lowered to her knees. "It's okay," she said. "I've got it."

As she leaned forward to pick up slivers of glass, the necklace swung side to side. On the third stroke, he grabbed the clay circle and yanked, freeing the leather from the shopkeeper's neck. Charlie bounced upright, turned, and ran out of Lavender's, leaving the glass door wide open and the woman seething.

"You stole from Zelima."

Seated, Rosaline leaned against the wheel, her palm holding up her cheek. The walking stick was wedged into the corner. The story was coming together, a mosaic of different colored and shaped tiles. Again, she thought of the shop owner's words. *The swamp can be a dangerous place for a young girl like you.* Zelima had been warning Rosaline about Charlie.

The girl sat up straight, one hand on the wheel, the other grasping the rifle.

"I wish I hadn't," Charlie said, his voice soft. He didn't seem to notice the change in Rosaline's posture. She was surprised by the regret in his voice. It seemed genuine. "I didn't know she was the real deal."

Rosaline swallowed, recalling how easily that alligator had crushed the bones of a deer. How little effort it would have taken Charlie to do the same to Poppop. "What do you mean?" she asked, keeping her voice emotionless.

"A witch."

If Charlie had told Rosaline this story a couple of days ago, she would have said he was crazy. But now. She had no reasonable explanation for any of this. And she still didn't know where Poppop was or if he was okay. Play along, she told herself. Keep him talking. "Zelima turned you into this?"

His large snout nodded.

"Why? How?"

Charlie gave Rosaline directions before answering her question. "I knew the amulet was authentic; what I didn't know was what it represented."

"Which was?"

"Youth. Whoever wears it is protected from aging."

Lines flexed in between Rosaline's eyebrows. "How long had Zelima been wearing it?"

"I'm not sure, but when she caught up to me she was all wrinkled; it looked like she'd soaked in a tub too long. And her skin had turned ashy." Rosaline asked what Zelima had said to Charlie. "She asked me if my father really beat my mom. When I said yeah, she told me that's what makes a lie believable, grounding it in truth. I told her I knew that. That lying wasn't new to me. Then she warned me that what was about to happen was going to hurt." His body trembled, his version of a shrug. "And it did."

"That's when she turned you?"

"She asked for the amulet back first. Said she'd be gentle with me if I did." His sentences strung together, breathless. "I had been carrying the necklace in my pocket for a week, never going anywhere without it. Hadn't found the right buyer for it yet, you know? I handed it to her and she snapped it in place around her neck. Within seconds, her wrinkles cleared up, her skin became smooth. She grinned at me like a freaking villain in a Disney movie."

Rosaline smacked her lips together before answering, "You gave it back to her and she still cursed you." I would have done the same, she thought.

"She likes to teach lessons to those who cross her. That's what she said. So they don't do it again."

Rosaline set down the rifle. She rubbed her temple, trying to help her brain absorb all of this. "Did you really mean it?"

"What?"

"That you wish you hadn't stolen from Zelima."

Charlie's reptilian form shrugged. "I did what I had to do."

Heat tingled across Rosaline's chest. "And look at where it got you." She couldn't believe this guy. A thief with a wild story about a witch and a curse. But what she couldn't figure out was why he would bother to lie about any of it. What angle could he be playing? And what did it have to do with her? With Poppop?

She sighed. The wheel was slick, her palm oiled. "What did it feel like? Turning into this?" Rosaline nodded toward him.

Charlie was silent for a few beats, the serenity of the swamp sinking in. "The first place I felt it was my nails; it was like someone was stretching them from the beds. Then a tail started to grow where it shouldn't. Next I had a horrible toothache. But instead of just one tooth hurting it was all of them. I thought I was going to pass out from the pain. Soon my limbs shrank and then thickened, and my skin changed into scales; it was like really bad sunburn and being stung by hundreds of bees all at once, everything hurt and was itchy.

"As I was transforming, the witch said, 'This will teach you to not steal from elders, especially me. You will be confined to this state, a young man trapped inside the body of an alligator, indefinitely. However, since you have returned my property, I have granted you a kindness. The curse can be broken.' I know, you're probably wondering if I'm making that up. I'm not. Promise. That's exactly what she said word for word. A guy remembers a thing like that. Anyway, I'm in agony, right, and I beg her to tell me how. She says if I can find a lady and make her fall in love with me like this, no con, I'll become human again."

Rosaline's forehead folded like an accordion, her cheeks on fire. She reached for Popopop's gun. "You're not saying—" The alligator nodded his head. "Are you really taking me to my grandfather? Or was that just a ruse to get me to come with you?" Her grip pulsed against the rifle.

"I have him. Promise. My friend's keeping an eye on him for me." Rosaline asked who his friend was. "Her name's Julia. We're almost to her cabin." She relaxed her grip on the wheel and the gun.

They had passed nothing but trees, alligators, and raccoons for nearly an hour.

"Julia Baudin." What was the old lady up to? she wondered.

"You know her?"

"She's my grandfather's neighbor. Of course I know her." Rosaline could just make out Julia's run-down cabin in the distance. How could that jail Poppop? "Julia's probably trying to get my grandfather to drink that tea she makes. We've seen her picking herbs when we've been out on the boat. The smell wafts across the swamp when she boils the plants. It always makes me think of death, or how natural death would smell. Musty, untamed. Not at all like the country morgue. Poppop believes root work is evil. Says Julia's a devil woman."

"She's a little eccentric," Charlie said. "But she's a nice lady. Poppop is fine. I trust her."

"You don't know her."

"She promised to help me break the curse if I help her get the amulet."

"What could she possibly want with that amulet?" An image flashed before her. Poppop's boat driving over Charlie, splitting his body like a seam. Rosaline at the wheel. There was only one way this story ended— Poppop alive and safe. Rosaline reminded herself that every tale about curses and witches had a hero. Why couldn't it be her? Rosaline made herself a promise: she wasn't going to help Charlie break the curse. She wasn't going to be any man's bridge.

"Cut the engine," the alligator said. "We're almost there."

A lopsided cabin with a small front porch sat in the middle of a dense forest of trees. The weathered wooden structure looked like it had been built on an angle. Raccoons walked around on their hind legs outside of it scavenging for food. It didn't matter that it was early afternoon—these normally nocturnal creatures were gluttonous. As the boat glided toward the dirt land in front of the house, the raccoons lifted their heads to peer at Rosaline and Charlie. They didn't see any food, so they shook their heads and continued their search in the woods.

As the boat slid into the sandy earth, a tiny, old woman hobbled out of the cabin onto the porch. She sat down on the steps, her body sinking with exhaustion, as she waited for her visitors to approach. Julia Baudin.

Charlie wriggled out of the boat more gracefully than Rosaline had expected. The girl watched the alligator, then looked around for something to tether the boat to. There was nothing. The boat, snuggly wedged into the sand, would be okay for a little while; she wasn't staying long. She checked her phone to see if she had reception. Zero bars. She sighed, slipping the phone into her shorts. Then she slung the rifle over her shoulder, Poppop's walking stick in hand, and climbed off the boat, onto the shore.

When Rosaline reached the porch, she took in Julia's head of wild silver curls shooting in every direction. The old woman's skin rippled with wrinkles. She wore a black shift that went to her feet, which were bare and leathery. Somehow Julia looked even more ancient than the last time Rosaline had seen her. Charlie was on the ground in front of Julia, his tail slapping the dusty ground. It reminded Rosaline of an excited puppy wagging its tail.

"Where's Poppop, Julia?" Rosaline said, not interested in chitchat.

"He's inside getting some shut eye. He's pretty beat from all the excitement," Julia responded. "It's nice to see you, dearie." She spoke with a deep twang. Her *i*'s sounded like *w*'s and her *e*'s like *a*'s. Rosaline saw the old woman was missing several teeth. The ones that remained were a dirty yellow.

"I want to see him. Now." She slammed the walking stick into the ground.

Julia swatted at the air as though there were a mosquito. "Go on in. Charlie and I have some business to chat about."

That seemed too easy to Rosaline, but she needed to make sure her grandfather was okay. She walked across the porch to the screen door, the only shelter between nature and the front of the home. The door creaked as the girl pulled it open. Once she moved into the threshold and let go of the door, it swung behind her, squeaking for several seconds before going silent and still. Rosaline had never been inside Julia's home before. Her grandfather and the old woman weren't the type of neighbors to invite one another over for meals. Instead they yelled at each other outside, their voices echoing off the swamp.

The cabin was filled with shadows, the only light seeping in from the screen door and a rectangular window directly across from it. It too only had a screen between it and nature. Straight ahead was a folding table made of fake wood, two plastic chairs, a stove, and a mini fridge. A sheet on the far right of the room separated the bathroom—a small sink, toilet, and shower head—from the rest of the cabin. To the left was a rotted pull out couch with down feathers peeking through the cushions. The mattress had a single sheet that may have been white once, but now was yellow with several round, brown stains. Poppop lay on that sheet, his once formidable stature curled into a ball. Rosaline choked back a sob.

She rushed over to her grandfather and knelt beside him. Placed the walking stick and rifle on the floor. "Poppop. Poppop, it's me, Rose. Wake up."

He mumbled something indiscernible. She nudged him until his filmy eyes opened. "What?" he snapped. "Rose? What are you doing here?" He grabbed a hold of her arm and started to sit up. He struggled. "My joints aren't what they used to be."

He allowed Rosaline to help him.

She leaned close to her grandfather and said in a hushed voice, "I've come to rescue you, Poppop."

"From that blasted alligator? Figures Julia would be involved in some voodoo mumbo like that."

"There's no time to explain, but we need to go. And now. Right now."

Poppop nodded and asked how they were going to escape. "That old bag never leaves her stoop."

"She's talking to Charlie right now."

The ridges and creases along Poppop's forehead and chin deepened. "Who the hell is that?"

"Sorry," Rosaline replied. "The alligator."

Poppop scowled.

"It's a long story. Now," she lowered her voice so Julia and Charlie wouldn't hear, "we need to get through that window."

"You're nuts. How am I supposed to get through there?"

The window was about five feet from the ground. Rosaline studied her grandfather; his skin was pale and ashy, and he appeared even smaller than he had a few days ago. She didn't know if he was strong enough to pull himself onto the ledge or climb out the window. But it was their only chance.

The girl looked around the small cabin. She walked over and grabbed the two plastic chairs. They would have to boost Rosaline and Poppop up. She placed the chairs in front of the window before climbing onto one to test its weight. The seat bowed. She bounced gently; the plastic moved with her but held. "It should work."

"Not very structurally sound," Poppop said from behind her, his words mirroring her own thoughts.

Rosaline turned and smiled at him. "It'll do." Then she stepped off the chair and put down the gun and walking stick. She helped her grandfather onto one of the chairs. Once he was stable, she said, "Okay, Poppop. You need to hoist yourself up and over."

He grumbled something indiscernible. Rosaline guessed it was something like, *I'm not a child or this isn't my first rodeo.* She ignored him. "I'll stay down here in case you need help." When he didn't immediately try to pull himself onto the ledge, she said, "Go."

Rosaline glanced back at the screen door directly behind them. If Julia turned for any reason, she would catch them. Poppop cursed under his breath. His muscles flexed as he pulled himself up. Once his feet were off the chair, hovering about a foot from it, Rosaline got underneath them with her hands and pushed. Together they were able to get Poppop onto the ledge. "Now hold on and—"

"I know what I'm doing," he spat. "Worry about yourself."

Rosaline looked at the back of Julia one more time, handed the walking stick to her grandfather, and hung the gun across her back before stepping onto the chair and pulling herself up.

One after the other, Poppop and Roasaline's feet landed on the soft grass behind the cabin. There was a small crunching sound from the girl and a smack from her grandfather. She hoped it wasn't loud enough to attract attention. She paused, listening.

"Whatcha gonna do? Keep the girl captive till she falls in love with you," Julia said.

"That's the plan," Charlie replied.

"Not a very fast one."

He scoffed. "What do you think I should do, Julia? Obviously, you have something better in mind."

Rosaline tuned them out. She didn't want to hear Charlie and Julia discussing her future as though she were nothing more than a key to unlock a door. She turned to Poppop. "If we can get to the boat, we should be able to get away."

Her grandfather was bent over, his hands on his knees, raspy wheezes rushing from his mouth. The walking stick was on the ground near his feet.

"The element of surprise is our best bet," she said the words she had heard many times in movies. "The gun is loaded," she continued. "I can go out first with it on them. You go to the boat and get it started. Okay?"

Poppop shook his head and coughed a low bark. He reached down and grabbed the stick, steadying himself on the wood. He cleared his throat. "You're faster. I'll go out first with the gun. You'll come right behind me and make a beeline for the boat."

Rosaline agreed. She handed the gun to her grandfather. They rounded the edge of the cabin, the boat in sight. Before Poppop walked into the view of their captors, he winked at Rosaline. She smiled; even if it was just for a moment, even if this plan went horribly wrong, her grandfather seemed himself—charming and playful—instead of an old man plagued with cancer who was being held by an old woman and her talking alligator compatriot.

"Don't come any closer," Poppop said, his voice low and raspy. "Give me a reason to shoot you, you blue son of a bitch."

Rosaline almost laughed at how cinematic this entire scenario was; she clapped a hand over her mouth. She watched Charlie's golden eyes narrow onto Poppop, jaw wide open, teeth covered in spittle. Rosaline imagined the alligator licking his long snout, salivating at the thought of such a large meal.

Julia stood before the steps to the cabin, her knees bent, shoulders hunched. Her hands stretched forward. It looked as though she were impersonating a cat, its claws drawn, ready for blood. It did not convey the fear Rosaline thought the old woman had meant it to. Julia looked like she might topple over if a breeze came through.

The old woman muttered a chant under her breath.

Almost to the boat, Rosaline ignored her. The girl just needed to make it another couple of feet and she could hop on and get the engine purring. She went to take another step, but her foot didn't move. She tried to take a step with her other foot, yet it didn't budge either. Only Rosaline's eyes could move, darting in their sockets at the scene before her. Julia remained in her crouched position, her chanting continuing like waves rushing from her tongue.

Poppop started backing toward Rosaline and the boat. Charlie advanced, his tail thrashing. Poppop reached Rosaline, her body a statue. He shifted the gun, pointing it at Julia. "Release my granddaughter from your spell, witch!"

Charlie sprang forward, his massive jaw cranking open, ready to feast. Poppop, a hunting veteran, turned with ease, as though this were a normal afternoon, and fired a shot before Julia turned her chanting in his direction. His hands froze around the gun.

The bullet hit the alligator's armor just above his right front leg. The beast flopped onto the ground with a dusty thump. With a huff, he lifted himself and continued his advance, this time at a slower pace, gait uneven.

Rosaline wanted to scream, but her lips and tongue wouldn't move. She could only see what was in front of her—Julia chanting—and in her periphery, her grandfather was stuck in the moment he shot the alligator. She could see Charlie approaching, a clay-colored liquid oozing from the round wound above his leg. This was it, she told herself. There was nothing she could do.

As she waited for him to attack her grandfather, breaking his bones, shredding the life out of him, Rosaline imagined what her life would be like with Charlie. Rosaline knew she wouldn't last long. She would never love someone like him, regardless of whether he was a man or a beast. She would never forgive him for killing her grandfather or kidnapping her, robbing her of college and a career and a life. Eventually, Charlie would grow tired of Rosaline and her disinterest in him; he was the kind of guy who got rid of what wasn't benefiting him. Sure, he'd taken care of his father so he'd never go after his mother again, but then Charlie had left her behind. He wasn't someone who deserved love, and when he realized Rosaline would never love him, never breaking the spell, he'd get rid of her too. A fisherman would find her body floating in the swamp, bloated and long gone. Or torn to ribbons of flesh and guts.

Or maybe, she told herself, maybe she would go with him, with a ploy of her own. She could convince Charlie she was growing fond of him. She might have to get creative, might even have to debase herself, but all she would need is the beast to let his guard down and then she could drive a hunting knife into his soft underbelly, disemboweling him until he was nothing but an empty carcass. His head would make for an excellent edition to Poppop's hunting trophies along the cabin walls, where Rosaline imagined herself moving. Yes, she told herself, she could survive this. If she had to, revenge would be her happy ending.

Rosaline watched the beast's jaw widened, preparing to take a bite out of Poppop when Charlie stopped. His mouth shut, his pursuit suspended. Julia's chanting halted. The air whooshed as swamp water whorled faster and faster. Poppop and Rosaline found their arms, torsos, and necks could move again. They turned toward the whirlpool as a figure emerged from the swamp.

Rosaline's tongue squirmed in her mouth. A soft whine spewed from her mouth, an echo of the scream she had attempted. Poppop's hand, still holding the gun, lowered to his side.

Before them stood a vision. The woman, if that's what she was, was exceptionally beautiful with a freckled, tanned complexion and eyes the color of the cloudless blue sky that melted into the water's surface. She had glimmering rose gold hair that tumbled to the ground in waves. It looked like liquified gold. She wore a sleeveless white empire waist dress that kissed the top of her bare feet. Somehow she was completely dry.

The apparition glided toward Charlie. She knelt before him and cocked her head, examining his wound. "That must hurt," she said.

Her hand against his snout stopped him from speaking.

"I don't take kindly to men who use women like pawns. Does this young girl look like a chess piece to you?"

He didn't answer.

"You always look for the easy way out, don't you, Charlie? That's what Zelima said."

"That bitch."

The woman stroked his snout. "Oh, honey, if you think she's a bitch, just you wait."

She turned from him then and stepped back into the water. Her eyes shifted from Julia, to Charlie, then Poppop and Rosaline, inviting them to watch. She clasped her hands before her breast and closed her eyes. Her body stretched until she was several feet above their heads. The dress she had been wearing shrank to a top, revealing the curves of her body. Rosaline's heart drummed in her chest, the tempo quickening. The percussion vibrated in her ears. She pressed her hands to them, as she watched the unimaginable reveal itself. The woman shed her hair like she had her dress, and the color of it stained her skin reflective and gold. Her ears grew large and acicular. Gills appeared along her cheeks. From just below her navel emerged a gilded fin. She flicked it before placing her hands on her hips. She smiled at them, revealing two rows of jagged spikes. Only the piercing blue eyes of the woman remained.

Rosaline glanced at Poppop, who had his hand pressed to his chest, his face stretched in a mixture of wonder and horror. He looked like a sailor bedazzled by the Sirens, half-woman, half-bird monsters from Greek mythology. One more note of that intoxicating song and he'd walk into the swamp to drown. Rosaline reached for his arm and squeezed it. "Stay with me," she whispered.

"Let me tell you how this is going to go," the shapeshifter said. "That girl and her grandfather—super cute by the way—" She paused to blow Poppop a kiss. "Are going to get in that boat and go home. And you'll never go near them again. Either of you."

"We are?" Rosaline stammered.

"Yes." She shot Julia a steely glance. "Zelima sends her regards. She wants me to remind you of your agreement and the consequences for breaking it."

Rosaline watched Julia's features shift from shock to terror. Her eyes, now glazed, bulged from their sockets and her teeth began to chatter. "You should be grateful she's willing to let this one slide."

Julia nodded her head and hobbled over to the cabin stairs to take her seat.

Rosaline felt the twitch of her toes in her shoes. Her feet and legs could move again. The shapeshifter had broken Julia's spell. Rosaline pulled Poppop to her. He winced from the pressure, then chuckled. "I love you, too, Rose."

The girl released him and smiled. She put her hand on Poppop's shoulder, unsure of what was going to happen next.

"I'll tell you what I'll do, Mr. Alligator," the shapeshifter continued. "I'll give you a head start because you're wounded. It'll be the race of all races."

Charlie didn't move. Sunlight reflected green off of his scales as his body trembled.

"Should I close my eyes and count to ten?"

Still he didn't move.

"You really should get going." She crossed her arms in front of her massive chest. "I've never lost a race before. And it's almost dinner time. I always swim faster when I'm hungry."

Rosaline shivered. This woman, whatever she was, was planning to murder and then eat Charlie, and the girl couldn't help but feel that there was blood on her hands.

"Well?"

Charlie tottered to the water's edge, leaving a trail of brown. He didn't look at Rosaline or Poppop. Once his body was in the water, he took off, his tail whipping the swamp's blue-green surface before disappearing.

"So, I guess that's it." The shapeshifter tilted her head to the right and then the left. Each crack sounded like a tree branch snapping. Before Rosaline and Poppop's eyes, she transformed into her original form, a beautiful maiden that belonged in a fairy tale.

"What are you?" Rosaline asked.

Before the woman could answer, Poppop collapsed. Rosaline dropped to his side, pebbles and old fish bones embedding themselves in the flesh of her knees. "Are you alright?"

Folded like that, Poppop appeared to be nothing more than a discarded pile of clothes. Where was the giant of a man he once had been?

Eyes closed, her grandfather shook his head. His face was beet red. "I need a beer."

Rosaline sighed. "Poppop."

He shrugged. "Alcohol will help this all make sense."

Rosaline couldn't deny that. "If we get you back to the cabin in one piece, you can have a beer. Just one."

He chuckled, a bark following each string of laughter. "Deal."

Rosaline helped her grandfather to his feet. They turned toward the boat; the shapeshifter had vanished. Rosaline and Poppop looked at each other, and then at Julia, who sat on the porch steps.

The old woman threw her arms in the air. "Beats me." She began to whistle.

"Neighbors," Poppop grumbled.

"Neighbors," Rosaline agreed.

Turning onto Bourbon Street, Rosaline's senses were littered with the stench of alcohol and garbage, and the percussion of loud music and shouting. She weaved through pedestrians and performers on the infamous street, shaking her head no when solicited for fortune telling or happy hour specials. It was only ten in the morning, and she was seventeen, but in the Big Easy, there were no limits. Her feet shuffled faster, picking up speed until the sign for Lavender's came into view. The girl opened the glass door, entering the shop. Zelima stood behind the modest wood counter, her braids pulled to the side, cascading to her hip bone. She wore the youth amulet around her neck.

"It's good to see you in one piece," Zelima said.

Rosaline nodded. "It is. I wanted to say thank you. After all, you did warn me about alligators acting strange."

Zelima's smooth face cracked into a smile, illuminating the small shop. "I suppose I did."

A myriad of questions flooded Rosaline's mind. Are you really a witch? Do you practice Voodoo? Is Julia a witch? What was that woman in the swamp? Is Charlie dead? Will Poppop live? Rosaline wasn't sure she wanted all of these answers, at least not yet. She smiled at Zelima and told her goodbye.

At the door, the girl paused, turning to face the mysterious shop owner. "Are you by any chance hiring? My mom will kill me if I don't get a job."

Zelima crossed her arms below her breasts. "Are you sure this is the kind of job you want?"

Rosaline looked around the shop, taking in the amulets, potions, and rabbit's feet. A shiver ran up her spine. She thought about what Zelima had done to Charlie. Before this Rosaline would have never accepted revenge as a solution. Yet hadn't she fantasized about eviscerating Charlie too? Rosaline reminded herself of what Zelima had done for her. And Poppop. She couldn't deny the woman's power and the kindness she had shown them. It seemed morality was even more complicated in a world with magic. Rosaline would have to learn more before she could judge Zelima. She swallowed, meeting the witch's gaze. "I won't pretend to know what you do or what happened these last few days, but I know you have the power to do good. To help people. And I want the chance to do that. I want the chance to learn."

"Then consider yourself hired." She offered her hand.

Rosaline started to think about how she could spin this new job to her mother. Maybe she didn't have to tell her. Maybe it was better to keep some things hidden. She took Zelima's hand. Electricity hummed where their skin touched, audible. The women grinned at each other then, a secret blooming between them, uniting them like Spanish moss pouring from a live oak at the swamp.

To Break the Curse,
Kiss the Siren

In the middle of Honey Island Swamp lay a sleeping maiden with flowing rose gold hair. Her name was Isabelle. She was on a small floating dock that had once been brown, but now was a slimy green in texture and color. Kids used the dock decades ago for diving and cannonballs or midnight rendezvous. Honey Island had once been a popular getaway for New Orleans locals and out of towners looking for a reprieve from the troupes of tourists parading through the French Quarter night and day. The cabins along the swamp's edge were brightly painted with mowed lawns and beach chairs set up by the shoreline. Where there weren't homes, the land was set up as a campground. A large fire pit, outdoor shower, and dozens of s'mores kits were at the ready.

It was like Airbnb before that was a thing. The owners rented out their homes and stayed with family in New Orleans or Baton Rouge.

But after Hurricane Katrina the campers and minivans full of families stopped coming. Honey Island was forgotten, a wasteland haunted by what it once was. The cabins along the shoreline fell into disrepair. Several residents of Honey Island remained in their homes; some worked to repair what was lost in the storm, others adapted to their new lodgings. Today there were only two full-time residents—Edouard Albert (who insisted on being called Ed) and Julia Baudin. They lived on opposite ends of the swamp, and besides one unfortunate encounter involving Ed's granddaughter, Rose, and a blue alligator—the two stayed on their respective sides of Honey Island.

Contrary to popular belief, there was no island on Honey Island Swamp. If there was, it would have been the perfect place to keep a sleeping maiden. But, since there wasn't, she slumbered on the dock. Her body was placed onto a reclining beach chair and was clothed in the quintessential sleeping beauty ensemble: a sleeveless white empire waist dress with yellow stitching below her breasts and along the hem. Not a wrinkle or imperfection in sight. The fabric stopped at her ankles, revealing two tanned feet. Her sun-freckled arms were joined by her clasped hands, creating a triangle, her head the top point. A piece of string looped around her left wrist, a piece of paper attached to it. It read, "To break the curse, kiss me." Like the princess in the famous story, her eyes were softly closed; in fact, everything about her look was soft and round and gentle. Her pale pink lips were slightly parted, her chest rising and falling with even breaths.

She was the sleeping beauty of the swamp.

As she appeared to slumber peacefully, a small engineless boat glided toward her. Through the tunnel of live oaks and their hanging branches dripping in Spanish moss, the boat continued. Aboard were two young men in their late twenties. They were half rowing with wooden oars, half letting the boat do whatever the hell it wanted. One had light brown hair shaved on the sides and long on top. He wore an aqua t-shirt, khaki shorts, and flip flops. His friend had wispy blond hair that hung around his forehead and the top of his ears. He wore a salmon tank, navy shorts with white anchors, and Sperrys. Isabelle knew the type. They had rich daddies and grandpas. Crashed luxury boats and cars without consequence. A lesson plan bloomed in her mind; Isabelle prided herself on being an excellent and effective teacher.

The young men had the boat full of bait, fishing rods, and beer. "Yo, that club was tight last night," the brunette said.

"Too bad the girls weren't," the blond replied.

They erupted into laughter that resembled a pack of hyenas; it vibrated along the still water, disturbing the tranquility of the swamp. The sleeping beauty guessed these two were several six packs in. Or maybe they were just tools.

"Hey, dude, do you see that over there?" the brunette said. He swatted his friend in the chest before pointing to Isabelle.

"Is that a chick?" the blond said.

"Looks like it."

"Let's check it out. You know there's nothing I love more than a—"

"Sleeping girl." His lips split into a grin.

"Right," he said, chuckling. "She lets you do whatever you want. Less fuss than a woke girl."

"I don't think that's the word you mean, dude. You mean awake. Or conscious."

"I'm not talking about what's right and wrong, Jake," the blond said. Clearly, Isabelle thought.

"That's your conscience, Matt, not being conscious," Jake said.

At least one of them wasn't a complete idiot. If Isabelle didn't have company, she would have stretched her neck. Her body felt like it was being pulled in half; she knew what it desired, but she told it to wait. The reward was always better if she waited. Isabelle inhaled the sweat, cheap beer, and horrible cologne spouting from the boys' pores. It wouldn't be long now. She was ready to wake up.

Contrary to what the bros believed, Isabelle was not just a sleeping maiden; in fact, she never slept. She could see far more with her eyes closed than when they were open. She watched the creatures and people who entered the swamp, the images rolling through her mind like a movie reel. If only there were snacks. She reminded herself there would be soon enough.

She studied her prey, her suitors as she liked to call them, to see if they were worthy of salvation or devouring. There were only two choices. Isabelle told herself she didn't have time for indecision, except of course, the irony was she had endless time. She was immortal now.

Hunger made Isabelle particularly impatient; her stomach echoed, *Hello?*, over and over, afraid she had forgotten about it. She told it to hush; the boat was bobbing against the dock. It was showtime.

Her eyes still closed, she watched Jake attempt a clumsy knot, trying to tether Matt and his boat to the slime-riddled dock. A giggle wanted to escape her throat, but she didn't allow it. She shifted her attention to Matt, who was on the dock, beer in hand, moving toward her. He stopped in front of her. "Dude," he said. "She's a babe."

Jake had finally finished tying the boat to the dock; his efforts would hold short term. "Damn." He stood beside Matt, ogling Isabelle. "What's that?" He pointed to the note attached to her wrist.

Matt rushed to Isabelle's side, as though they were racing and she was the prize. Finders, keepers. He jerked the piece of paper from her wrist, lifting her hand an inch before it dropped like dead weight. This was something Isabelle had practiced to further sell her curse-induced slumber. She wanted those who found her to believe she was a sleeping dead girl, completely unresponsive, save for a magical kiss.

"What's it say?" Jake asked, leaning forward.

"I can wake her up by kissing her."

"It says *you* can wake her up?"

"Pretty much."

Jake scrambled to Matt, ripping the note from him. "You jackass. It says, 'To break the curse, kiss me.'"

Matt shrugged his shoulders. "Same thing." He took a long swig from his beer, emptying it of its fermented liquid. He crushed it in his hand and tossed it behind him into the swamp.

Isabelle fought the urge to rip his throat out.

"Why do you get to kiss her?" Jake asked.

"Because I found her," Matt said.

"I'm pretty sure I saw her first."

If Isabelle's eyes had been open, she would have rolled them. Can one of you kiss me already? she thought.

She always waited until a suitor tried something, whether that was a tender kiss, curious fondling, or further violation. Usually, they started with a kiss. After all, the kiss seemed innocent enough in Disney classics like *Sleeping Beauty* and *Snow White*. Kiss the sleeping or dead girl, she'll wake up and be yours for the taking. Isabelle had seen firsthand how the ideal of a submissive woman, one silent and unconscious, a living doll to play with, could sour. Her once perfect peach skin had worn the bruises to show just how nasty it could get. At the time, she had believed she deserved it. At the time, she had believed she needed Tommy's love.

"Ding," he breathed in her ear. His voice was husky and humid. It made the baby hairs on her neck perk up. She had thought he would be with the boys most of the day. She stood in the rundown garden behind Tommy's shotgun house. She shivered even though it was nearly one-hundred degrees outside. "How's my bell?" he asked.

Her voice shaky, she said, "Fine."

"Just fine?" He tongued her ear.

Her head tried to move away from the whiskey-soaked muscle flicking her ear drum, coating it in saliva. He gripped the back of her neck in his hand to keep her in place, the callouses like sandpaper against her flesh. She closed her eyes and waited for him to finish his licking and sucking.

"How about now?" he said, his tongue back in his mouth.

"I'm good, baby. Real good." Her voice was mechanical, detached, but Tommy didn't seem to notice.

He took her by the shoulders and turned her to face him. "I have something to show you. Something special." His black eyes looked her up and down.

Like a child on her birthday, Isabelle beamed. "You do?" Her voice filled with glee.

His tongue glided over his chapped upper lip. "Wait until you see this." He picked up a cardboard box by his feet. Isabelle hadn't heard him put it down or noticed it until then. Her eyebrows lifted, waiting for the surprise. She rehearsed in her head, "Oh, Tommy baby, for me? You shouldn't have," like she'd seen in movies and T.V. shows. She liked the idea of her life being like either of those mediums. So did Tommy, but they were interested in different genres. She liked romances and comedies, he liked thrillers and horror.

Isabelle remembered this when he pulled the item, what was supposed to be her present, out of the box. Tommy held it in front of her as though it were a rare piece of art or a diamond ring, an offering fit for a lady. It was smaller than she had expected, a yellow and black box no larger than a plate. Tommy's latest toy was inside.

Her light brown eyebrows knit together. Her chin began to tremble. She knew what this meant. "I don't know, Tommy."

"C'mon, Bell, you know you like it."

She took a step back from Tommy and the item. "Last time—"

"Last time had its issues. That's why I got this."

"A defibrillator."

"Yeah, to ensure you'll come back to me. No more trips to the ER." He bent down to put the defibrillator back into the box. Then he stepped toward her and took her hands in his. "You know I can't live without you. You're my bell." He smiled, revealing his one golden tooth. "Ding. Ding." He chuckled to himself, pleased.

He was sickening, as was his fetish. At that moment Isabelle hated him, yet knew she'd let him do it to her. She always gave in even though she was pretty sure giving into Tommy was going to kill her one day. But Isabelle loved him; Tommy was the only one who'd ever had her back. And, as he constantly reminded her, he was the only one looking out for her. She was nothing if she wasn't Tommy's girl.

There was protection and respect when you were in with the gang. Out of it, you were on your own. Tommy had saved Isabelle from her cop daddy who liked to beat her; at first it was only after bad days—when a murderer got away or a kid died—but soon he got a taste for it and knocking around Izzie, as he liked to call her. Then it became his way of celebrating. Like the prince in fairy tales, Tommy saved Isabelle. As the boss of a Bywater District street gang, he alone could protect her, and because of his position, Tommy got exactly what he wanted. It didn't take long for Isabelle to learn she was no exception. If you were Tommy's girl, you gave without hesitation and he took with little to no gratitude. If she played her part, it was like a seesaw, balancing perfectly. If not, Tommy would let her fall to the ground, tossing her away like he had to dozens of girls before. She couldn't go back to her daddy. Tommy's fetish was dangerous, but it hurt less than Daddy's fists.

It had started in bed as these things usually do. Tommy liked to experiment; his unpredictability made Isabelle hot and wet. He was on top, his eyes wide and searching. He wanted to capture it all. "Like a movie," he said. "You're so goddamn beautiful. You're my goddess. My movie star, Bell."

His arms bookended her shoulders. She glanced at the lean, tight muscles in his arms. The skin was peppered with tattoos, no rhythm or reason to the placement or pieces. She felt safe there in Tommy's arms. "I love you," she said.

A mischievous smile spread across Tommy's face. "You love me?"

"I do."

"You trust me?"

"With my life."

"I'm going to try something," he said. She nodded, consenting. He shifted his weight to his left arm and lifted his right. He brought it to Isabelle's throat. His eyes on hers, Tommy's fingers closed around her neck. She swallowed but nodded to say she was okay. He could keep going. Tommy's angular face glistened with sweat. He licked his lips. Put pressure on Isabelle's esophagus, his fingers gripping her neck. She felt her jaw open and her tongue push against the back of her lower teeth. It was like having a tickle in your throat but larger. Tommy pressed harder, his nails digging into the soft flesh of her neck. She started to dry heave, her chest leaping forward. He maintained eye contact. Isabelle felt his erection growing inside her, straining against her dryness and tightness. "C'mon, baby," he said, panting like a dog. "Get wet for me, baby."

Isabelle started to cough. She lifted her hand and grabbed Tommy's arm to try to tell him to stop. She'd met her limit. But he ignored it or thought it was her way of egging him on. "Don't worry, baby, I'll keep going."

Her eyes filled with tears. Her lips trembled, turning blue. Tommy tightened his grip and amped up his pumping. "Fuck, yes," he said.

Then he started to growl and moan.

White stars flickered as the room and Tommy slipped away. Isabelle coughed again, saliva speckling her lips and chin.

He kept going.

The stars faded to black.

Isabelle woke up coughing, her lungs desperate for air. Her face was slick from crying. Her thighs and crotch soggy with semen. Tommy was in the bathroom talking to his reflection in the mirror. She heard him complimenting himself. Smug bastard, she thought. Isabelle patted her chest, loosening the last dry coughs from her throat. She fingered her neck to make sure she was still in one piece. Her skin uneven and on fire, she winced. Maybe now, she thought, Tommy would be satiated.

She was rubbing her throat when Tommy came back into the bedroom. "You're awake. Hey, Bell."

He walked over and leaned down to kiss her. She pulled away.

"You choked me unconscious," she spat the words at him.

His eyes glimmered with excitement.

"You could have killed me."

His face and his words showed no remorse. Tommy said he'd never come like that before. That he couldn't wait to do it again. The erection pressing against his boxers proved that.

Isabelle slid off the bed, leaving a streak of semen. She walked past Tommy and went into the bathroom. She cleaned herself up, her hands brimming with rage. After she finished washing herself, she stood in front of the sink staring into the mirror at the bruises setting into her neck. They looked like deep red vines, as though she'd gotten a peculiar sunburn.

Tommy came up behind her. She flinched at his breath on her ear. He put his arms around her and said, "I'm sorry. I didn't mean to hurt you."

She swallowed and said it was okay. He kissed her. Then he went into the bedroom, leaving Isabelle alone with her bruises.

After that, they went back to less experimental and rough sex. Isabelle could tell Tommy was bored; he closed his eyes now instead of trying to capture the moment. He had trouble finishing. Their sex life suddenly seemed like work; Isabelle knew Tommy would go find someone else if things didn't get better. If he hadn't already. She couldn't stand to lose him. Who was she without him? Where could she go if he kicked her out?

One night when they got into bed Isabelle asked if he would choke her. "It turns me on," she told him.

Six months later he gave her the defibrillator.

For months, he choked her until she blacked out. It happened every time they had sex. Sometimes he didn't stop after she was unconscious though; Tommy had realized he liked to feel her pulse weaken to a dull hiccup. He pushed the limits with her life, and each time he did this, he pushed her further into the Other Place.

Isabelle wasn't religious; she didn't believe that death equaled ending up either in heaven or hell. She nicknamed where she went the *Other Place* because it was just like reality yet it existed in shadows and fog. Shades of gray washed over everything and everyone. The first time she blacked out she woke to find herself on the edge of a swamp. It was vast and quiet. The fog was thick; the Spanish moss played peek-a-boo, appearing like limp, dismembered arms. She heard nothing but the crunch of her body moving on the grass. She pawed at herself as she had after the first time Tommy had choked her to make sure she was in one piece. Her usually peach-toned skin was a light gray. She rubbed at her skin to remove it, believing it to be make up, but the color didn't smudge. She stood and began to walk on the outskirts of the swamp. Eventually, she came across swamp dwellers—alligators, raccoons, and snakes. All were gray like she was. Isabelle jumped at the sight of three full-grown alligators coming toward her, but they waddled by, disinterested.

It wasn't until the tenth time she awakened in the Other Place that the swamp creatures spoke to her. A raccoon welcomed her in a raspy voice. It said to follow her this way, jerking its furry head to the right. A snake slithered in between the raccoon and Isabelle. It said, "Don't listen to him. Unless you want to stay here." Its long forked tongue flew from its mouth and back in like a cuckoo bird in a clock. "Forever."

"You can go back, if you want," one of the alligators interjected. Its massive body appeared from the fog, gray scales resembling a suit of armor. The alligator's nostrils flared. "You might not always have this choice." Isabelle asked what it meant by that. "One day you may have to follow the raccoon."

"To where?" she said.

"To the graveyard."

The snake wiggled on top of the alligator. It didn't seem to mind. The snake said, "A mortal body can only take so much. Yours is expiring." It flicked its tongue forward then drew it back inside its mouth. "Fast."

Each time Isabelle went to the Other Place she spoke to the creatures for longer, learning more about her fate. Her limited options. She felt like Alice, the Other Place was her Wonderland; it was erased from her mind as soon as she woke up in the real world. Even though she didn't remember going there, the roots of fear reached deep. She could feel Tommy becoming omnivorous, his thirst deepening; he wouldn't stop until he killed her.

Three weeks after he gave Isabelle the defibrillator he was dead, and she was no longer human.

When Isabelle woke, she found herself changed. She grew ravenous when she thought of Tommy or her father. Her rage at these men, who had battered, used, and killed her, had transformed her into something entirely different. Something unkillable. A monstrous creature with an appetite for retribution in the flavor of male flesh.

After several minutes of arguing and a brawl that led to Jake falling into the swamp, Matt and Jake had finally come to an agreement. Since Matt was the winner of their drunken duel, he would get to kiss the sleeping beauty first. While Jake swam back to the dock and struggled to get onto it, Matt went to the boat and took another can from the cooler. He sucked down beer, the amber liquid spilling down his chin every time he chuckled at his friend's struggle. Isabelle knew he was the perfect prey. She just didn't know yet if his friend was too.

Matt finished the can and tossed it into the swamp. Not only was he a jackass, he was a jackass who littered. Isabelle was ready to end his drunken, garbage existence. He sauntered over to her, his chest puffed up. Isabelle stifled a snort. He dropped to one knee and took her hands in his; this was how elaborate and romantic proposals usually began. His hair was frizzy from the humidity and some of it was pasted to his forehead from sweat. His pale skin was reddened from the sun. Isabelle didn't take him for the sunscreen type; he probably still said ridiculous things like YOLO and thought he was original. Matt's chest rose furiously, and a wheeze whistled from his parted lips.

Get on with it, Isabelle thought.

"Dearest maiden," he said, "I crown you fine as hell. You don't know this yet, but I'm about to bring you into a reality sweeter than any dream."

Isabelle wanted to spit on him.

Matt looked over his shoulder at Jake who was sitting on the edge of the dock, his feet in the boat, a beer in hand. She knew Matt was grinning at Jake, rubbing his triumph in his friend's face. When Matt turned back to her, the corners of his mouth were still raised. He fingered a strand of Isabelle's rose gold hair with his thumb and pointer finger. "I wonder if the carpet matches the drapes," he said to himself.

He didn't even bother to stand up; he used his other hand to pull the white fabric covering Isabelle's lower half toward him. She wore white underwear, made of the same material as her dress. Matt's pointer finger started to lift the fabric over her hipbone to sneak a peek. Jake bounded over and pushed his friend, throwing Matt's body to the surface of the slimy dock. The right side of his body was covered in the green substance. His salmon tank was streaked, the color dark brown. "What the hell, man?" Matt said as he tried to shake the slime from his bicep and forearm.

Panting, Jake knelt beside the sleeping woman, his hands on his knees. "That's not okay, Matt. I don't care how fine she is or that she's asleep or that she has that string around her wrist telling you to kiss her. You have a sister, bro. What if this was her?"

"So, you what? Want to leave her here? A prime piece of meat out in the open."

Jake straightened his legs, standing tall. He nodded his head. "When we get service, let's call the cops. They can help her better than we can."

Isabelle's stomach churned. The organ had become an empty tomb. Soon beetles would crawl and worms would slink out of it, looking for food, for life. She waited to see what the drunken fools would do. There was still a chance she could have them both.

The friends looked at each other; Matt appeared to be eyeing Jake up, trying to decide if they should go for round two. He shook his head. "Fine. Let's go. But you're buying more beer."

"After we get back to town and call for help, I'll buy you whatever case you want."

A crooked smirk stretched Matt's right cheek, causing his eye to squint. "Deal."

Matt and Jake walked to the boat and climbed in. Jake's knot had thinned, barely keeping the boat attached to the dock. He only had to twist it to release them. He dipped an oar into the water. The boat started slipping away from the sleeping beauty on the dock.

Matt cracked a beer open and gulped it down. "She was fine," he said when he took a breath from drinking. He clucked his tongue.

"Let it go, man," Jake said. "Hand me a beer?"

Matt grabbed a can from the cooler by his feet. As he held it out to his friend, his body went flying backward. Isabelle had transformed into her preferred form, a towering, golden monster with a long fin and jagged teeth. Her monstrous body rose from the swamp, her hairless head skimming the clouds. The sun reflected off of her blue eyes, making them sparkle. She was the mermaid-like creature no one wrote fairy tales about.

Isabelle held Matt up by her shoulder, the dagger-like claws extending from her fingers skewering his back. She grinned, the pointed edges of her teeth gleaming with saliva. Then she drove her fangs into Matt's flesh, tearing him to pieces as his heart continued to pulse.

When she first latched on, she could feel his pulse racing, but soon it slowed until it stopped altogether. Once Matt was dead, and Isabelle had had her fill, she tossed his limp, bloody carcass into the swamp, creating a loud splash before the water grew quiet and still again.

She licked her lips and cracked her neck. She glided to the boat where Jake stood frozen, his face plastered in horror. She raised her hands, her golden palms out to him. "I'm not going to hurt you," she said.

"Why not?" he stammered.

"Because in the end you protected me from your friend. Though I do hope you've learned an important lesson. Consent is not optional. And sometimes women fight back."

Jake cocked his head to the side, his forehead ridged with horizontal lines.

"Let me slip into something a little more familiar," Isabelle said.

She began to change, her gargantuan frame shrinking to human size, the gold tint of her skin fading away to a freckled tan, and flowing rose gold locks spilling from her head. Only her bare shoulders and head were above the blue-green water.

Jake took tentative steps toward the edge of the boat. He went to speak, but nothing coherent came out.

Isabelle smiled, her teeth small and rounded, the pointed fangs gone. "Are you more comfortable with me like this?"

Jake mumbled something indiscernible.

"As you can see, I am perfectly fine. You don't need to call the police. I appreciate the thought though. And if you want to call the police for your friend, I won't try to talk you out of it." She moved closer until her small hands gripped the edge of the boat, inches from Jake. "Sorry about your friend, Jake. I'm sure it wasn't easy to watch him…expire."

Jake frowned, but he didn't move away from her. "What are you?" he managed to say.

She pulled herself up, her face in line with his. "Men have called me many things. Bitch. Slut. Witch. Monster. I prefer siren." She leaned closer to him, her breath on his lips. "It's a sexier title, don't you think?"

He screamed and threw himself backward. Grabbed an oar and frantically began to paddle. The boat circled as he thrashed. Isabelle let go, floating on her back in the water. She cackled as he tried to get away from her.

After a minute, Jake was able to straighten the boat. The siren closed her eyes, the sunlight warming her flesh, and watched the movie projected in her head: Jake paddling away from the she-monster who would haunt his nightmares, panic etched into his young face, sweat glistening on his forehead and by his sideburns. He certainly would never forget this.

She stretched her arms overhead, full and happy. "Another asshole bites the dust."

Lady Mariticide

The blood dripped gloriously off his chin, pooling on the white tile floor. She exhaled, elation settling the unease in her veins. Her heartbeat slowed, stabilizing to a thump instead of the rapid rattling that had shook her body like a sputtering dryer. It was done, and she was the better for it. Wherever he was now, well, who the hell cared? That prideful bastard deserved it. She saw through his dimpled chin and magnetic smile, his deep blue eyes and smooth yet strong hands, and delivered him to his necessary end.

She had watched how he talked to people, his broad chest puffed out like a male frigate bird, hoping to attract admirers. It hadn't been all about sex for him, but that was certainly part of it. His pursuit. He had pursued women and men, even children, everywhere he went. He had craved the attention, the near-drooling women who had tossed themselves at him, the men that praised his business sense and his beautiful wife, the children who reflected in their large, naïve eyes and round, freckled faces how he saw himself: a hero, a role model, someone to look up to and aspire to be.

Lorelai had seen it all, every dull moment of these idiotic people thinking Caleb was anything more than a foolish, prideful man. She spent too much time waiting, lurking in the background being ignored, until Caleb needed to parade his beautiful, wealthy wife around. The whole thing mildewed quickly. She knew she had to do to him what she had to the others.

Lorelai knew she wasn't a typical murderess. Women usually sought poison and other neat and tidy ways to dispose of their husbands, while Lorelai enjoyed the blood, reveled in untucking parts of their bodies, exposing her husbands for their true, grotesque selves. She liked to make a mess of a beautiful-seeming thing.

The one typical aspect of her killings, however, was who she killed: her spouses. But we can't be original in every way, can we?

47

Still she believed her vision, her purpose, distinguished her from the others. She saw men for what they were—wild, unfiltered, urinating everywhere and jumping on everything. Like dogs, could be trained, at least to a certain extent. They could feign obedience for a while. Yet at the end of the day men were nothing more than four-legged beasts who walked on their hind legs, fooling society into believing they were something more. They craved dominance, and weren't always so crass to attain it via humping. Some of them were lazy and some proud, others angry and greedy. Some were just plain hungry.

Lorelai didn't seek out men with these attributes, but they had a way of sniffing her out. So far, each one had a very specific vice she found particularly vile, and so she had rid New Orleans of his sin. She saw herself as a modern day Bluebeard, a husband slaying hero and crusader of the wicked. Lorelai accepted this as a private opinion, of course. One to hide in order to protect herself. To protect her work.

Her now-deceased husband was slumped in a sitting position against the wall. His blue eyes were wide and staring. She bent before him, her hands on her knees. He looked like a taxidermied animal; there was something feral about the expression on his face. For a moment, Lorelai considered removing his organs and mounting him. He would look good in the dining room over the peach wingback chair by the piano. He was a beautiful beast, after all. She cocked her head, musing it over for a moment. Then she sighed and stood tall.

She decided to wait until tomorrow to begin cleaning up Caleb. She had a dinner party to attend with her recently—just minutes ago, actually—dearly departed husband's friends from the gallery. When asked where her dashing, larger than life husband was, Lorelai would sigh deeply and begin to snivel. She'd lower her head to hide her embarrassment over such a public display of emotion. Marti, the owner of the gallery, and Trish, the wife of one of the other curators, would excuse the three of them from the group and pull her aside. Trish would rest a hand on Lorelai's slender shoulder. Marti would fold her sculpted arms in front of her chest.

"What happened?" Trish would say.

Lorelai would fake cry for several moments before responding. "He left me."

Marti would say, "What?"

"For one of his whores."

"Veronica? Was it Veronica?" Trish would say. "I knew she was a slut. Homewrecker."

Lorelai would shake her head, tossing her perfectly blown out hair back and forth between her shoulders. "I don't know."

"He wouldn't say?" Trish would ask, reaching to console Lorelai.

Lorelai would shake her head again, her face crumbling in her hands just as she'd practiced in the mirror dozens of times.

"Bastard," Marti would say. "I guess this means he's stepping out on me, too."

Lorelai would pull her face from her hands just enough to show her misty eyes and the bridge of her nose. She'd nod. "I'm so sorry, Marti," she would say. "I know he owes you—"

Marti would swat Trish's hand away and grip Lorelai's shoulders with her hands. "Don't you worry about that," she'd say. "He'll get what's coming to him."

"Amen to that," Trish would say. "I'd kill Peter if he did that to me."

Marti would nod, staring deep into Lorelai's eyes, seeing pain and betrayal reflected in them (an act much harder than fake crying). "I'd kill Sarah, too," she'd say. "Don't you worry though, Lorelai. It'll all be okay."

Lorelai would pull Marti in for a hug, clutching the back of her as though she were a life preserver and Lorelai had been drowning. Marti would inhale her lavender perfume and imagine their bodies intertwined in a different scenario. She'd stop herself and pat Lorelai on the back.

When they were done embracing, Trish would throw her arms around Lorelai, rocking her. Lorelai would be seen as the victim, the doting wife Caleb left behind for something newer and shinier. More plastic and stupider than she.

The newly thrice-widowed Lorelai stood before the cylindrical mirror in the master bathroom of her three-story townhouse on Royal Street. She smoothed the lace fabric where it tended to bunch at her upper thighs. She wore a fitted navy dress that licked the top of her calf muscles. The garment was sleeveless, revealing her thin yet toned arms and shoulders. She wore navy four-inch pumps that were pointed at the toes. She had blown out her shiny medium-brown hair; the longest tresses traced her pronounced collarbone that made a wide v across the top of her chest. Her makeup was simple and flawless. Nude eyeshadow with a hint of shimmer, black mascara that made it look as though she naturally had long, fluffy lashes, and a pink lipstick two shades deeper than her lips' natural color.

She studied her reflection intimately, checking for flecks of blood or sweat. A hair out of place. Satisfied with her appearance, she practiced crying one more time.

Three months later, Caleb's corpse was found in Honey Island Swamp by a Miss Julia Baudin, an old woman who lived on the swamp and was believed to be a witch. Or, rather, the witch found what was left of him. Caleb's head remained, blue and rubbery, and lopsided with only one ear. It was attached to an uneven section of neck that looked like a jagged line on a graph. The police dragged the swamp and found his left hand and what was supposed to be his right knee. Both were slabs of blotted, serrated meat. A gator must have gotten to him and some fish too.

He was the first husband Lorelai had disposed of in this manner. The first she had buried in the backyard—she had been sentimental at the time and wanted to be able to visit him. The second she had put in an acid bath. She kept a jar of his teeth in a safe place. Every so often she took them out to remember him; she didn't consider this to be a maudlin act, but instead one of pleasure. These keepsakes were her trophies. Her first two husbands had been greedy and lustful, which she had found abhorrent, but Caleb was prideful, and she found that far worse, so she treated his murder and disposal differently. She wanted his once beautiful face and exceptional physique made ugly. She wanted him to roll over in his grave; her latest dog doing a trick.

Lorelai had been asked to come to the police precinct on Royal Street to identify the body. She came as soon as she received the call, in black yoga pants and a long gray pullover. Her hair was pulled back into a tight bun. Her face makeup-free. The coroner was a woman in her early to mid forties. She introduced herself as Dr. Albert and assured Lorelai she would only show her Mr. Knight's face. She said, "There's no reason you should see the state of the rest of him."

Lorelai frowned. If only this woman knew what Lorelai had seen. What she had done. Lorelai remembered herself and nodded, sniffling, and thanked the woman for saving her from such an atrocity. "The police think he might have been murdered. They say they have no suspects," Lorelai told the coroner. She shook her head, her bun remaining perfectly in place. "I just can't believe it. Who would do such a thing?"

Dr. Albert sighed. Her brown eyes were kind and the crow's feet bookending them deepened in sadness. "Mrs. Knight, if there's anything I've learned being a coroner in this city, it's that monsters look like you and me. They fool us with their people skins. Convince us we're safe. They get off on wreaking havoc and causing pain." She shook her head, the blue and white horizontal stripes on her scrub cap blurring, wave-like. "You'll never get the answer you're looking for about why this happened. Not from a monster."

Lorealai appreciated the term *people skin*. It described the performance aspect of her work. She knew Dr. Albert could never understand why she had murdered Caleb or her previous husbands. Lorelai reminded herself that the show wasn't over. She was still playing the role of the grief-stricken widow. Her face broke into despair, her forehead lined, lower lip and chin trembling, eyes filmy with tears. This face was a mask she pulled on and off, as natural as a flick of a switch. "Thank you, Dr. Albert," she said.

Lorelai sat in the wine cellar of Brennan's. It had been almost six months since her husband had died. The former stable of the historic building and now restaurant was a hideaway from the loud patterns, colors, and people above in the dining room known as the Chanteclair Room. She found the dim lighting, warm brick walls, and exposed wooden beams of the cellar soothing. She sat at the head of a long table, her back resting against the leather of the tall-back chair. A glass of merlot before her, dark and bloodlike. She hadn't sipped from it, hadn't even palmed the glass yet, and she wouldn't until he arrived.

Marcus walked in a few minutes later. He was tall and dark like Lorelai's favorite chocolate. His eyes were rust-colored and round, resembling a lion, which Lorelai thought made his gaze seem carnal. But then again she found everything about him erotic. He kept his black hair short with just enough length to show its curly texture. It faded into the start of a beard, also black, tinged with gray and white. Marcus had the brightest, largest smile she'd ever seen.

Their relationship had started as business: Marcus owned a small boutique hotel outside of the Quarter that had just opened in the last month. Lorelai was one of its investors. Between her multiple husbands and her trust fund, she had endless assets to play with, and she knew she wanted to play with Marcus as soon as she saw him. They had met at a gala two months ago. With the discovery of Caleb's body, she knew it was risky to begin pursuing Marcus, but she couldn't help herself. She had to have him.

Marcus bent down and kissed her on the cheek before sitting in the chair to her left. "Bonjour belle. Ça va?" The French words rolled off his tongue smooth and without effort, velvety. His accent was authentic with a hint of the Caribbean, as though it were spiced with cayenne and nutmeg.

"Ça va bien," she said. She eyed him, pausing on his chiseled cheekbones that looked endless, like water, when he tilted his head toward her and the light.

"You haven't touched your wine."

She grinned and took the stem in her hand. "I was waiting for you."

He grinned, pleased. "I'm here now," he said.

"Yes, you are." She lifted the glass to her lips. She paused and looked at him before tipping it, drinking the dark liquid. She put the glass back on the table, the wine still in her mouth, tonguing it, feeling the graininess on her teeth.

A waiter entered the room, interrupting their foreplay. He was a young man, no more than twenty-two, with blond curly hair and fuzzy patches of yellow on his jaw and cheeks. "What can I get you, sir?" he said to Marcus.

Marcus watched Lorelai. She swallowed her wine and smiled, her cheeks flushed. Without taking his eyes from her, Marcus said, "I'll have what the lady's having."

"Very well, sir," the waiter said and turned, walking out of the room.

Over the next hour and a half, Lorelai and Marcus polished off two bottles of red wine. Their laughter bounced off of the brick cellar walls, encasing them in warm elation. It took a lot of self-control for Lorelai not to have him right then and there. She licked her upper lip and grinned. Their bodies would be entangled soon enough, she told herself.

For the first time in a long time, Lorelai felt happy. There was a lightness in her gut, illuminating her innards like a flashlight switching on in a dark cavern, that begged to expand and shine outward. She felt it pull at her tissue, at her skin, in an attempt to break free and share itself. And she was starting to think she wanted it to. Maybe with Marcus she could be in the light.

She couldn't remember feeling this way about her late husbands. Sure, she loved them at one point or another. She could faintly remember wanting to marry each of them, but the weddings themselves were gone from her memory, a collection of loose balloons drifting up to the clouds. Sometimes in the middle of the night when Marcus breathed heavily, sound asleep beside her, Lorelai would imagine their wedding. Her dress—a fitted white cocktail-length with a birdcage veil, his suit—dark gray with a white shirt and navy silk tie, the setting—Jackson Square Park, on the other side of the controversial Andrew Jackson statue, with St. Louis Cathedral, white and gray and formidable behind them, surrounded by no one but strangers, tourists from all over the world and street performers in their various getups and body paint and tools to create or fool passerbys. Or both. The street jazz musicians would serenade their ceremony, and maybe even an impromptu second line would begin, weaving through the square, heading down St. Peter Street and deeper into the belly of the Quarter.

Sometimes, while Lorelai envisioned their wedding, Marcus would roll over and his eyes would flitter open, appearing tawny in the shadows. He'd ask why she was awake. What was keeping her up? "Nothing," she'd say. "It's nothing. Go back to bed." Then he would say, *Okay*, and press his lips to her arm before drifting back to sleep.

If Marcus had to have a flaw it was his jealousy. He was smooth and charming and his ability to read people was instinctual, like he were playing darts and hit the center of the corkboard every time. Lorelai believed his new hotel would be successful because of these traits, but he threw it all away like a tempestuous toddler smashing a tower made out of rainbow-colored blocks whenever he saw someone talking to Lorelai. It didn't matter male or female; he thought Lorelai was everyone's desire.

At first, it was endearing, even a little hot. Caleb had been a philanderer, as had John and Stuart, Lorelai's first and second husbands. Pride, greed, lust, it didn't matter. All three needed something extra, something to prove they were as extraordinary as they believed themselves to be. Hookers, women at bars, Lorelai's former best friend, Stacia; they took it wherever they could get it. Lorelai didn't stroke their power balls enough, or so they said. At least that's how she remembered it.

Lorelai was determined a man wouldn't write her story. No matter how much she loved him.

She and Marcus had been dating for nearly a year now, and she knew he had bought a ring. The jeweler, Darla, was a friend and a relentless gossip. It was surprising to Lorelai that Darla didn't ruin all of her clients' engagements. "It's a little too soon after you-know-what," she said to Lorelai over cocktails one evening.

They were sitting at the bar in Josephine Estelle, an Italian restaurant attached to a boutique hotel in the Warehouse District. Lorelai studied the Corinthian column sandwiched between two bookshelves full of every bottle of liquor imaginable. She adjusted on her stool, crossing and uncrossing her ankles, her stilettos catching on the footrest. Lorelai was tired of playing the grieving widow; it was as though someone had pressed the two vertical lines on a remote, pausing her life indefinitely.

Darla, a bottled blond in her early forties with dark eyebrows painted like the curves of parentheses, was divorced, happily half of the time, begrudgingly the other. The divorce had only been finalized a year and a half ago, yet Darla continued to broadcast her husband's issues in bed and her unfulfilled desires. She used to hang on Caleb, stroking his arms and batting her false eyelashes as Lorelai watched. In fact, Lorelai didn't know with certainty whether or not Darla was one of many women with whom her husband had cheated; Lorelai hoped Caleb had had more restraint, or at the very least, more dignity.

Silence wasn't a situation Darla understood or tolerated. When Lorelai didn't respond to her first comment, she sucked on the olive in her half empty martini before saying, "Love waits for no one, I guess. When he's ready, he takes you."

Lorelai turned to face her friend and arched her eyebrow. "He? Love is usually female, like the earth."

"Yeah, sure. Whatever, Lore."

Lorelai hated when people shortened her name. She wasn't a Lore, a story or tradition or omen passed down orally, and she wasn't a Rory, a doe-eyed young girl. She had never let anyone call her by a nickname as a child, and she wasn't going to start now as a thirty-five-year-old woman.

"Elai," she finished her name for Darla.

Unaware of her mistake, even though Lorelai had corrected her dozens, maybe even hundreds of times, Darla spat, "What?" Her lips glistened with the clear liquid from the martini she had finished slurping.

"My name is Lorelai. Please call me that."

"Fine, Lorelai." Darla emphasized each syllable of the name, making the *e* sound like a frustrated sigh. "The ring is gorgeous. Stunning. Marcus has great taste."

"Don't give anything away, Darla. I'd like for it to be a surprise."

"You're going to say yes?"

Lorelai pursed her lips, a smile beginning to rise in her cheeks.

"Can you even still be surprised after so many proposals?"

Lorelai's jaw tightened, her cheeks dropping. She imagined herself slamming Darla's heavily contoured face into the glossy bar top. She would grab her empty martini glass and break it against the back of Darla's head. With the stem and a little of the glass remaining in her hand, she would take the jagged edge and dig into Darla's skinny neck, like a child frantically searching for treasure at the beach.

She clenched and unclenched her fist, letting it rest against her lap. She opened her mouth to tell Darla off when her phone vibrated. It was sitting in her clutch on the bar, buzzing against the marble surface. Lorelai unzipped the bag and pulled out her iPhone. It was Marcus. She lifted it to her ear and shifted her body away from Darla, her shoulder and part of her back to the woman. "Hi, honey."

"What are you doing?" he said.

"Just grabbing a drink. I'll be home soon."

"With whom?"

Lorelai frowned, smelling gasoline ready to explode. She wasn't in the mood for a blowup. "Darla."

"When will you be done?"

"Soon," she said through clenched teeth.

"I thought you'd want to grab a drink with me after work."

She sighed. "I do. I'll be home soon."

He cursed and hung up.

Lorelai said, "Bye. I love you," before putting the phone back in her clutch. She didn't want to give her friend further ammunition for gossip. Darla didn't need to know that Marcus' unchecked jealousy made Lorelai feel like a possession, a prize he had won. That Lorelai thought Marcus would prefer to keep her behind a sheet of glass like an expensive, breakable doll. His very own untouchable bride. Darla didn't need to know anything other than Marcus was planning to propose and Lorelai was thinking about saying yes.

"Should we get the bill?" Lorelai asked. "I didn't realize the time."

Lorelai Moreau, formerly Knight, Rousseau, and White, married Marcus Dumont on a breezy afternoon in early November in Jackson Square Park just as she imagined. After the ceremony, Marcus officially moved into the townhouse Lorelai had lived with her previous husbands. She had worried it would exacerbate his jealous tendencies, and she hadn't been wrong.

Less than a week into Lorelai and Marcus living in holy matrimony, Marcus brought up redecorating the house. At first, he suggested it during their morning coffee and eggs. He acted as though it had just popped into his brain. "Hey, babe."

She murmured in response, her attention focused on the newspaper.

"What do you think about redecorating our bedroom?"

Lorelai looked up at him, a line forming between her eyebrows. "Excuse me?"

"I know it's your house—"

"Our house."

"Okay, it's our house, but you've lived here for years, so I don't want to propose any changes that would make you uncomfortable."

"Okay…" She raised her eyebrows.

"I was looking around the kitchen and thought, wouldn't it be nice if we did some renovations? Modernized the house." He bit his lip. "Made it ours."

"Does it not seem like ours now, as it is?"

Marcus opened his mouth, then closed it. He sipped his coffee, swallowed and shook his head. "Don't worry about it. We can table it for now."

For now, Lorelai said to herself. She opened her mouth to tell him they were going to talk about it now, but before the words could come out she closed her mouth. Silence filled the space between them. Lorelai's body felt itchy and expansive, as though fiery hives were erupting along her flesh as she sat there with her new husband. She checked her arms—they were clear except for their usual freckles. Marcus didn't need to spell it out for her: she knew this was insecurity taking over. Envy of what once was, of who came before. With how jealous he got about her grabbing coffee or a drink with a girlfriend, it was inevitable he would be envious of her late husbands. This jealousy would come to the surface sooner or later, a nasty ingrown hair that could threaten their marriage.

And his life.

Lorelai could feel it slithering through her gut, along her intestines, her lungs, toward her heart. It was similar to feeling both arousal and terror. Like having goosebumps and hot flashes simultaneously. When it reached her heart, it was as though she were slipping on a new skin.

This sensation, a homicidal parasite, had come before. Each husband would showcase his sin, flaunting it in front of her, and the parasite would come, ready and with an appetite for carnage. Each time Lorelai had welcomed it, until now. Marcus' sin was clear and visible, but was it a deadly one? Could she live with it, overlooking it as so many other women did with much worse offenses? Could he change? Be broken of it like a bad habit? As a child, Lorelai sucked her thumb and ring finger so vehemently her parents thought her digits might become indented and misshapen. So they placed wooden popsicle sticks to both sides and taped them tightly over her fingers. Every time she went to pop them into her mouth, she got the papery, grainy taste of tape and stick. After a month, she stopped sucking on her fingers. Lorelai wondered if she could do something similar with Marcus.

Marcus may have said the issue could be tabled, but Lorelai could see it seething under his tongue and his skin, ravenous to tear at the seams and spill out. A part of her admired his self-control; another was troubled by the impending eruption.

The eruptions didn't take long. They started small like lava foaming, bubbling at the mouth of a stretching volcano that had just woken from a long nap. Lorelai heard him mutter *our house* under his breath in a gurgling growl. His resentment and pain were so clear, yet she tried not to react or call him out.

Then Marcus began pocketing items that belonged to Lorelai's past husbands. A vintage pocket watch, a glass figurine of an alligator, a first edition of *Leaves of Grass*. Lorelai found them shoved in the back of the closet, behind Marcus' suit jackets a week after the items had gone missing. When confronted, Marcus snapped at Lorelai, saying she was crazy. "Why would I move them? They mean nothing to me. Clearly," spit sprayed the air in front of him as he spoke, "they mean plenty to you."

No matter what she said, Lorelai couldn't convince her husband that he was the one she wanted a life with. A few nights after the blow-up about the pocketed items, she surprised him with a new comforter and set of sheets for the master bedroom. To make more of a statement to Marcus, a declaration of her commitment to him, she had shoved the old sheets and comforter in the trash in the courtyard. Marcus couldn't miss it; he had to pass it to come into the house.

Once he was inside, he called for her and she told him to come up to the bedroom. "I have a surprise!"

Lorelai stood in the doorway of their bedroom, in a black lace negligee and matching robe, smiling ear to ear. This would work, she told herself, full of confidence and a touch of pride. This would make her husband feel more at home. This would put an end, or at least a pause, to his jealousy.

Marcus trudged up the narrow stairwell to the third floor, where the master bedroom was. He could have taken the small elevator for an easier and faster trip—Lorelai was always telling him this—but her first husband had put it in; therefore, Marcus refused to use it. Lorelai stuck her neck into the hallway, listening to the thump made by her husband's every step. Thump. Thump. Thump. Lorelai could tell he was taking each stair one foot at a time. Her smile began to shrink, folding in on itself. She didn't want to consider what might happen, what she would do, if this demonstration didn't work.

Vanilla, cherry, and earthy spice wafted up the stairs. Lorelai knew her husband had gotten into the bourbon. She braced herself, her hands flexing and curling into fists. When Marcus finally arrived at the top of the stairs, she forced her face to stretch back into a full grin. His eyes seemed like a stagnant river; instead of fish, squiggly red lines floated around his irises and pupils.

"Hi, baby," she started.

He huffed a greeting and went past her into the bedroom. He flopped face down onto the bed. Lorelai stayed in the doorway; she turned her body to face him, her brow furrowed.

"Marcus?" she said after a minute.

He rolled onto his side and said, "Big surprise, huh?"

"I thought you'd be happy about this. I know it's small, but it's a step toward making this room, this house, feel like ours."

"Yours and mine."

"Yes."

He laughed, a booming, mocking roar that filled the room. He didn't look at her, his eyes trained on the two-toned burgundy baroque pattern on the comforter. "Did you really think a new pair of sheets was going to make me feel okay about sleeping in the same bed you did with your other husbands? The same place you fucked them?"

Her face twitched at the vulgarity spewing from her husband's mouth, his tongue bloated with liquor and insecurity. She cleared her throat. "Like I said, it's small, but it's a start." She took a step toward him, her hands out before her, cautious, as if she were sneaking up on a sleeping bear.

He sprang up then, standing a few feet from her. His body loomed large and threatening. Lorelai's legs trembled but she didn't move away from her husband. His face was set in sharp angles. Marcus shook his head before speaking. "Don't you get it? I won't feel like this is our house until I burn it down and rebuild it." His eyes were wild, bulging from their sockets.

Lorelai's legs gave out and she crumbled to the floor. The negligee rode up to her hips; she left it where it was, allowing the flesh of her thighs and the black silk thong she was wearing to be exposed. The wooden floor was harsh on her sit bones, but she didn't move. She wrapped her arms around her legs and rested her chin on her knees. She eyed her husband with fear and disgust. Marcus took a deep breath, and when he exhaled, it was like watching an evil spirit leave the body of someone it had been possessing, like he was washed clean and everything was back to normal. A happy ending. He frowned, his chin quivering, and took a step closer to his shrunken wife.

Lorelai remained in a ball on the floor and told Marcus to not come any closer. Her eyes were wet and ready to spill over. Snot slid down her lips. She willed herself to get up. Wiped her nose and eyes. She wasn't going to allow herself to become this woman. Lorelai stood and backed toward the doorway, shielding her body in the robe. She swallowed and cleared her throat, her gaze set on the angles and curves of her husband's trembling face.

"This is not acceptable. I don't accept this kind of behavior. This treatment. I am your wife." Her pointer finger struck the air like lightning as she spoke. "You are my husband. My one and only. And if you can't see that, if you can't get over yourself, then maybe I will find myself a new one and only."

Lorelai turned and walked across the hall into the guest bedroom. She slammed the door behind her without looking at him, and with a click, locked it.

⚜

Marcus was addicted to envy, to the inferiority complex he had created and the paranoia that followed on its heel like a loyal dog. Instead of trying to get better, to reel that green-eyed monster in, he seemed to be giving into the obsession, to the delusion. If Lorelai left the house for even a minute to grab the mail or to pick up something from the store, he interrogated her upon her return. *Where were you? Who were you with? Are you lying to me?*

Even when he was at the hotel, he'd call and text, demanding answers to his unending questions. Her answers never seemed to satisfy him; Lorelai started to believe Marcus wanted to catch her in a lie.

Sometimes, however, the charming, sexy Marcus Lorelai had fallen in love with reappeared. Sometimes Lorelai would come downstairs to find a four-course dinner on the table with a bottle of her favorite red wine open and breathing. Sometimes Marcus would surprise her with gifts—jewelry or chocolates or flowers. The usual suspects. The showering made her feel shameful. Guilty, even. It reminded her of a story she'd heard about a young girl whose father was a cop and beat her when he didn't find a missing kid or when he lost a suspect. Then he got a taste for it—the adrenaline, the power, the romance of taking something good and beautiful and destroying it. He started beating her when he found the lost kid and when he didn't, when he caught the bad guy and when he lost him. Lorelai couldn't remember where she heard this, but she did remember asking why the girl had stayed. The storyteller had said, "Eventually, she left. She realized she had to in order to survive. But for a while, she stayed because he always apologized after. He came to her on his knees with fat tears sliding down his shadowed face. He brought gifts—flowers, chocolates, teddy bears like the ones she liked as a little girl. He said it wouldn't happen again, even though it always did. And they both knew it."

"What happened to her after?" Lorelai had asked.

"She was killed by her boyfriend."

The young girl had struck Lorelai as sad and pathetic. Even somewhat responsible for her fate. Lorelai wouldn't allow herself to become one of those weak women who hungered for affection no matter the price. She loved her husband despite his major flaw, but Lorelai wouldn't be limited or ruined by it.

She started dreaming about killing Marcus, a knife puncturing the black stubble and flesh on his neck, then gliding across, unzipping his throat like a suitcase. She could almost smell the acidity as the blood seeped out, dripping down his torso and legs to the white subway tile floor in her studio. She imagined peeling back the skin as far as possible to see his gullet, his vocal chords, and the other purplish muscles inside. Some nights she dreamed of cutting Marcus in other places, slicing into his bicep or calf muscle, opening him up and taking a peek inside. Other nights she saw herself smearing his dripping, warm blood onto her arms, her face, her chest. In these dreams, the blood felt electric on her skin. It seeped into her flesh and began to course through her veins. She felt her body transform, stretch and strengthen, until she was rejuvenated. She stepped toward the gold-rimmed oval mirror on the far end of the room. Just before she got close enough to peek at her metamorphosis, she woke up.

This went on for several weeks before Lorelai decided to turn her dreams into action. Things with Marcus were worsening by the day, quickening like a terminal illness in its last stage, wiping out the vital organs and lifeforce of their romance. She couldn't move or breathe without Marcus interrogating her. They were in a long lasting tug-of-war, and she, exhausted and bruised, no longer cared about victory; she simply wanted the battle to end.

After Marcus had fallen asleep one night Lorelai tiptoed down the stairs to the basement where her studio was. She had decided against using the elevator outside the master bedroom until she had him where she wanted him. Marcus was never allowed to enter this space; she had told him she was horribly shy about her work. He had assured her that he wouldn't judge her art—he added that he wasn't an art dealer like her last husband—he just wanted to see what his beautiful, genius wife was creating all those hours she spent locked away in the dungeon of their house. "It's not a dungeon," she'd said. "It's a sanctuary. A place for privacy. For a break from all of this." She had raised her hands above her head and moved them counterclockwise several times to reference the bustling outside their house and throughout the city.

"Fine," he'd said with the hint of a smile. "I think you are keeping me out to maintain an air of mystery for your new husband."

She had laughed at that remark, knowing on some level he was being serious. "You got me," she said and raised her hands in surrender. "Would you mind giving me an hour or two of sanctuary?" She twisted her face in the way a child does when she is asking her parents for something she knows they don't want to give.

Marcus frowned, but then nodded and said, "Of course. I have to check in with the hotel anyway."

"Great. I'll just be an hour. Two tops. I promise." Then she had taken the brass skeleton key from her pocket, fit it into the lock, and turned it. She slipped inside without opening the door more than a couple inches, so Marcus wouldn't see more than a sliver of white backsplash.

But tonight while Marcus slept upstairs, Lorelai stood cloaked in darkness. She gazed up at the pale blue moonlight filling the floor above her. She felt for the lock, placed the skeleton key inside, and turned it. The door to her studio creaked open as she twisted the doorknob. She put the key into her robe pocket and went inside, pressing the door closed without making a sound. The bright fluorescent lights hummed on as they sensed her motion. She blinked a couple of times to adjust, then walked over to a glass cupboard on the right side of the room.

There were two glass doors framed by a dark oak about four feet tall and wide with two identical key holes. The holes were on the inside of the wooden outline, almost kissing. To open the right side of the cabinet, she produced a small key, no larger than her pinky finger, from the pocket of her robe. It had a forest green ribbon tied at the end. She inserted the tip into the hole and flicked her wrist to the right. The glass door eased open, swinging outward. Inside were dozens of small vials with handwritten labels. Lorelai left the key in the lock and began scanning the bottles.

After looking at a handful, she grabbed one with a blue label. There was faint, smudged evidence of handwriting having been on the label once upon a time. Lorelai didn't need to read the handwriting to know this was the bottle she wanted. She hadn't held it in her hands in over a year, and the weight of the bottle in her palm made her body buzz with heat.

"Hello, old friend."

She dropped it into the pocket of her robe, closed that door to the cabinet and locked it. She then removed the key and fit it into the left door's lock. She twisted it to the right and the door inched open, gliding left. Dozens of syringes and an open leather pouch full of medical equipment filled this side of the cabinet. Her fingers hovered over the syringes before grabbing a three millimeter one. She added it to the pocket with the vial before closing and locking the cupboard. She dropped the key into the other pocket of her robe, pulling the larger one out.

Before exiting the room, she studied it for a minute. The room was covered from floor to ceiling in white subway tiles. It wasn't visible, but the walls were soundproof. To the right, there was the oak cupboard full of syringes, medical equipment, and vials in the glass top. Knives and saws in the lower wooden section. To the left of the room was a plain wooden desk painted white with one long, narrow drawer running the length of it. Before it was a dark cherry chair with no cushion. Propped against both sides of the desk were a series of paintings. Some done with oil, others with watercolor. Most of them were abstract and used a dark palette. In the center of the room was a steel easel with a tripod design. A blank canvas rested on its ledge. Lorelai sighed and opened the door, stepping into the corridor. She shut the door, flooded by shadows, and felt for the lock with the skeleton key. Once in place, she turned it to the left. Then she removed it and put it with the other key in her pocket.

Back upstairs, she stood behind her slumbering husband, the syringe loaded with the contents of the blue-labeled vial in her raised hand. She watched him breathe, his shoulders flexing with each inhalation and exhalation. The parasite had slinked through her body all day, slowly working its way to her heart. Lorelai had felt the pangs of hunger deep in her gut and groin. She wanted to kill her husband, to let her dreams play out. In her studio, the desire had grown, leaving her breathless and panting as she climbed the three flights to the bedroom. Now, as she observed Marcus sleeping, she wavered. The hunger was still there, yet it had become stagnant, no longer brimming over.

This was a new experience for Lorelai; before when she had decided to drug and slice open her husbands, she had done it that same day. There had never been hesitation. Her appetite had never leveled off. She put the syringe back in her pocket and bit her lip. Dammit, she thought.

Lorelai hung the robe in the bathroom and climbed back into bed. A part of her hoped her husband would find it, that maybe if Marcus found the syringe it would propel her into action. She lay on her back, her head turned toward her husband. She loved him, but she didn't know if she could live with his sin. This wasn't how she imagined her life, being married to a man she loved but couldn't stand. She replayed all the damning moments of their relationship—the paranoia, the deception, the raging jealousy. Lorelai believed Marcus deserved to die, just as her previous husbands had. Yet something in her wouldn't allow it. At least not yet. She tried to shut her mind off, and with it the hunger churning quietly in her gut and in between her legs.

When that proved impossible, Lorelai sighed loudly. She waited to see if her husband would stir. He didn't. A grin spread across her face. She knew how to satiate the hunger. Lorelai slipped out of bed and into her closet.

Several minutes later she came out in a black fitted dress with a deep v in the front and back. She adjusted her push-up bra to maximize the fullness of her cleavage. In one hand she held a pair of black strappy stilettos; she would put them on when she got downstairs. In the other a black clutch. Before heading out, she went to the bathroom and fluffed her tousled bedhead. She slid creamy red lipstick on and a hint of black mascara. Grabbing the syringe and the two keys from her robe, she slipped them into her clutch.

It didn't take long to find one.

Lorelai milked her drink, taking tiny sips every ten minutes or so as she surveyed the bar. Her purse rested beside her glass. Several men approached her, wearing their sleaziness on the sleeves of their suit jackets. Sleaze was what she was after, but not just any brand. The one she would choose had to parade a specific flaw. Twenty minutes later she found her guy. His name was Raymond; he insisted Lorelai called him Good Time Ray. He called her Lori, which she didn't even bother to correct. He had a very specific purpose, and she didn't want to waste any time.

Good Time Ray was a venture capitalist originally from New York City—a downtrodden part of Queens. Lorelai guessed he was in his mid-fifties. He was aggressively overweight, so much so he waddled as he walked over to the bar to greet her. He was on the shorter side—no more than five-six. His round, red face was clean shaven and his gray hair was slicked back. Colonies of sweat clustered around his ears, nostrils, and hairline. He wore a Ralph Lauren salmon t-shirt that made his face appear even more crimson, khaki shorts, and tan loafers. When he talked, his tongue hung from his mouth like an overheated dog. He did most of the talking. Good Time Ray told Lorelai he'd been living part time in New Orleans "going on" three years.

"I came down for some business, saw that it was a never-ending party here, and didn't want to leave. So I didn't."

"Fascinating," Lorelai chimed in. She gave him just enough to appear interested and to keep him talking. She was pretty sure what his vice was, but she needed to be certain before she acted. She was nothing if not disciplined when it came to her very specific cause.

Lorelai sipped her wine in a disinterested fashion. Good Time Ray didn't seem to notice. He was too busy sucking down every kind of drink imaginable. He had a beer when he first came over to Lorelai. Then an old fashioned, a dirty martini, and now a Hurricane, a New Orleans rum concoction sure to intoxicate. He was also scarfing down food—shrimp cocktail, then two dozen oysters—Lorelai watched with disgust as he sucked on the slippery mollusks, making a slurping sound after each one before licking his glistening lips.

In spite of his gross consumption of everything in sight, Lorelai listened with interest to his life story—how he had come from nothing and rose to the big leagues. How he wanted for everything as a child and now insisted on wanting for nothing. If he desired something, he got it. That was his motto.

And it was that very motto that sealed his fate.

She didn't even have to convince him to come home with her. She knew the moment he waddled over that he wanted her. All Lorelai had to say was, "Let's go to my place," and Good Time Ray said, "Hell, yes." He paid his tab—$150.00—and put a twenty down for Lorelai's unfinished glass of wine. "Keep the change," he said to the bartender. Lorelai grabbed her purse and followed him out of the bar.

It was nearly 3 AM when they arrived at Lorelai's townhouse. In the courtyard, she told Good Time Ray she had family staying with her and that they had to be quiet. He swayed with inebriation, giggled, and put his pointer finger to his lips.

"Don't worry, I'll be quiet," he said, nearly shouting.

She forced a smile onto her face, as though he were endearing, and said, "Shh."

Unlocking the front door, the shadowy foyer filled with light from the courtyard's lanterns, creating a spotlight on the black elevator door. She took the key out of the lock and placed it back into her clutch beside the needle. She closed the door behind them and the room went black.

"This way," she said in a whisper, and grabbed his arm with her free hand, leading him toward the elevator.

"Where are we going?" he asked once the door had closed and the elevator vibrated as it descended. "Is it a surprise? I like surprises."

"You have no idea," she replied.

The door opened to the corridor outside Lorelai's studio. "This way," she said and walked toward the door. Good Time Ray lumbered after her. She fished inside her purse, this time for the skeleton key. She had it in the lock as the elevator doors shut and darkness enveloped them.

"What's down here?" he said, excitement in his voice. "Some kind of play room?"

"You could say that."

Lorelai flipped on a switch to the left of her; a black steel lantern illuminated the door before them. She turned the key in the lock. The door creaked open. Taking the key out, she put it back inside her clutch. Her hand remained there, gripping the syringe. "After you," she said.

Lorelai stepped aside to let Good Time Ray enter ahead of her. She couldn't wait any longer, the sensation was snaking its way through her veins, her flesh ignited in hunger. As soon as he was past the threshold, she pulled the needle from her bag and stabbed her new acquaintance in the left side of his neck.

"What the—" He craned his meaty neck to look at her.

She grinned and shoved him into the room. As soon as his head entered the space, the fluorescent lights flickered on, displaying his demise. He toppled with a smack that echoed off of the subway tile. His face was smashed into the floor, and like dough being kneaded, his cheek rose from the impact. Lorelai closed the door as swiftly and soundlessly as possible. She took out the skeleton key and fit it into the lock. She was about to turn it, locking them in, when Good Time Ray moaned.

The fat bastard wasn't completely knocked out.

"Shit."

She opened her clutch, searching for the blue-labeled vial, but it wasn't there. It was the one thing she hadn't packed for her nightly prowl. And now it might be her undoing.

"Fuck it."

Lorelai rushed Good Time Ray, her stilettos click-clacking, and kicked him in the head, hoping to knock him out. He went still for a few moments, but then started to groan again. She looked around, unsure of what to do next. Her eyes landed on the cupboard. She hurried to it, yanking the small key from her bag by the green ribbon. Her hands shook as she tried to get the key into the lock and open the cabinet full of vials. There had to be something in there to knock him unconscious.

Once open, Lorelai bit her lip, cursing herself, as she scanned the vials. She grabbed one that read *phenobarbital* in cursive letters. Unlike the blue-labeled bottle, this writing was clear, as though it had recently been labeled or hardly ever used. In fact, Lorelai hadn't used it before. She'd never needed to. She unscrewed the lid and dipped the needle into the clear liquid. She went to pull back on the plunger and her fingers slipped. She tried again to grip the end of the needle.

"Get it together," she told herself. She clenched the plastic plunger between her thumb and middle finger and pulled until the drug filled the entire syringe.

The bottle in one hand, the needle in the other, she turned and ran over to Good Time Ray, who was struggling to get up, her heels clattering on the tile. He tried to prop himself up with his hands, but the left one kept crumbling under him like putty. Lorelai jammed the needle into the right side of Good Time Ray's neck before he could get control of his left hand. He melted to the ground, face down once again.

Lorelai sighed. "Okay. Okay. You got this."

For safe measure, she reloaded the syringe and emptied it into his neck. She let the syringe, bottle, and clutch fall to the ground. Lorelai would clean up later. Then she kicked him in the head three times, the circular bottom of her stiletto leaving an impression on his right temple. She didn't want any more surprises.

The hungry parasite tingled inside her gut and groin. Adrenaline coursed through her veins; Lorelai thought she could see it swimming along her arms, like fish in a river. She was ready to satiate the desire, to purify the world of this gluttonous pig of a man. Balancing on one foot at a time, she peeled off her stilettos and tossed them at the door. Barefoot now, she moved to the cupboard without making a sound. The subway tile was cool on the clammy pads of her feet.

Lorelai walked to the left side of the cupboard and reached into the crevice between the back of the piece of furniture and the wall. She felt the key with her middle finger and hooked it through the bow. She slid her arm out. The key was even smaller than the green-ribbon one, about half of the size. Lorelai went around to the front of the cupboard. She sat on the floor in front of the lower half, which consisted of two large oak doors shut with a silver padlock. She fit the key into its opening and twisted clockwise until the lock popped. The wooden doors opened with offbeat vibrations, like two cymbals sounding at once. The doors themselves even wavered as they went right and left. Two shelves ran the length of the interior. Lorelai's weapons sat organized like plates and bowls in a kitchen cabinet. Her hand skimmed the air above the weapons on both shelves. She picked up a butcher knife and held it up; the fluorescent lights gleamed off the long, serrated edge.

Lorelai left the door open, the weapons exposed, and walked over to Good Time Ray. Standing over his unconscious body, she nudged him with her bare foot. He didn't stir. His bulk shifted on the floor, creating a whooshing sound. She bent down, the butcher knife in one hand, and lifted his right arm with the other. She pressed the silver blade to his flesh and began to go back and forth. Leaned into the blade, putting her weight behind her. The skin on his arm opened, resembling the jagged, bloody mouth of an alligator after a meal. She let the blood run down his arm and onto the floor.

She wanted to try the butcher knife on his gut next, but she couldn't manage to flip Good Time Ray. His body was stiff and heavy, corpselike, even though he was still breathing. She tried without success for several minutes.

Lorelai wasn't sure how long the phenobarbital would keep him unconscious. "Screw it." She examined the knife and then Good Time Ray, her eyes shifting from the weapon to her victim, back and forth. She decided the butcher knife wasn't going to be the best tool, so she took it back to the cabinet and pulled out an 18-volt cordless reciprocating saw. She cupped her right hand around the handle and pulled back with her pointer finger and thumb. The saw roared to life, vibrating in her hand with a loud buzz. This would do the trick.

Lorelai released the trigger to turn off the saw and went back to where Good Time Ray lay. She hiked up her dress and knelt down, angling the jagged edge above the back of his neck. Before it met his flesh, she looked around the room and thought about her purpose. Good Time Ray was about to be the first man she had killed that wasn't her husband. Lorelai had expected it to be more difficult to take the life of a stranger. Yet something about it seemed easier, as though the parasite could flow through her body with more ease, not weighed down by the silly violin strings of love, plucking at the soft and gushy parts of her core, or the tricky endeavor of murdering and getting rid of her husbands without causing suspicion or getting caught.

Good Time Ray had no public connection to Lorelai; she would never be suspected. She hadn't used her real name when she introduced herself and he had paid for her drink. If someone happened to see her with the man and accurately describe her to the police, she knew Marcus, her overprotective, obsessive husband, would say under oath that she had been home all night, even if his insecurities didn't believe it. She was his, and he wasn't going to let her go anywhere without him. Not even prison.

She grinned. Maybe Good Time Ray had shown her a good time after all. This could be her future. Maybe he had shown her the way to rid the world of these terrible and hungry men without having to kill those closest to her. Maybe she could even cure Marcus of his all-consuming jealousy. Lorelai felt warmth radiating in her chest. She imagined the sun rising over a new day, the deserted streets of New Orleans bathed in glowing white, the luminescence stretching to her door. For the first time in a long time, she felt hopeful. Maybe she could have it all—a purpose and a living husband. She tugged on the saw; once again it howled to life, blocking out all other noise. She brought her left hand to steady her right and lowered the blade into Good Time Ray's neck. Blood sprayed through the air like a sprinkler, speckling her face, dress, legs, and the tile floor in crimson. She turned off the saw for a moment, and holding the tool in her right hand, she lifted her left arm to wipe her face. When Lorelai opened her eyes, Marcus stood in the doorway in his boxers, his eyes filled with horror and his jaw agape.

"Hi, baby," she started.

Penumbra

Blood dripped down his chin. Caleb imagined it collecting on the white tile floor of his wife's studio, a small crimson pond. She would detest the mess in her pristine sanctuary, a place he had been forbidden to enter, or at least he thought she would. He wasn't sure of anything anymore. Somewhere in the room, his killer exhaled. Caleb's vision was nothing more than fog with twinkling stars. He could feel the beats of his heart decreasing, slowing to a soft pitter-patter.

Two faces materialized. Both male. One was round and freckled, with ridges along his forehead, eyes, and mouth. It was obvious from the lines he had lived life to the fullest, and the skin covering his face was used to wearing a grin. The other face was long with a tan complexion. A perfectly manicured goatee hung a few inches past his chin, peppered with middle age. Caleb squinted, trying to see them better. Somehow he knew them. Somehow they were familiar.

Thin breaths escaped in huffs from his mouth. His spine stabbed the tiled wall; the sharp, ice cold surface stabbed back. This wasn't how Caleb had imagined dying. The faces of the men disappeared, shadows in their place. He stared forward, unable to see anything with clarity, and waited for death.

Lilly's head rocked against the cracked concrete, a heaviness blooming at the back of her skull. She rolled off of her side, pressing her hands to the ground. Weeds and pebbles tickled the lines on her olive palms. Her eyes fluttered open, revealing tawny, reptilian irises. Her eyebrows formed one long, thick line that curved at the edges. She blinked as she looked around, the morning sun bright in her eyes. She was in front of a boxy mausoleum with a triangular top. Exposed clay-colored brick encased the front, as well as the sides, where the stone had worn away. Around her were dozens of aboveground tombs like this. Some had crosses carved into their surface, others *X*'s, most with common Creole names. Dupart. Glapion. Mercier. Trudeau. Valdez. She sighed. She had awoken in the cemetery again.

The sleepwalking had started on Lilly's twenty-first birthday. At first, she wondered if it had to do with sleep deprivation or her increased alcohol consumption. She didn't know any other college students experiencing anything like this though and it had become difficult to convince Taylor, her roommate, that she was up studying late or had slept at Jake's again. All Taylor had to do was ask Jake, and he'd tell her Lilly hadn't stayed over in months. In fact, since her birthday Lilly had been ignoring his calls and texts.

She wasn't concerned with Jake though; something was happening to her and it was bigger than her on-again, off-again college boyfriend. The only thing that made her feel less crazy these days was believing her subconscious was trying to work through something and Honey Grove Cemetery was at the center of it.

Lilly pressed herself onto all fours and then up to standing, resembling an accordion lengthening, stretching its bellows. She ran her fingers through her dark chocolate hair, pulling pebbles and blades of brown grass free. She fluffed the ends; they settled at her collarbone in loose waves.

As always, she woke barefoot and in her pajamas. From the layer of black coating the bottom of her feet, she must have walked here. So far all of this was ordinary, even expected. Lilly had given up on screaming or panicking when she woke here weeks ago. Instead, she researched sleepwalking and dream analysis in search of answers. Though, of course, she never remembered her dreams; it had always been that way.

Lilly headed to the section in the back of the cemetery where the iron gate was bent. This was how she squeezed in and out undetected; Honey Grove Cemetery, a city for the dead just minutes from Honey Island Swamp, an area teeming with lush plants and wildlife thirty-five miles outside of the French Quarter, didn't officially open until 9 AM. If everything was as it usually was, it would be about a quarter to eight. For whatever reason, the one thing Lilly never managed to bring was her cellphone. She weaved through the cluttered aboveground tombs made of stone and brick, bidding good morning to the deceased whose names she'd learned from passing their graves the last few months. "Hello, Monsieur Arnaud."

Sometimes she heard a bird chip or a distant bell in response. Otherwise, there was only silence and the soft crunching of her footsteps on the broken gravel. This morning, however, she heard something else.

"Good morning, Lilly."

Lilly jumped at the sound of a human voice. She looked around, her hair whipping her shoulders. A woman appeared from behind a white crypt surrounded by a low, rusted iron gate. She had a blunt bob dyed dark gray that resembled flappers' haircuts in the 1920s and choppy bangs high on her forehead. At its longest, her hair grazed her cheeks, which were both at once angled and full. Under a pair of thin, painted gray eyebrows her eyes were green. The woman wore a high-waisted black floral skirt that skimmed the bottom of her calves, a black scoop neck t-shirt, and black gladiator sandals. Mouth closed, cheeks lifted, she smiled at Lilly as Lilly studied her. The woman seemed to be waiting for Lilly to speak.

"Do I know you?" Lilly finally said.

"Not quite," the woman replied.

Lilly shook her head and folded her arms in front of her as a shield. "How do you know my name?"

The woman nodded, her face smooth of worry. "Let me put it to you this way. I know why you keep waking up here because it's a part of my destiny, too."

"What the hell are you talking about? How did you find me? Did Jake send you?" She rubbed her temples, then scoffed. "This is some prank."

The woman took a step toward Lilly. Lilly stood her ground, her arms still crossed in front of her. "I assure you it isn't," the woman said.

"Why should I believe you?"

"I'm going to tell you a few things—intimate, private things—that I know about you, and if I'm right, you'll know that I know you. That we are," her hands went out, palms open, "connected."

"Okay," Lilly's voice wavered. "Go ahead."

"Your earliest memories are of finding dead and dying creatures—bugs, birds, stray cats, and rodents. You were what? Four. Perhaps it's not accurate to say that you found them but that they found you. There was that one tabby cat with a limp that followed you the ten blocks to school. It waited outside of the schoolyard under the shade of a tree for you all day. And then it followed you home and died at the foot of the stairs to your house." The woman sighed. "There's always been something about you and death."

Lilly's hands gripped the soft flesh of her arms, trembling. Her eyes were wet. How could this woman know any of that? She swallowed. "I thought if I could have just gotten that cat into the house I could have saved him." Her forehead wrinkled. Tears streamed down her tan face. "I tried to save so many. Spiders, butterflies, baby birds, raccoons, cats. It's like they needed to find me before they could die. And I watched all of them go. Have you ever seen a naked, pink baby bird wheezing, gulping for its first and final breaths? Do you know how many times I went to get something to pick it up with and when I got back someone had stepped on the bird, its guts spattered on the pavement?"

"It happened four times before you learned how heedless people could be."

Her forehead still folded, Lilly nodded. The woman was right. Lilly started carrying a plastic bag with her after that. She was seven at the time. "How do you know all of this? I never said anything after—"

"After your mom told you to stop making up stories for attention."

Lilly's lips parted to speak but nothing came out.

"I know all of this because I've been there with you. I was there when the tabby cat died and when you started to bring plastic bags with you and when you tried to tell your mom about an alligator that followed you when you were at the house off of Honey Island Swamp." Her pale face cracked into a smile. "I have to give it to your mom on that one. It sounded a little far-fetched." The smile vanished from her face, a steely look in its place. "Yet you were telling the truth. I saw the alligator follow you out of the water and waddle toward the picnic table. I watched it die, its large yellow eyes wide open even after it had stopped breathing."

Lilly swallowed. She remembered that. The large beast's jaw had shut like a nutcracker's when someone cranks the wooden lever down, yet its eyes remained open, observing the young girl. It reminded her of King Kong dying at the end of the original film, the stop-motion animated ape saying goodbye to his beloved Ann before tumbling from the Empire State Building to the pavement below. Lilly remembered staying up late to watch the black and white movie, promising her mother she wasn't scared. Night terrors of looming planes firing at an innocent creature plagued her for weeks.

Lilly didn't know what to make of the woman before her and all that she said. All that she knew. How could she know these things unless she had actually been there? Lilly frowned. This brought another question to mind. "If what you're saying is true and we're connected, why didn't you talk to me sooner? Why didn't you try to help me?"

In a nonchalant tone, the woman replied, "It wasn't time."

"Time for what?"

She smiled. "Let me ask you a question. Did you wake up in Honey Grove Cemetery before your twenty-first birthday?" Lilly said no. The woman nodded. "See? It wasn't time."

Lilly scoffed at that response. She crossed her arms. "Look, lady, for months I've been waking up in this cemetery. I have so many kinks in my neck and shoulders I think I might end up with a hunchback. I haven't had any coffee yet today, I don't know where my shoes are, and here you are talking in riddles. Some lady whose name I don't even know who seemingly knows everything about me. So, if you're here to kill me and steal my identity, go ahead, or let me go."

The woman's painted eyebrows lifted, an amused expression on her face. "My name is Deanna. I can suggest a great masseuse on Chartres. There's a good little coffee shop not far from here, though we may want to go get your shoes before heading there. They're in your apartment by the way. Where you always leave them. Same with your phone." She clasped her hands together in front of her chest. "Like I said, we're connected. I'm always there in the shadows or among a crowd, hidden in plain sight, watching over you. It is my destiny to be your companion and to guide you through the plane between the living and the dead."

Lilly's hands gripped her hips. "Okay, now I know you're crazy. And so am I for listening to you this whole time. I have to go. I have class. The plane between the living and the dead will have to wait."

She turned away from Deanna and walked to the opening in the gate. Lilly half expected the woman to call after her, but Deanna didn't.

Lilly kept going, ignoring the heat emanating from her face and ears and the moisture gathering in the corners of her eyes.

Hands outstretched before him, Caleb stumbled through the shadows of the plane he had been wandering since death had come for him. He narrowed his eyes in an attempt to see past the pervasive fog. He mumbled, careful to keep his voice down. Something about this place felt dangerous; it rippled through his skin in the form of goosebumps and a hot whisper on the back of his neck. His words were clumsy half-sentences and phrases, but he didn't stop. He couldn't. Caleb could feel his memories slipping away. Brown hair, rich in color and shine. To her shoulders. Green eyes. Light, with a yellow tint. Lips that were neither thin nor full. The perfect combination. Square bone-white teeth that looked filed, and ready to bite, ripping into flesh. Don't forget, he told himself. Don't forget what she did. Cold blade to throat. Pressure, then a gust of air. A spilling. Darkness. The men. Darkness again.

Deanna sat cross legged on the concrete in front of Lilly. She wore black jeans and a dark denim button down. Her hair was pulled into two coin-size buns on the top of her head, loose hairs sticking out and beginning to frizz from the morning humidity. Lilly pressed her hands to her face, wishing this was a dream.

"Good morning, Lilly," Deanna said.

Lilly groaned in response.

"It's nice to see you, too. I come bearing gifts."

Lilly kept her hands over her face. "No, thank you."

"You sure? I brought coffee and shoes."

Lilly peeked through her fingers. She removed her hands from her face and propped herself up to sit. "What'd you get?"

"Iced coffee with coconut milk."

Lilly's favorite. She put her hand out and Deanna passed it to her. "And the shoes? Tell me you're not only a stalker but a burglar too."

Deanna smiled and lifted a pair of flip flops from the ground beside her. "I popped into a tourist shop on the way and bought them. Size eight."

Lilly sipped her coffee, already feeling more awake. She reached for the flip flops, and after Deanna gave them to her, immediately slipped them on. "Thanks."

"You're welcome. Just so you know, I've never been inside your apartment. Believe it or not, there are boundaries to this whole companion thing."

Lilly nodded, studying Deanna. The woman's eyes were bright and she had a soft glow surrounding her. There was something inhuman about Deanna, something magical. "What about you? Did you get coffee?"

Deanna shook her head. "I don't drink caffeine. Ministers don't need sleep or energy boosts the way humans do."

"Ministers?"

Deanna nodded. "Yes. A Frieda's companion."

"And a Frieda is?"

"You, Lilly. A Frieda's job is to help the newly dead reach a place of rest."

Lilly's forehead wrinkled. She sucked down more coffee before standing. She began to pace. "You're saying my destiny, my job, is to help dead people crossover." Deanna gazed up at Lilly as she spoke. The woman nodded. "And your destiny is to help me do this?"

Deanna stood in one swift, graceful motion. "My destiny is to watch over you and guide you through Penumbra, the plane between—"

"The living and the dead. You said that yesterday." Lilly stopped pacing. "Tell me, why do I need help if this is *my* destiny?"

"Because you're mortal."

"And you are...?"

Deanna shrugged, a closed mouthed smile blooming, further illuminating her. "I am somewhere in-between."

"What the hell does that mean?"

"I came to be when you were born. This is how it's always been. When a new Frieda is born, a new Minister comes to be. And when a Frieda dies, her Minister's task is complete and so she ceases to be."

"So you're not immortal?"

"No."

"But you're not human?"

Deanna shook her head no.

"You're," Lilly paused, eyeing up the woman before her, "in-between."

"I am."

"What about me? I'm human, aren't I?"

"You are. A human with a special purpose."

Lilly nodded even though she still wasn't sure what this all meant. She continued to pace. "And because you're not quite human, but not immortal, you can guide me through Pen-whatever?"

"Penumbra. That's right. Since you are human, your body and soul are not meant to be in the plane between the living and the dead for an extended period of time. Each time you venture there to guide a person to their resting place, your soul becomes further attached to the plane. The more times you go, the higher your risk of being stuck there permanently."

"In limbo."

"Yes."

"That seems to be a pretty big flaw in this plan, don't you think?"

Deanna answered her question without hesitation. "A human must help other humans find rest. I may be on this plane the same length of time as you are, but I was not born and I do not die. Think of me as a piece of clay molded into a woman; just because I look like a human, doesn't mean I can relate to the mortal experience. And since I am not human, I cannot become stuck in Penumbra. There is no resting place for a Minister. We simply fulfill our destiny and stop being. So, you see, Lilly, it is the perfect plan."

"The more you talk, the crazier this all seems." Lilly finished what was left of her iced coffee. "If I need you so that I don't get stuck in limbo, why are you just coming here now? Haven't I been in danger for months?"

Her face somber, Deanna nodded. "I cannot come until I am called for."

"Who called for you?"

"You did."

"Me?" Lilly waved the empty plastic cup around. "I did not. I didn't even know you existed before yesterday. Or that I was a Frieda." The word felt awkward and heavy in her mouth.

Deanna pressed her palms together in front of her. "Being a Frieda is your destiny. No one had to teach you how to bring the recently dead to peace. You've been doing it on your own for months. However, you've been struggling to get back to the plane of the living and that is why you called me. A Minister is a companion for her Frieda, however, only if she seeks her." Lilly asked how she knew to summon Deanna. "There is a shapeshifter, a siren, who exists on all three planes."

Lilly crossed her arms in front of her. "How is that possible?"

"Isabelle was once a human woman like you. The world was cruel to her, or rather, the men of it were. She had a cop father who beat her and then a gangster boyfriend who liked to play with the line between life and death. Murderer and savior. The game eventually killed her. But before that happened she wound up in Penumbra. Many times, in fact."

Lilly couldn't believe what she was hearing. "What happened?"

"That many trips to Penumbra fractures the soul. When Isabelle died, her soul was gone, but her rage was thriving. It transformed her into something else."

"Something undead." Lilly's eyes widened. "I can't believe this stuff is real."

Deanna nodded.

"Does she just hate the world now? Everyone and anything in it?"

Deanna shook her head. "No, her rage has bounds."

Lilly raised her eyebrow, waiting for Deanna to continue.

"Men who don't respect women."

"What does she do to them?"

"She eats them."

Lilly stopped pacing. "What the fuck."

Deanna shrugged. "It's a part of her destiny. And Isabelle has a strict moral code."

Lilly scoffed. "I'm sure she does." Soft lines by her mouth and eyes deepened. "I think I've heard enough about this monster mermaid lady and her man-diet. What does she have to do with me? Why would she tell me to call you?"

"She is empathetic to women in trouble and would never wish her fate upon another."

"You're telling me she's not happy being a man-eating sorceress. C'mon. It sounds like every angry feminist's dream."

Deanna's lip twitched before she replied, "Let's just say Isabelle has adjusted to it."

Lilly tongued her upper lip, the gears in her brain cranking, trying to make sense of this puzzle of information. "So I have to help all of the men she murders crossover."

"Not necessarily. You'll understand better tonight."

At 10:57 PM, Lilly's eyelids grew heavy. Once closed, she had the sensation of being scratched or tickled by someone who hadn't cut his fingernails recently. Whatever was scraping against her skin was uneven, sharp in some places, rounded in others. Her arms and ankles were itchy and chaffed from it. She swatted with her hands and it crunched in her palms. Her eyes flickered open to find gray blades of grass clutched in her fists.

Sprawled on her side; she pressed herself up to a seated position. Her polka dot nightgown slid up her thighs. She tugged at the end until it was stretched as far as it would go just above her knees. Lilly looked around. There was a body of water roughly two feet in front of her. She couldn't tell if it was a lake or pond or swamp; there was a fine gray mist hovering just above the surface. It was impossible to see the water below, but she could hear something gliding smoothly through it and smell its heat and moisture, along with something else. A sour, rotten stench. She leaned forward, her hands finding the grass before her. Her legs untangled and she pushed onto her knees. On all fours now, Lilly rocked toward the water, her nostrils just above the water's edge. The odor was heavier here. She inhaled the smell, trying to place it. It seemed familiar, and that familiarity was frightening.

"I wouldn't get any closer if I were you," Deanna said.

Still on all fours, Lilly craned her neck to glance back at her Minister. Deanna appeared more ghost-like than corporeal. The grooves and roundness of her face were filtered in shadows. Her golden eyes shined like distant train lights at night. The rest of her was washed in gray. With her eyes like this, she certainly seemed to be something in between human and other. "What is it?" Lilly said.

"The putrid corpses of those who weren't put to rest."

Lilly scurried away from the water and turned to face Deanna. She stood, her face twisted in disgust. "How long have they been here?"

Deanna's shadowy form rose in a shrug. "Some have been here for hundreds of years. Others, much shorter than that."

"Why didn't they crossover?"

Deanna stepped closer to Lilly until she became solid in form. She wore a long dark dress with bell sleeves and her hair was down, the ends curling by her cheekbones. Her eye makeup was dark, as were her lips. Lilly thought Deanna resembled a witch.

"Because they were damned to this plane for their actions in the living world," Deanna said. "They will never stop rotting. Never pass on."

"That's awful."

"Yes."

"This is what you meant about the siren's victims," Lilly said. "If their souls were stained in the living world, they don't get to crossover."

"Yes." Deanna cleared her throat. "We should get going. We only have until the living world begins to awaken."

Earlier that day, Deanna had explained to Lilly that a Frieda only worked during the hours she slept. Once asleep, Lilly's body left the plane of the living and entered Penumbra. Then she had until dawn to help as many people find their final resting place as possible. Those she was unable to assist would have to wait until the following night or the one after that. Lilly thought this was atrocious. "So, they're stuck here until I can get to them. How will there ever be enough time to get to all of them?"

"You do your best," Deanna had said.

"Let's go," Lilly said. She was about to ask Deanna for guidance on what direction to head in when she found her feet already walking her along the water's edge. She saw a large gray form emerge from it and drag itself onto the grass before her. Up close, she saw a long, thick body with four stout stumps, and a long pointed tail. It was covered in what looked like armor—an alligator.

"Deanna," she said, her voice shrill and panicked.

Deanna stepped beside her. "Hello," she said to the scaly beast as though this were a totally normal interaction. "Have you two been properly introduced yet?"

Lilly looked at Deanna, her jaw open. Deanna glanced at her before turning her attention back to the alligator. The reptile shook its head. "Okay, then. This is Lillith, the new Frieda. She goes by Lilly. I am Deanna, her Minister." She grinned, proud of her title, her teeth gleaming in the twilight. "And you are?"

The alligator's jaw opened, cavernous as Penumbra. "Truman," he said. His voice husky and human-like.

Lilly stared at him, unable to form words. Deanna glanced at Lilly before telling Truman, "I guess this is her first time meeting anyone down here besides the recently deceased. Give her a minute. She'll warm up."

Truman the alligator nodded his gigantic head. "It always takes some getting used to. I'll see you later. It was nice meeting you, Lillith." He started past them.

Lilly watched his tail flick side to side until he disappeared into the mist. "Animals can talk here," she said once he was gone.

"They can."

"And they don't try to kill me? Us?"

Deanna shook her head. "They have no interest in human flesh or violence. They need only to exist to receive nourishment. You see, they feed on memories. Those of the recently deceased, those trapped here, and Friedas. They are the reason you won't remember this when you wake up."

"And I'm supposed to be okay with that? With my memories of this plane being gator food."

"And raccoons, snakes, rodents, turtles. All swamp creatures, really." Deanna sighed. "You have to be okay with it. For it is the design, and there is no changing it."

"Yeah, yeah. Destiny. Design. I get it."

Lilly started walking, letting her feet be her guide. Deanna kept pace with her. A jumble of words flowed from the Minister's lips. To Lilly it sounded like gibberish. Within seconds, however, she understood their purpose. Two torches appeared in the Minister's hands, the tip of them aglow with flames the same shade as Deanna's eyes.

"Handy trick," Lilly said.

Deanna kept her focus forward as though she could see something up ahead despite the thick fog. "A necessary tool for a Minister to guide her Frieda."

"What were those words you said?"

"An incantation to call forth my torches. They only exist when I'm in Penumbra."

Lilly nodded, too stunned to question this. Her ears perked up. She heard something just beyond the fog. A gentle rocking. Her feet moved with determination, each step of her bare skin crunching the dirt earth. Lilly noticed that Deanna's feet made no noise. It was as though they weren't even touching the ground, but Lilly didn't bother to inquire about that either. She had a job to do and asking Deanna every question that popped into her head would only serve as a distraction.

Her feet stopped. After a few seconds the thick fog began to clear, revealing a dock with a small motorless boat tethered to it. An oar rested against each side of it. Lilly had been here before. The mist, the boat, the dock. It was all familiar. "I know this place," she said.

"Yes." Deanna stood beside Lilly, her arms stretched parallel to the ground, torches blazing.

"This is where they meet me."

"Yes. One is approaching now."

Lilly wondered if the torches served as another set of eyes for the Minister, allowing her to see ahead in time.

Out of the shadows came a young boy. He had a bowl cut, freckled cheeks, and dark eyes. As soon as she saw him, Lilly knew everything about the boy. His name was Evan. He was eight years old and in third grade. He lived in the Bywater District with his mom and dad and pet gerbil, Harry. He had been riding his bike when he died. Hit by a tourist unaccustomed to the heavy bike traffic in New Orleans and in a rush to get to the French Quarter.

Lilly walked forward and kneeled before Evan. She offered her palms to him. He brought his hands just above hers, hovering so their flesh didn't touch. "My name is Lilly." She smiled at him. "Do you want to go on a boat ride?"

The boy looked around the shadowy swamp land. His eyes lingered on Deanna and her torches. "She's a friend," Lilly said, gauging his hesitation and fear. "Her name is Deanna. She is going to help us get to a safer, happier place. We just need to go on this boat over here and I promise you'll feel much better."

Evan let his palms rest on Lilly's. He asked where his parents were. "They're at home." And Harry? "He's at home, too." He then asked where he was. "You're in a place between home and Heaven."

"You'll take me to Heaven?"

Lilly nodded. She didn't know how it was possible, but just as she had known his name and how he had died, she could sense his faith.

"Will Grandpa be there?"

"There's only one way to find out," she said.

She squeezed Evan's hand gently, testing his trust. He squeezed back. "Are you ready to go, Evan?"

He nodded and together they walked to the boat. Deanna followed, her torches glowing on their backs.

"They're gone," Caleb said, forgetting to keep his voice low. He blinked back the tears in his eyes.

"Trust me, they're in a better place," a raspy voice answered.

Caleb's breath caught in his throat. "Who's there?"

"The name's Truman." A deep chuckle bloomed in the shadows ahead of Caleb. "We haven't been formally introduced, but I know you real well."

Caleb took a step back, trying to decide if he should flee. What good would that do though? He couldn't see more than a foot in front of him in any direction. He balled his hands into fists, and raised them, prepared to fight.

The laughter grew louder, its owner getting closer.

"Down here," the voice said.

Fists still raised, Caleb looked down. He jumped at the sight of the creature. It was a massive alligator.

"Hiya," the alligator said.

Caleb swore the lips—if you could call them that—of the alligator had parted, sound coming out. Was he losing his mind in this place?

As if hearing his thoughts, Truman, the alligator, replied, "No, you're not crazy. And, yes, I can talk. All the animals here can."

"What the—" Caleb took a step away from the reptilian beast.

"What can I say? Penumbra doesn't work the same way as other planes."

Caleb stammered questions about Penumbra and whatTruman meant when he said he knew Caleb well. Sweat pooled in his armpits, beads dripping down his biceps.

"Think of this place as limbo, a space between the living and the dead."

"But I'm dead. Aren't I?" The lines between his eyebrows flexed.

"Oh, you're dead. Have been for a month or two now." Truman's pupils dilated as he studied Caleb. Caleb swallowed. "Do you remember how you got here?"

Brown hair. Shoulder length. Green...green what? Eyes? Faces. Darkness. Caleb's forehead wrinkled as he tried to recall the memory of his death. "What color are my eyes?" he asked Truman.

"Everything here is gray, man. But they look light. Maybe blue. Or green."

Caleb rubbed his temples. Remember, he told himself. Please remember.

"Hey, you know what? Don't worry about it. All that matters is you're here now. I don't dwell much in the past anyway. Not my own, at least."

Caleb wanted to ask what that meant. Instead, he said, "What happened to my friends?"

Truman seemed to know a lot more than he let on. Caleb pictured the talking alligator with a cloud of mist floating around him. In that mist resided all the secrets of this place.

"The Frieda took them."

He took a step forward, hungry for an explanation, any explanation. "What is a—?"

"You'll meet her soon enough. Best of luck, man," Truman said, disappearing into the shadows.

Lilly and Deanna stood by the dock waiting for the next person to be put to rest. So far they had guided two. A seventy-eight-year-old widow named Marie and a thirty-seven-year-old street performer named Leo. Marie had died from a heart attack in her sleep, and after two decades of smoking two packs a day, Leo had died from lung cancer.

"Eighteen this week," Lilly said.

Deanna didn't respond.

"That's pretty good."

Silence.

"Isn't it? Last week I only did fifteen."

Deanna sighed quietly. "It's not a competition, Lillith."

She hated when Deanna insisted on calling her by her full name. "But if I don't help them, they're stuck here. Waiting until I can put them to rest."

"True."

Lilly watched Deanna examine her torches with care. Her Minister accepted everything about her destiny and the world without question. She had an answer for everything, though usually it was philosophical mumbo jumbo. When asked why Lilly couldn't have her memory of Penumbra when she was awake, Deanna said, "Your memory has no effect on you performing your destiny." When Lilly asked why Deanna had her memories in both planes, she said, "Because that is the will of the Creator. A Minister is tasked with protecting and guiding her human Frieda in every plane."

It had only been five days, fifteen hours, and thirty-two minutes since Lilly had learned her destiny. She had accepted her role as a Frieda; it made sense to her after being surrounded by death and the dying for so long. Being a Frieda gave her a purpose, but it didn't give her peace. She knew she was helping people; she could see it on their faces and sense it when they reached their resting places. It was like the sun shining down, caressing your skin after a cloudy day. Lilly wanted to close her eyes and bathe in it.

The feeling never remained for long though. Almost immediately after saying goodbye and *have a good rest*, Lilly would hear the boat rocking against the dock, signaling it was time to return to the other side of the swamp to guide the next person. If she tried to linger, her eyes closed, soaking in that feeling, Deanna would interrupt, her torches blinding, blazing in Lilly's face.

What Lilly found most frustrating about her destiny, however, was the lack of free will she possessed. Nothing about being a Frieda was offered as a choice. Each morning she awoke in Honey Grove Cemetery with no memories of who she'd helped during the night, or Penumbra. Each night she would awaken in the plane between the living and the dead and the memories of that place would return. Then her feet would guide her to the first person she was to help. It was a cycle of being led by her body and her destiny devoid of her own decisions.

Lilly heard the familiar crunching of someone walking on the grass nearby. Out of the mist came a man. His hair was light and trimmed sharply into a crew cut like grass freshly cut. His eyes were a pale gray, and from his dimpled jaw, Lilly knew his smile would melt anyone he shined it on.

"Hello," she said. She opened her arms, palms facing up.

He said hello back, his voice shaking. Up close, the man looked ragged, his pupils darting left and then right, his lips ashen, hands raised in fists. How long had he been here?

Lilly took a small step forward. Seeing how scared the man was she didn't want to startle him. "What's your name?" Lilly asked, even though she knew it already.

When he didn't answer, she said, "My name is Lilly." She gestured to Deanna, who stood beside her, torches glowing yellow. "This is Deanna."

His lips parted to speak, then closed, as though he had thought better of whatever he had planned to say. Lilly took another small step toward him. "I know this place is strange and full of shadows. But I'm here to help you. I'm going to take you away from the shadows, to the light."

He tongued his chapped lips. "Do I know you?" he said to Lilly. "Did I know you before?"

She smiled without teeth. Moved another step closer. "We're meeting for the first time now. But I'm very glad to make your acquaintance. And, if you'll let me, I can help you find peace."

Lilly walked up to him, offering her hands.

"What are you?" he asked.

"A Frieda. I help people reach their final resting place."

He jerked his head toward Deanna. "What about her?"

"She's a Minister. Her torches help guide us."

The man frowned, his eyebrows knitting together. "I know that word," he said. "Frieda. I don't know where from though."

"That's okay. I can help piece things together for you," Lilly said. Again, she offered her hands. He took them and she squeezed his hands gently. "How about we start with your name?"

He told her his name was Caleb. "I don't know anything else. I don't know what I did for work, or if I worked. Or where I lived."

"Do you remember how you died?"

"Brown. Shoulder. Green," he muttered. Caleb sighed, shaking his head. "That's it."

"That's okay." Lilly reassured him with a small smile. "I can see it."

Lilly experienced the deaths of those she guided. Most often through flashes of images or like a reel of film, playing before her eyes. As Caleb moved toward her, she didn't see or watch his death, but experienced it. She tasted metallic and then she felt it tear into her. The flesh on her throat peeled open like someone opening a package of sealed meat. It was effortless, a lazy, banal pressure and release. A breeze hit her Adam's apple, the cartilage pink and exposed. She tried to cry out, but her larynx failed her as it too was cut into, splintered and meaty. Her instincts told her to clutch at her throat with her hands, to hold the flaps of skin and cartilage together. Her hands were numb and unmoving as was the rest of her body. She heard a humming in her ears and a faint tingle on her lips. Otherwise she felt nothing but herself draining from her throat, blood and life and her identity spilling out. She would be dead soon, and she knew by whose hand.

Caleb's killer was his wife. Lorelai.

She pulled her hands away from him, wrapping them around her waist.

Lilly hadn't been a Frieda long, and she'd heard of wives offing their husbands before, but it seemed more like an episode of *Criminal Minds* than reality, forty-five minutes of dramatic, fictitious storytelling with moments of humor and heart and triumph over evil. At least until next week's episode, that is. This murder, on the other hand, was raw and tangible. She had felt her own throat cut open and pulled back like a pair of curtains. It wasn't a crime of passion, but a calculated, surgical procedure. Lorelai was precise, composed. Her killing was sophisticated, as Lilly imagined her persona to be. She had a feeling Caleb wasn't Lorelai's first kill, or at the very least, her last.

"Lilly," Deanna said. One of her torches had disappeared into thin air and she was using the free hand to grip Lilly's shoulder. She squeezed it. "Are you okay? What did you see?"

Lilly had noticed Deanna follow her, expecting her to still be several steps behind. Lilly swallowed, the mucus in her throat swirling around. She grimaced. It was sour. Tangy. She turned to face Deanna, and mouthed, *Murder.*

Deanna's usually smooth face was full of ridges and peaks. Lilly shook her head, meaning she'd tell her Minister later. Lilly met Caleb's gaze, his eyes watering. She took his hands again and gave them a squeeze. "I am sorry for the ugliness your life ended with. I can promise you it's all behind you now. Lorelai cannot hurt you again. Not here."

The veins under Caleb's eyes twitched. "Lorelai?"

"Your wife. Do you remember her?"

Tears streamed down his face. He shook his head. He didn't remember.

"That's okay," she said. Lilly fought the tears building. She nodded, trying to reassure him. "That's all over now. Come with me, and you'll find eternal peace."

His hands trembled in hers. "What now?"

"We go on a boat ride," she answered.

Lilly leaned her head in the direction of the boat. Caleb told her he was ready. She smiled, showing all of her teeth, and walked toward the boat. He followed, as did Deanna, torches ablaze.

They glided along the silent water for nearly an hour before reaching the cemetery. The boat seemed to serve as its own compass. Caleb thought about asking Lilly about it, his lips parting, tongue hovering, but instead he closed his mouth, and studied this strange place. The plane and its magic mystified him.

Lilly rambled throughout the trip, attempting banter. She asked Caleb all about himself—where he went to school, what he did for work, his favorite color, favorite dessert, and so on. He shrugged, grunting in response. She knew Caleb didn't have any answers to those questions, since his memory was bereft of his previous life, save for a few glimpses. He sensed that she was nervous, like she were training for this role as a Frieda and was subject to criticism. From Deanna? From Caleb? He wasn't sure.

Lilly had said one thing that stood out to him. "Immersing myself in their humanity, protects my own." She said it under her breath, in a whisper. He wasn't sure who *they* were, but he guessed she meant people like Caleb. The ones she was helping to cross over, or whatever it was that they were doing. There was a sense of pride, too, in her voice, as though she felt accomplished. Special. And Caleb couldn't really argue with that. He didn't know anyone else like Lilly.

Caleb remained silent, gazing down at the water, watching the wretched, decaying shadows moaning and sputtering water and bubbles.

"The soulless," Lilly said, reading his mind. "The ones who haven't been saved. Who won't ever reach their final resting place."

Caleb nodded, unsure of how to respond. Deanna, her partner, didn't seem to notice the writhing creatures. She stared forward, her torches outstretched, casting off flickering light. The woman looked like a goddess of protection or war, her dark-outfitted form a silhouette against the shadows and firelight.

The boat nudged the muddy embankment, trying to secure itself.

"We're here," Lilly said and rose to her feet, graceful and with ease.

Deanna was already on the moist ground. Her skirt was matted to the muddy earth, and from the boat, it looked like Deanna's body extended into the ground. Lilly followed, her feet slurping with each step, and turned, waiting for Caleb. He stood and stepped off the boat, careful not to fall overboard as it swayed side to side. When he was in front of her, Lilly took his arm and began walking.

They passed a series of wooden crosses before they came to the bent back gate of a cemetery. Lilly told him it was called Honey Island Cemetery. He nodded, his eyes sweeping the aboveground tombs shrouded in mist. Deanna went through the gate first, then Lilly, and finally, Caleb. In the shadows and mist, the tombs and mausoleums looked like creatures ready to pounce. It was hard to imagine people resting inside, in serenity.

Lilly turned to Caleb, and said, "I promise you this isn't a scene from a horror movie." She placed a reassuring hand on his arm. That close, her breath was minty fresh. For the first time, Caleb studied Lilly, realizing she was dressed in pajamas. She couldn't be older than twenty, he thought. How human she seemed, how alive, if only in that moment.

He swallowed; he would never brush his teeth or don pajamas again. He was dead. This woman was taking him to his final resting place, whatever that meant.

Caleb cleared his throat. "How do you know which one is mine?"

"Your soul is showing me the way. It knows where you belong."

They came upon a stone crypt with a wide opening at the bottom. Deanna bent down and inspected the space with her torches. Then she stood and nodded, satisfied. Lilly and Deanna's eyes met. She nodded.

"Caleb, this is where we'll leave you."

He took a step back. "Here?"

Both women nodded.

He crossed his arms in front of his chest. Shaking his head, he managed to stammer, "I'm supposed to climb in there and do what exactly?"

Lilly beckoned him closer to the grave. "You climb in and allow your soul to rest."

"It's easier than it sounds," Deanna chimed in. She stood beside Lilly. "Your soul wants to be here. It wants to be at peace."

Lilly smiled at him. "When you're ready, Caleb. I promise you it's as easy as breathing."

Caleb looked around, his forehead ridged with zigzag lines. What could he do? It wasn't like he had other options. "You're sure it's as easy as breathing? That I won't ever have to roam this place again?" He gestured with his hands.

In unison, the women said yes.

He bent down before the hole to inspect it. Crumbly stone and darkness awaited him. He nodded, psyching himself up to crawl into his own grave. He wanted to laugh at the absurdity of all of this. Instead, he said, "Okay," after a beat, trying to keep his voice level.

Caleb gripped the opening with his hands, the stone sweating in the Louisiana humidity. He turned his head to the side, then straightened it. He turned to face them, balancing on his legs in a frog-like position. There was one thing he wanted—needed—to know. He swallowed, his Adam's apple jutting forward.

"Those things we saw in the swamp...are they damned?"

"Yes," Lilly said. She clasped her hands in front of her.

"Is that where she'll end up? My wife?"

Lilly tongued her upper lip. "When Lorelai dies, yes, she'll end up here."

Caleb frowned. "What will happen to her in the meantime?"

Lilly opened her mouth to answer, but seemed unable to find the words.

Deanna cleared her throat. Her torches were gone now, her arms in front of her like Lilly's. "Unfortunately, we don't know. It is not our destiny to become involved in affairs of the living world."

Anger rose in his chest and throat, burning them with its heat. He let out a barking laugh that made the women shiver.

"Of course not," he growled. He shook his head. "My wife murdered me. How is that okay? How is it fair that she gets to live while I am here?"

"It isn't," Lilly said, her voice cracking.

"So, she can go about her life, kill another husband. And then another, like some horrible dominos game."

The words stung his tongue with familiarity. What if he wasn't the only one she had killed? What if that was what he had been trying to remember this entire time?

He stood, wiping his hands on the front of his pants. "I don't think I was the first."

Lilly asked what he meant. His eyes darted from one woman to the next. He shook his head, thinking about what he was going to say. It was insane, but there was something sour about it. The way an awful truth can taste like vinegar on your tongue.

"I can't be certain, I can't remember, but I think maybe she was married before. Maybe she's killed other husbands."

"Oh my—" Lilly started.

"You're saying you weren't her first kill," Deanna said, her voice even, void of surprise.

"No, I don't think I was." Caleb cracked his knuckles and pressed them to his lips. When he removed them, he asked what could be done.

"Nothing," Deanna said. "As previously stated, we don't get involved in human affairs."

Lilly looked at her partner with contempt. "We will look into it. We promise."

Caleb wanted to believe the sincerity of her words and the sadness in her eyes.

"You rest now," Lilly said. "Lorelai and your former life are in the past. Peace is your future."

Tears spilled down Caleb's cheeks. He let them. He swallowed and nodded. What more could he do? He was dead, after all. He hoped Lilly would honor her word. He bent down, glancing at Lilly and Deanna one more time before turning and climbing into the opening of his tomb.

"We have to do something."

Lilly and Deanna sat in the boxy mausoleum with the pointed top, where they ended each night. In the living world, the old tomb was closed up, covered in exposed brick. But in Honey Grove Cemetery in Penumbra, the entire front was open, the clay-colored bricks only forming the sides. They gazed at the swamp. In the distance, they could see some of its memory-sucking creatures like Truman and Rocco, his friend raccoon. They could hear the shrieks of the damned. But past all that light rose. Dawn was blooming, its glow spreading across Penumbra and the plane of the living, which meant Lilly and Deanna were done helping the recently deceased find rest until the sun dipped below the horizon the following evening, brewing night and all its shadows.

Deanna's arms were clasped in her lap. On one wrist a white string was tied. Facing forward, she said, "We are not tasked with intervening in these kinds of human problems." *Human* twisted in her mouth like something bitter.

Lilly's face hardened. Her palms rested on her outstretched legs. She glanced at her Minister, a woman she had started to think of as her friend. "What about my problems? I'm human, aren't I?"

Deanna didn't respond.

"Tell me if I'm wrong, but don't your job description include guiding me with my mortal problems?" She crossed her arms in front of her.

"I have never intervened in your life on Earth. It is not a Minister's duty to affect her Frieda's waking life. I watch, but I do not act. That is how the Creator planned it."

"So, you're saying that even though we know there is a woman who's murdered her husband—maybe even others—we can't get involved because of destiny. Because of some big plan. Because of how things are." She quoted the last sentence with her fingers for emphasis.

Lilly watched Deanna's nod, the one pigtail bun she could see moving with Deanna's head. "It is not for us to decide," the Minister said. "We do not manage Destiny."

We'll see about that, Lilly thought. She folded her arms in front of her chest again and pushed her shoulders back. She opened her mouth, preparing. When she spoke, her voice was deeper, steady and assertive. "When I wake up in the cemetery tomorrow you will tell me what Caleb told us. You will not get in my way of trying to bring this woman, a murderer, to justice. As your Frieda, this is my will, and I command you to do as I say."

Deanna didn't say anything in response. Lilly yawned, feeling exhaustion enveloping her like a blanket. She lay back, her body melting with stone, her eyes drifting closed and then open. Then closed again. At the cusp of dawn, Lilly always fell asleep. She was, after all, only meant to exist on Penumbra during the shadow hours.

To ensure her Frieda made it back to the plane of the living with her soul intact, Deanna remained by Lilly's side in the tomb. As soon as they entered the mausoleum, the Minister removed the string from her wrist, fastening it to Lilly's wrist. As soon as she fell asleep, Deanna lifted her Frieda's wrist, her hand in a loose fist, and flicked it one, two, three times, as though she were in a bell choir. This motion slithered to the bell on the outside of the tomb. The ringing woke Lilly up in the cemetery of the living world. Deanna would pull Lilly out of the grave and put her body on the cracked concrete ground, where Lilly preferred to awaken. Deanna had let her wake in the aboveground tomb once; Lilly shrieked until she was red in the face and couldn't breathe. Deanna promised that would never happen again.

Lilly knew that consciousness was slipping away from her. She would awaken in the cemetery that was full of color and light. She would be back in the plane of the living any moment now. She heard Deanna say, "I apologize, Lillith. It is not my intention to upset my Frieda—in fact it is my opposite objective—but I cannot allow you to start some kind of investigation of this woman, even if she is a murderer."

Lilly frowned. She mumbled, trying to yell at Deanna for her insubordination, for her inhumanity, but she couldn't form the words. She willed her eyes to open, to keep her awake and aware. To hold onto her memory of that night and that killer.

Lilly was on the ground of the cemetery, the familiar weeds and pebbles scratching her bare arms and legs. She kept her eyes closed for a moment, feeling the warmth of the sun. She inhaled, breathing in the heat and moisture of the day. She exhaled and opened her eyes. As usual, Deanna sat crossed-legged before her.

"Good morning." Deanna wore a black sleeveless maxi dress. Her hair was down and curly.

Lilly sat up. "Good morning. What happened last night? Anything notable?"

The corners of Deanna's lips twitched. Lilly watched her push them into a closed mouth smile. "Not much. A typical evening in Penumbra."

Lilly raised her eyebrow, examining her Minister. Deanna's lips remained pressed into a smile. Lilly told herself she was half asleep and seeing things—what would Deanna possibly have to hide?

"A typical evening in Penumbra," Lilly said, her arms crossing before her in a sweeping motion before dropping to her thighs. She grinned. "That should be the title of a movie or something. Can you picture it?"

Deanna swallowed, then shrugged. "I suppose I can."

Lilly laughed. "Deanna, you are too serious. Lighten up."

"Okay," she said. "I'll try that."

"Good. Now let's go get breakfast."

Lilly stood and wiped her palms of pebbles and dust. She left the accumulation on her knees.

Deanna stood and held out a pair of flip flops for Lilly. She took them and slipped one on at a time. Then Lilly started walking in the direction of the bent gate. She didn't hear or sense Deanna behind her, so she stopped and turned around. Deanna was still in the spot where she'd given Lilly her shoes. Her hands on her hips, Lilly asked. "Are you coming?"

Deanna nodded. "I am," she said, and walked toward Lilly.

The Avenger of Evil

She didn't have a name, at least not a real one anyway. The Avenger of Evil was what the shop owner, a witch named Zelima, called her. It sounded made up though. Like it was folklore. So she called herself Me. It made more sense than Avenger of Evil. Everyday she heard those in the shop saying, "Me this," and, "Me that." Or "But what about me? Why did this happen to me?" So, she thought, what about *me*?

She gazed out from her black button eyes. They shined in the light, reflecting those passing by. She thought it was morning from the lack of shadows in the room; whatever time it was there was a lot of commotion in the shop. It sounded like how outside did during one of the city's many festivals. Mardi Gras was by far the worst. It was like explosives going off in her ears for eternity, even though she didn't have any. Ears, that is. Her body was made of wax and stuffed with Spanish moss and magical herbs: cinnamon, dill, ginger, and mugwort. Or so the witch had said.

Me didn't know when she came into existence, when Zelima had made her, but she knew she was here now and she wasn't exactly happy about it. And not just because of the current raucous. The witch poked and prodded her, stuffed and then emptied her only to do it again before sewing her back together. Zelima did it as though it were nothing. As though it didn't hurt Me.

The truth was it did hurt. Me might not have a heart and lungs and intestines of her own, but that didn't mean she didn't feel pain. Every pin was a hot sting, like she was being set on fire repeatedly; the witch had burned her many times, and she remembered the wax of her body blackening, an acrid, earthly musk floating into the air.

A hush fell through the shop and the group walked over to the table Me was on. Zelima stood closest to her and leaned down. Me noticed a gold needle in the witch's hand and locks of gray curly hair. She wanted to scream when the witch began to sew the hair into the top of her head. Of course she had no mouth to do so.

It felt like a spark igniting.

"It's time," Zelima said. She looked at Me's button eyes, oblivious to the presence that existed behind them. "Are you ready my little Avenger of Evil?"

"No, I'm not," Me said, but, as usual, no one was listening.

There was a beat before Zelima began to chant a spell that sealed the fate of the doll to her target. A young woman opposite the witch whispered to the girl next to her, "I can't believe she thought she could cross Zelima."

Me didn't know who *she* was, but the doll was used to not knowing things. Maybe She was the person's name.

The girl responded, "I know. Helping him after what he did to Zelima was suicide."

They looked young to Me; their faces were smooth and without lines. They both had their hair pulled back in colorful turbans. The patterns on the head wraps were mesmerizing to Me, and she tried to concentrate on them, hoping they would distract her from the impending pain.

"Taking her amulet? Definite suicide," the one across from Zelima said.

The girl next to her nodded and pursed her lips.

"That's enough, girls," said a woman with a raspy voice. It came from the direction of Me's feet, out of her sightline.

Zelima continued to cast her spell, the words undulating from her lips like a series of waves, ignoring the women around her and their gossiping. After a minute, she said, "It's finished. Now for the fun part."

The witch turned away from the table for a moment and when she turned back she had a small dish in her hands. Zelima passed it to her right and instructed each woman to take one.

Me didn't have to see inside the dish to know what it contained—shiny, silver steel pins with prickly points.

When the dish made its way back to Zelima and she took a pin in her hand, the other women raised their hands, the needle pressed between their thumbs and pointer fingers. The shop lights reflected off the slender tools.

The shop owner stood luminous and monstrous above Me. She had her long black braids pulled into a giant bun on top of her head. She wore a black cotton dress with a thick gold necklace that looked like a collar around her throat and tear drop shaped earrings that were twice the size of her eyes. When she leaned over Me, the doll caught sight of the witch's circular medallion, tucked into the top of her dress. There had only been one time Me could recall her creator not wearing it, but she told herself to stop thinking about that. She didn't like remembering how angry the witch had been. The curses her wicked tongue had spewed. Me shivered, but, of course, no one noticed.

"When you're ready, ladies," Zelima said, her voice smooth like velvet with a hint of spice and mischief.

Me braced herself.

Dozens of pins sliced into the doll. Me focused her black button eyes on the girls' colorful turbans. Some of the pins were jammed deep inside and left there, while others were ripped out and inserted again. Me could hear She howling and could feel the woman's body twitching, convulsing with each stab, a wounded beast in the wild left to die. Me heard She whine and grunt, felt her seize and contort, and envisioned dozens of tiny pinpricks of blood covering her body as though She were tangled in a rose bush, the thorns spiking her flesh.

The wicked enchantment wouldn't kill its intended, but the marks would remain for several days. Zelima cackled at the thought. Me wept for She and for herself, yet no tears slid from her button eyes. She screamed when the girls with the head wraps—a particularly cruel pair—dove their pins into her stuffed insides and twisted them deeper, right and then left and back again. They were splintering She and Me, inside out. The holes gouged in their flesh would remain open for the rest of the day, blood and pus oozing from the one, herbs and moss the other.

"That's enough for today," Zelima said.

"Thank god," Me whispered, unnoticed by the group. She heard She's breathless howling and felt her leaking, trembling body wind into a ball.

At once the women yanked the pins from Me's body. It felt as though her guts were being ripped out.

"Thank you for coming," Zelima continued. "We'll do another session tomorrow."

Me began to sob. She couldn't take another round of this. Me didn't know if she could survive it. If She could.

The doll lay there raw and exposed, utterly forgotten, as the women said their goodbyes and left the shop. She counted the flecks of dirt and water damage on the ceiling, waiting for her creator to close up for the day. Me didn't know how she was going to do it, but she would find a way to escape. She wasn't going to be the Avenger of Evil any longer.

The Monster of
Honey Island Swamp

"**S**tep right up. Don't be shy. You will witness something you've never seen before. Never even thought possible. The stuff of imagination and nightmares, folklore and horror stories," a young woman said, her voice bravado.

A group of tourists crowded into an alleyway outside of Jackson Square, the woman at the center.

Her name was Mathilda. She was in her mid-twenties with milky skin and large almond-shaped eyes like moonstones. Strawberry blond locks undulated halfway down her bare back in loose curls. She wore a blue halter dress with a low back. Her feet were unconfined, the pads forming to the curves and angles of the cobbled street. Mathilda looked like she belonged in a fresco.

She stood in the only patch of direct sunlight in the alley, a natural spotlight for the performer. Mathilda lifted her fleshy arms into the air as though she were about to conjure a great and terrible storm. Her eyes narrowed to combat the sun's rays. "Are you ready to see the monster of New Orleans' nightmares? The elusive, mysterious predator born of Honey Island Swamp, just thirty-five miles outside the city?"

The group murmured yes, heads bobbing as they nodded. Some shivered. Others looked at one another, their eyes betraying their unease. Mathilda's left eyebrow raised, a perfectly practiced arch that asked if the group was really, truly ready. Satisfied the tourists were, she grinned, two dimples like half-moons cutting into the base of her flushed cheeks.

"Behold," she said, "the Monster of Honey Island Swamp!"

The crowd gasped as she transformed. Mathilda's eyes lifted, drawn to the sun. They were almost translucent in the scorching light. Her hands changed first; the pale, slender fingers of each appendage fused together, creating three thick digits connected by slimy webbing that glistened in the sunlight. Mathilda's once freckled skin was now stained a brilliant green. Curled claws like potato peelings hung from each digit.

The green traveled down her arms as though another street artist were smoothing paint onto Mathilda's skin. Scales popped up where fine blond hairs and brown moles had previously been. They continued down her body until Mathilda's bare feet morphed into green webbed feet with six toes. At the end of each toe was a triangular toenail, also green.

The last part to change was her head. Her golden locks contracted into her scalp until she had no visible hair. Bald, her head shone in the daylight. A speck of green appeared on her forehead. The crowd gasped and cried out as the vibrant stain grew into a circle that spread down the crown of Mathilda's head to her chin. Gills fluttered along each side of her face. Her mouth appeared like a fish's, rubbery and lipless. Her eyebrows blazed neon yellow instead of dark blond. Everything else was moss green. Before the group stood a monster of mythic proportions. The kind that inspired fake documentaries and cult followings.

The blue dress had become tight around the monster's body. It shrugged off the garment, revealing its bottom half to be flat and smooth like a Ken doll. Utterly exposed, the creature's eyes lowered from the sun to survey the observing crowd. Its eyes still resembled moonstones, yet they were rimmed in black as though all that existed behind those irises was darkness. The Monster of Honey Island Swamp reached toward the audience.

The tourists shrank at the motion, retreating. Several shrieked like teenage girls in horror movies. Some took off, running from the crowd. A handful remained, their bodies drawn back, afraid of the creature yet curious to see what would happen next.

The monster's eyes darted, landing on the steeples of St. Louis Cathedral impaling the cloudless sky. Its dimples deepened as it swallowed, unnoticed by the group. The members of the crowd saw what they wanted, projecting their own fears and beliefs and fantasies onto the monster, turning it into a caricature of itself. The creature's jaw dropped and a high-pitched howl escaped its spinach-green lips. The remaining crowd cheered; some turned up their chins and howled like they imagined werewolves did.

When the monster was done howling, its jaw closed, a marionette at the end of its act. It bent to pick up the dress from the ground and pulled it to its chest, holding the garment in place with its arms. Then the monster's arms rose to the sky as the street performer had done minutes prior. The creature morphed into the beautiful young woman as effortlessly as a snake shedding dead skin. Mathilda grinned at the crowd, her dimples revealing themselves once again. She fastened the strings of her halter dress and placed her hands on her hips.

"There you have it, folks. The Monster of Honey Island Swamp. In the flesh. More or less." She winked. A few members from the audience chuckled. "If you enjoyed what you saw today, tips are appreciated. Otherwise, enjoy the rest of your visit in the Big Easy, have a Hurricane or two, eat some beignets, and keep an eye out for the Monster of Honey Island Swamp. Contrary to belief, he doesn't only prowl the swamp." She let out a dramatic laugh, the kind that erupted from obnoxious, drunk men slapping their sweaty thighs in tandem. Mathilda's lips curled into a snarl, the laughter empty, an echo of the joy it was meant to express.

The crowd, already disillusioned, dissipated, more interested in food and booze and the nearby shops advertising personalized t-shirts. Crawfish, fleur-de-lis, and alligators were only the beginning of the options. Mathilda accepted tips from the tourists that remained and thanked them for coming.

One member of the audience hovered in the back, waiting to approach until the others were gone. Mathilda counted her tips for the day, unaware of the woman. Her lips moved in a hurry, her voice sounding like the whispering rush of a river through rocks. "This is how we make a living, Mathias. I play my part, you play yours. We have a roof over our heads. That's the deal. You're impossible. That's not possible. No, listen to me. You're—"

"Talking to yourself?" a woman said, her voice like velvet.

Mathilda looked up from the small stack of coins and bills in her hands. "Excuse me?"

The woman before her was tall and curvaceous with long, midnight braids trailing down her back. Her dark skin held no lines or crevices. She wore blue and white striped linen capris that flared at her calves and a white tank top. Mathilda couldn't guess the woman's age. She almost sparkled, a hint that something magical was behind her youthful complexion. Mathilda always recognized a fellow illusionist.

"You were talking to yourself. Or, rather, to your other half." The woman spoke as though this were a casual conversation about the weather or one of the city's upcoming festivals.

Mathilda grimaced. She shook her head, a wave of blond lapping at her back and arms. "I don't know what you're talking about."

"Of course you do. You're quite rare." The woman stopped herself. Smiled. "I'm sure you know that. A stranger doesn't need to tell you what it's like to be born as you were."

Mathilda's cheeks blazed. She ignored the voice in her head and its pleas to be careful. She took a step closer to the stranger. "Look, lady, I know my act belongs in a freak show and I cater to a particular group of people, but that doesn't mean I have time for crazy delusions like yours."

The woman crossed her arms in front of her chest, her face stone. "Are you always in control? Or do you sometimes let your other half out?" She clucked, her tongue against the back of her teeth. "I have a feeling he or she doesn't get let out much."

The voice in her head grew louder. Not now, Mathilda wanted to say. Instead, she placed her hands on her hips. Leaning forward, she snapped, "You don't know anything about me."

The flicker of amusement sparked in the stranger's eyes. "I know that you're a Muoro. Half-human, half-beast. I know that wasn't an illusion just now. That was your other half showing itself. I've never seen one before. Only heard about your kind in stories my mother used to tell."

Mathilda's hands dropped to her side. She stepped back. Beads of sweat pooled in her armpits. How could this woman know what I am? she wondered. What we are? Mathilda's eyes tilted to the sky. She spoke in a hushed voice to the voice in her head.

"Okay, okay," Mathilda said. She met the stranger's gaze. "You know what I am, yet I don't know what *your* kind is. Or who the hell you are."

The woman smiled, revealing straight, milky white teeth. "My name is Zelima Delacroix and I am a witch."

Every fortune teller and tarot reader in New Orleans claimed to be a witch. Mathilda had never witnessed any real magic besides her own. "I'm Mathilda," she said, wanting to move along this interaction.

"Your other half?"

"Mathias."

"It's nice to meet you, Mathilda, Mathias." The so-called witch raised her pointer finger in the air. "You should know that I created the story of the Honey Island Swamp Monster. It was many moons ago with a very specific purpose in mind. I applaud your ingenuity, and as long as your angle doesn't interfere with mine, you can continue to do as you are."

Mathilda scoffed. "Whatever you say, lady."

Unfazed, Zelima responded, "One last thing before I leave you. If you and Mathias ever decide you don't want to be a Muoro anymore, come see me. I might be able to help."

Mathilda pulled her lower teeth along her top lip. Her eyes tilted up at the sky again as she listened. "You would consider that, Mathias? Really? It's probably a scam."

Zelima cleared her throat, disrupting the argument Mathilda and her other half were having.

The young woman glared at the witch. "We're not interested."

Zelima shrugged and lifted her hands in surrender. "If you change your mind, come by Lavender's. And I am the real deal, honey, just in case you were wondering." A smile stretched across the woman's face. It reminded Mathilda of a rubber band, ready to snap. She watched Zelima walk away, her braids bouncing and slithering.

Mathilda sighed and shook her head. "Mathias, we can't trust anyone but each other. We're a team, right? It's always been you and me, and it's always going to be."

Mathias lay awake, concealed in the shadows of Mathilda. She slept, her breath soft and even. A troubled sleeper, Mathias' insomnia had increased since they had met Zelima. Mathias didn't care what Mathilda said, there was something about that woman. Her energy. Mathias believed Zelima to be a witch capable of doing what she had offered.

Mathilda and Mathias were born in the Bywater District of New Orleans. Mathilda, always the dominant half, showed herself first. She came out of cooing, with a full head of blond hair. The young mother held Mathilda, her blue eyes misty, enamored with her daughter's beauty.

As she rocked the baby, however, it began to change. Exhausted and dehydrated from the delivery, the new mother thought she was seeing things. She squeezed her eyes shut to focus. When she opened them the golden-haired child was gone; in her place was a green, scaly monster with webbed feet and hands. The mother screamed and almost dropped the newborn. Mathias wailed. The cries sounded just like a human baby, and their mother, feeling the pull of maternity in her chest, drew the green infant to her body and rocked it until soothed. When she peeked at the child a few minutes later, it was once again the baby girl of her dreams.

This could drive any mother crazy, and this one was no exception. She was single—her boyfriend leaving when he found out she was pregnant—and only twenty-one. Mathilda always said their mother did the best that she could. She was kind to Mathilda, doting on the little girl. With Mathias, however, she withdrew her affection, refusing to even name the child. By the time they were four, their mother had left. Mathilda took over then, saying she was the eldest. She named Mathias after herself, choosing a masculine version of Mathilda. It had never been a discussion; Mathilda was in charge and she wanted a baby brother, so Mathias stepped into that role, without questioning who or what he was.

The last time their mother had come up, Mathilda said at least she had stuck around longer than anyone else. "You would say that," Mathias said. "You were her favorite. Her princess. A dream come true. You weren't the monster of her nightmares."

"You're a lot to get used to, Matty," Mathilda replied.

"You're not a walk in the park yourself."

When they talked to each other, one half to the other, one spoke out loud, corporeal and in control, the other nothing more than a voice inside of a head. A ghost of a self. At first, Mathilda had taken control, as her half appeared ordinary to the world. It wasn't safe for Mathias to be out. After all, Mathias was an *other*, seen as nothing but a monster. Mathilda told Mathias, "You are more than that." For a while Mathias believed her.

Of course Mathias did. Who had protected them from disinterested or cruel foster parents? Mathilda. Who had worked odd jobs to rent a crumbling studio apartment once they turned eighteen? Mathilda.

Who had stolen restaurant scraps or charmed men to get them dinner? Mathilda. She knew the world and its sharp edges better than Mathias ever could. And because she had been dominant for so long, because she had taken care of them for so long, Mathilda was too strong for her other half to deny, in any capacity.

Mathias couldn't even shield personal thoughts or feelings from Mathilda. Nothing was Mathias' alone. Not Mathias' body, identity, or sexuality. Mathias appreciated that sex and gender were complicated when you were human, but as a Muoro, as half-human, half-beast, it sometimes felt impossible to define either. Mathilda, by naming Mathias and assigning him the role of brother, had made her other half male, even though Matthias did not have that anatomy. In fact, Mathias had no genitalia. However, he had agreed, taking on the role his sister presented. Following Mathilda's lead, Mathias started to refer to himself as *he*, even though it never felt quite right. Because there were no secrets between the two halves, Mathilda was aware that Mathias was attracted to men and identified as non-binary. When Mathias attempted to bring it up, wanting to talk about sexuality, wanting to try out she/her pronouns, Mathilda said, "You *are* female. At least half of you. And I have been with men. You're there too. For all of it."

"When you let me."

Mathilda chuckled to herself. "When I let you."

"It's not the same as being kissed or going on a date with someone I like and am attracted to," Mathias countered. "You act like I am only attracted to men because you are. That I only see myself as female because you do too. It's not fair, Mathilda, to whittle me down to your shadow half, a monster without my own feelings and desires."

"I never said you didn't have feelings, Matty. But I don't get how you can be so sure of your identity when half of it is mine." Her voice softened. "I'm not me without you, just like you're not you without me."

Mathias didn't know how to explain it, but she knew who she was. Who she wanted to be.

Mathias' other half had never had to question her identity. Mathilda had had many lovers, even some boyfriends. As a femme-bodied person who was traditionally beautiful and vivacious, Mathilda moved through the world with ease. New Orleans' tourists and suitors lay in her palm.

Mathias longed to feel the warm press of lips on her flesh. According to Mathilda, their mother had kissed Mathias as a baby, but Mathias couldn't remember it, couldn't picture the woman she had horrified loving her back. No matter how many times Mathilda said they were two halves of a whole, Mathias knew her other half would never understand what it meant to be lonely, desperate to be seen and accepted. Maybe even loved.

The idea to pretend to be the Honey Island Swamp Monster had been Mathilda's idea, of course. She had heard the lore and said this was their chance. "Our way to both be a part of the world." Mathias gave in, not because she agreed with her sister, but because Mathias gave in to Mathilda's every whim. She didn't understand how this spectacle objectified Mathias, perpetuating the myth that she was nothing more than a sideshow to exhibit for profit.

The Honey Island Swamp Monster had been making appearances for two years now. Mathias hated every second of it, and Mathilda knew it.

"How else do you expect to see the world, Matty?" she said the last time Mathias tried to reason with her. "We're simply working with what we've got. We have to survive somehow, right?" When Mathias didn't respond, Mathilda continued, "I hate to say it, but who will accept you? Who will take the time to get to know you and not just judge you by your appearance?"

For twenty-five years, Mathias had believed Mathilda was the only one who saw Mathias for who she truly was. Who saw past the green skin and scales. But now Mathias knew the truth: she was just a pawn for Mathilda to maneuver, her advancement the only objective.

The only time Mathias' thoughts and feelings were truly private was when her other half slept. Mathias knew what she wanted: to find a way to separate from Mathilda permanently. It was time for Mathias to step out of the shadows, into the light.

Mathilda adjusted the black strapless dress Mathias had pulled on seconds before. She smoothed her hair to one side and grinned at her audience.

"Our audience," Mathias reminded.

She ignored her other half, smiled, and said, "If you enjoyed what you saw today, tips are appreciated."

A middle-aged couple in matching visors came up to Mathilda and placed a five-dollar bill in her hand.

"Thank you so much, y'all," she said.

Once the group left, Mathilda let out a sigh. Then she began to count her tips for the day, her tongue twisted to the side, its pink nub poking out of her mouth.

"Bravo, bravo," a husky voice said. Three slow claps echoed off the brick walls and cobblestones of the alleyway.

Mathilda jumped a little at the sound. She looked up to see a small man, bent over at a ninety-degree angle as though he carried a heavy load on his back. He wore an old tuxedo, dusted in cobwebs and stains of various colors. There was a hole by his left collar—it looked almost like paper snowflakes with its pattern and perforations—clearly moth ridden. His leather boots had once been black, yet now were a dark gray peppered with scuff and weather marks. Mathilda thought the old man might have used shoe polish to both stain and style his hair. It was poorly dyed black with streaks of white and silver—appearing skunk-like—and was pulled and glued across his head, giving it a shiny quality. She wrinkled her nose. The old man resembled a haunted, disheveled butler.

He pressed his hands together. The nail beds were jagged, cut extremely short, so much so that the flesh was pink and puffy around each nail. Mathilda's eyes lingered there before rising to meet his. The man's eyes were dark gray, almost black, beady in size and nature. His features resembled both birds and vermin; his nose was large and pointed, resembling a beak. Mathilda watched his pale lips form a thin line, waiting for her to speak. She tried not to show her repulsion at the black spots and shallow divots along his ashy olive face.

"Thank you," she said. Saliva swished in her mouth as she swallowed. "I didn't notice you in the crowd. Did you come in later?"

"It isn't difficult to be invisible if you want to be," the man replied, the hint of a grin on his face.

She nodded, the flesh between her eyebrows twitching. Something about this man made Mathilda's chest tighten. Mathias said the man gave him the creeps.

"You want to be seen. Obviously." The old man's tone was sharp, meant to wound.

Mathilda lifted her eyebrow. "I am a performer."

"You have showmanship, I'll give you that," he said. "But you are performing no great act, no magic. You simply set loose the other side of you."

Mathilda's chest constricted further; it felt like a rock pressing against her chest, slowly crushing her. She could feel perspiration forming on the back of her arms. "I don't like this," Mathias told her. Mathilda didn't either. She exhaled an audible sigh.

The old man waved his hand in the air, a flippant, sluggish motion meant to mollify her. "I don't mean to frighten you, dear. I simply don't believe in bullshitting."

Mathilda pressed her shoulders back and crossed her arms in front of her chest.

"I've been looking for one of your kind for decades."

Again, someone referring to them as a *kind*. It made Mathilda think about creatures locked in cages, tucked away from society as though they were a monstrous plague. "What do you mean?" The veins at her temples pulsed.

"You're a Muoro."

It was strange to hear that word again. One Mathilda and Mathias first came across in Tulane's rare book section several years ago. The term for what they were. *Muoro*. It was the second time the siblings had heard that word used by a stranger.

"Why have you been looking for a *Muoro*?" The word felt foreign in her mouth. Mathilda could smell her fear, ripe and salty on her goose-pimpled flesh.

"Call it professional curiosity. I am a collector of the rare and bizarre. I have a shop on Royal, near Bienville. J. Allister's Oddities & Antiques." He bent further, bowing, and rolled his right hand. "J. Allister at your service."

When J. Allister looked up at Mathilda, he beamed, revealing a smile made up of missing and crooked yellow teeth.

Mathilda forced her cheeks into a smile, her lips sealed shut, a mask she had perfected after years of performing in the streets of New Orleans. "It's nice to meet you," she said after a beat.

The old man loomed closer, now only a foot away. His eyeline at Mathilda's stomach. J. Allister twisted his neck, pointing his chin to the sky. "You have no idea how nice it is to meet you."

Mathilda imagined a boulder above her chest now, threatening annihilation. She remembered hearing that Incubi, male demons from Mesopotamian mythology, were known to squat on their victims' chests, suffocating them to death. Sweat ran down Mathilda's arms in small rivers.

"You would fit into my collection very well."

Phlegm thickened in Mathilda's throat. She gulped it back. "Look, Mr. Allister, it's been really nice talking to you, but I'm afraid you have the wrong idea about me. I'm just a girl with some tricks. A magician, if you will. I'm not a *Muora*, or whatever you said I was." Her heart thumped against her ribs.

J. Allister nodded, his mouth open, his fat, speckled tongue floating, as he sized Mathilda up. He grabbed one of her arms, still folded across her chest. Surprised by the old man's strength, Mathilda strained against him, her skin sizzling beneath his touch.

J. Allister sneered, his rodent eyes trained on her. "You, my dear, aren't fooling anyone. You are a *Muoro* as plain as day. There is another inside of you—a brother, sister—I'm not quite sure how you see one another, but I see you. Both of you. And," he squeezed her arm, "I will have you for my collection."

At that, he let Mathilda go and hobbled down the alley, disappearing into the crowd of tourists, locals, and street performers.

"What the hell was that?" Mathias said. "I have a bad feeling about that man and his *collection*."

Mathilda studied the handprint on her arm; it was red and indented. How was it possible an old man had done this to her? The pain and its resulting mark reminded Mathilda of an oil burn she got as a child, her foster mother flinging her spatula in the air to teach Mathilda to not come into the kitchen until dinner was ready. Tears rolled down her face. The scar would fade in a few hours, Mathilda's gaze lingering on her arm in the meantime, checking to see if the mark was still there.

For the next three weeks, Mathilda saw J. Allister every time she and Mathias performed their Monster of Honey Island Swamp routine. Sometimes the old man stood up front, the leader of the pack of tourists. Other times, he stood in the middle, almost invisible among the crowd. Even then Mathilda knew the collector was there. She could feel his eyes exploring her. Could hear the saliva popping on his tongue and lips as his face split into its sinister smile.

One time Mathilda swore J. Allister was in the building behind her, watching from above, a Peeping Tom with a bird's eye view. Her shoulders broiled under the heat of his black eyes. Her ears rang with the sound of his smile. His salivation.

The collector approached her after every performance, saying, "Bravo, bravo," accompanied by three slow claps. Then he would waddle closer, stopping a foot from Mathilda. "Are you ready to join my collection?"

When she said no, as she did every time, he shrugged and said, "I'll have you soon enough. Whether or not you give your consent is of no matter."

J. Allister hadn't touched Mathilda since that first afternoon. She waited for it, to feel that searing pain, to bear his mark again for several hours. At night she woke up screaming, her arm stinging where the old man had grabbed her. Mathias tried to calm Mathilda, telling her it was just a bad dream. The old man wasn't there.

But he was.

"He's inside of me," she cried to Mathias. "Inside of us."

After weeks of nightmares, Mathias said, "Maybe we should reach out to Zelima. Maybe she can help us."

Mathilda sniffled. "Is being attached to me so awful, Matty?"

"That's not what I'm saying. It's always been you and me, right? It's always going to be you and me, regardless of us inhabiting the same body." Mathias paused. "I'm thinking about our safety. If we're no longer a Muoro, we'll be free of J. Allister. We'll be free to be whatever we want to be."

Mathilda could hear the sticky sweet hope in her brother's voice. For several years now, she had known her other half identified as non-binary. Mathilda wanted to support Mathias' self-exploration, but she didn't know how he would begin to unbraid his identity from hers. They were a gnarled tree trunk, tangled roots growing together for so long it was impossible to tell where one stopped and the other began. A part of Mathilda knew, however, that Mathias would never live an authentic life until they were separated.

Neither of them would.

"You wouldn't have me to hide within," Mathilda quipped.

Mathias sighed. "Maybe that's for the best."

Tears stung her eyes. "Matty," she pleaded. Mathilda wanted her other half to be free, but Mathias didn't know what the world was truly like, how ugly and cruel it was. Mathilda wanted to protect him.

"Let's visit Zelima tomorrow and hear what she has to say. It's our only option," Mathias said.

"We could run away."

"And go where? I'm sure some other collector of freaks will find us." Mathias' voice trembled. "I'm tired of hiding, Mathilda."

"Okay," she said. Mathilda swallowed and wiped leftover tears and snot from her face. "We can go see the witch in the morning."

The bell above the glass shop door chimed, announcing Mathilda and Mathias' presence. Zelima was behind the register, her back to them. They watched her braids whip around as she turned.

"This is a surprise," she said once she saw them, hands on her hips. The shop owner wore a black maxi dress accessorized with a clay, circular necklace that just brushed her cleavage and a series of gold cuffs on both of her arms. The jewelry clanked each time she moved, bumper cars crashing along her forearms.

Lavender's was one long, narrow room. Tables and shelves displayed incense, good luck charms, potions, and herbs. Mathilda looked around the shop in silence. Mathias, on the other hand, chattered away, remarking on the various magical items for sale. "Do you think that's a real rabbit's foot? How do you think she got it? Is that really an alligator's head? Maybe she's the Honey Island Swamp Monster."

Mathilda ignored her other half. She picked up a small clear jar labeled *Lavender* in handwritten cursive, studying the tiny purple buds.

"My favorite."

Mathilda looked up to see the woman approaching, her braids swaying as she moved closer.

"Offers protection, purification, healing. It can even help with love," the self-proclaimed witch continued. "Is that what's brought you in today? Or can I help you with something else?"

Mathilda put down the glass of lavender. "There is a man," she said. "J. Allister. He owns an antique shop."

"J. Allister's Oddities & Antiques."

Mathilda looked at the ground. "He's been coming to the show. Every time I perform—we perform, sorry, Mathias—no matter where we are in the Quarter, he's there. Watching. Waiting. He said he wants us for his collection." She paused to listen to Mathias. Her face flexed with worry. "And he touched me. Or burned me. I don't really know how to describe it."

Zelima studied Mathilda, her forehead lined. "He marked you."

Mathilda nodded. Her insides churned at the thought of what it had been like when the old man had grabbed her, how his hand had branded her flesh.

"It's a magical enchantment. A binding spell. He does it to those he wants for his collection."

Mathilda rubbed her temples. "So, he's a—?"

Zelima shook her head. "J. Allister was not born magical. But he is a collector of the mystical, the strange, and unique. He has amassed powers—spells, knowledge of witchcraft—over the years. He deals in dark magic, mostly."

The skin between Mathilda's eyebrows wrinkled, resembling slender accordion bellows. "A binding spell? He bound himself to me? To Mathias and me."

Zelima nodded, her eyes apologetic. "I'm afraid so. How long ago did he do it?" Mathilda stuttered that it had been a few weeks. The shop keeper's face grew long, her eyes full of shadows. "He will come for you soon if the binding spell isn't broken."

"Can you break it?" For the first time since meeting her, Mathilda hoped Zelima really was a witch.

"It's not that simple. I have the magic, yes, but I don't have the spell Allister cast."

Mathias suggested they ask Zelima about separating them. "Maybe that could work," he said to Mathilda.

"What if you separated us? Mathias and me. You said you could do that."

The witch clucked her tongue as she thought. "That could work. He bound himself to you as a Muoro. If you aren't one anymore—if you are two separate beings—the spell should be broken. Besides, the old man won't want only half of you. To display a truly unique being, a Muoro, in his collection, he'd need you both. And, no offense, Mathilda, but on your own you seem nothing more than a pretty white girl."

Mathilda glared at Zelima, but she was relieved. She would be safe.

Zelima continued, "Mathias, however, is rare with or without you."

"What are you saying? That J. Allister might still come for Mathias?" Mathilda's cheeks reddened with shame. How could she feel relief without considering what this might mean for her other half?

Zelima nodded. "We can prepare for that. Protect him. Or is it her?"

It felt as though every inch of Mathilda's body was atrophying at once. She had never been without Mathias. The possibility of being without him was inconceivable. But would Mathilda keep him chained to her, when it could risk both of their safety?

"What do you want to do, Matty?"

"I think we should try."

"Okay," Mathilda said. "Let's do it. Can you do it today?"

The witch paused before saying, "I'd like to speak with Mathias before we continue."

The skin of Mathilda's forehead creased. "He wants this as much as I do. It was his idea to come to you." Mathias corrected Mathilda. She sighed. "Sorry. She."

"I want to hear Mathas say it. I want to meet her face to face." Zelima stressed Mathias' preferred pronoun. "She deserves to be out of your shadow."

Mathilda huffed. Even though she agreed with Zelima, she didn't appreciate the woman's tone.

Zelima lifted her hand as though she were about to recite a pledge. "It's hard giving up control. Trust me, I understand that, Mathilda. I know you're trying to protect Mathias. You need to understand this, though: I will not perform any spell without talking to you both. So give her control. Let her come out."

"Fine." Mathilda closed her eyes, balling her hands into fists. The appendages morphed green and webbed. Scales encased her body like armor. Her shift dress tightened against lean muscles and broad shoulders. Fully transformed, Mathias' eyes darted around the shop, in search of prying eyes.

"You don't have to worry, dear. The shop is enchanted. If anyone looks inside, they'll think I'm talking to Mathilda. You are safe here."

"Perhaps," Mathias said. "For now." She met Zelima's gaze. The witch's eyes didn't blink or widen. Nor did she flinch at Mathias' appearance.

"For now." Zelima smiled. "It's nice to finally meet you."

"You too."

"Tell me, do you like being trapped inside your other half?"

Mathilda groaned. "What a witch."

Mathias smiled.

"I imagine Mathilda doesn't see what she's done to you as entrapment," the shop owner said. "But it is. She's kept you prisoner, your half hidden, except for when it serves her."

"It has helped us," Mathias countered.

"Has it?" Zelima crossed her arms in front of her chest. The cuffs clanged against one another, a cacophony of bells. "Tell me, Mathias, what do *you* want?"

"To be safe from the old man."

The witch shook her head, smirking. "That's not what I meant."

Mathias' cheeks spiked with heat.

"It's okay," Zelima said. "Mathilda's just a voice in your head right now. You can ignore it." She winked at Mathias. "She's done it to you many times."

"I'm going to kick that witch's ass," Mathilda sniped.

"She's my sister. My family." Mathias hugged herself. "I love her."

"Of course you do."

"There is no me without her. It's always been Mathilda and me."

"Damn right."

"Mathilda, let me talk." Mathias sighed. "Thank you. Look, I love my sister. She's the most important thing in the world to me. But," she paused, "I want to be free to live a normal life. To be able to be me, you know? Not just a fake monster. Not just one half of a whole. I guess what I'm saying is I want to become the most important thing in my world."

Mathias expected Mathilda to jump in, but she remained quiet.

"I can't guarantee this will work," Zelima said. "And I can't promise you'll be totally free and safe."

Mathias nodded, her chest rising and falling.

"I promise I'm going to help you feel whole. Whatever I can do, I will."

"Thank you," Mathias said, eyes misty.

"Don't thank me until I've done it. Now," the shop owner said, clapping her hands together. "There is one more matter to discuss before we schedule the spell."

"Schedule? What does she mean by that?" Mathilda finally spoke. Mathias voiced her sister's question.

"I may be a witch, but I don't do magic on demand. Payment must be made first."

Mathilda bared her teeth. "That witch."

"Mathilda," Mathias urged. "How much? We don't have a lot, but—"

Zelima held up her hand. "Let me stop you there. I don't want money. I want a favor."

"What kind of favor?"

"Go to Honey Island Swamp and collect two vials of its water."

"That's it?" Mathilda asked what the catch was.

"Yes." Mathias asked why the witch couldn't go herself. "There is a witch who lives on the swamp, Julia Baudin. She is the real Monster of Honey Island Swamp." Zelima stared off into the distance, her nose wrinkling. "Anyway, she and I have an arrangement—she stays in the swamp, I stay in the Quarter. We do not intervene on the other's territory."

"But...?" Mathias could sense it coming.

"The swamp is a magical hub. Separating you will take a lot of magic. I'll need to harness the power of all three planes, that of the living, dead, and in-between. And I need you to get it for me."

"I can't believe you agreed to this," Mathilda said.

They approached a thick copse with leaves every shade of green, Mathilda in control. Lopsided, half-rotted wooden markers littered the ground. *1915* was etched into a marker near the front of the sylvan area. A forgotten graveyard.

"We're nearly there," Mathias said. "Zelima said when we reached the cemetery with the 1915 marker we would be only feet from the swamp."

"Remind me, why did we agree to this?" Mathilda's face shriveled with revulsion. She hated graveyards. She tiptoed around the crosses, wary of snakes or other swamp critters.

"Zelima is going to protect us from J. Allister. All she's asking for is two vials of swamp water. It's the least we can do," Mathias answered. "She even used magic to drop us on the outskirts of Honey Island Swamp so we didn't have to drive all the way out here. She's asking very little, Mathilda, and giving a lot more."

"I don't trust it. Not her, or Allister, or this supposedly magical swamp water."

"Do you hear that?" Mathias whispered.

"Hear what?"

"Be quiet. *That.*"

Mathilda's ears perked up. Rustling to the left. It sounded like a dog was padding through the wooded area, his paws crunching leaves and sticks. She hoped it was only a stray dog.

The noise swelled, its maker coming closer. Mathias instructed Mathilda to hide behind a nearby tree. Fat, stout limbs came into view. A long U-shaped head, electric yellow eyes, with slits for pupils. On its back and tail rows of spikes of leathery armor. A fully grown alligator, only a few feet away. They could reach past the tree and graze the beast's snout.

"Holy shit," Mathilda said.

"Mathilda!"

The reptilian beast's eyes landed on them. It lunged, jaw opening. Mathilda stared at its crooked teeth, bits of reeds and meat clinging to the creature's fangs. "Mathias, do something," she cried before squeezing her eyes shut. They were going to die because of a witch's stupid game. Mathilda imagined the alligator's triangular teeth tearing through her flesh. Their flesh. She didn't believe in god, but in that moment Mathilda prayed to him, asking for her and Mathias to be together in the afterlife.

The annihilation of their flesh never came, however. Mathilda blinked her eyes open. The alligator stood inches away, its yellow eyes trained on her. "Mathias," she started, before realizing her other half had taken over.

"It's okay, Mathilda. This alligator isn't going to hurt us."

"You took control," she said. "You never take control."

"I thought we were going to die. And then I thought, why not try something? Maybe the alligator would think I was one of them."

"And it worked."

"At the very least it confused the gator. It seems pretty stunned."

Mathilda couldn't help but smile. "Yeah, seems that way."

The reptile studied Mathias for another moment before turning and padding away. The ground rustled with each step before the swamp welcomed the alligator with a small splash. Mathias followed the alligator to the water's edge, kneeled, and filled the vials for the witch. She paused to take in the sun reflecting the trees and clouds onto the blue-green surface. Heads of alligators floated along the surface like slabs of stone. Birds chirped their cheerful, saccharine songs.

Mathias had never seen anything so beautiful.

"Is this what you really want, Matty?" Mathilda asked.

"Yes, it is."

"Alright, we'll try it," Mathilda said, before taking over, banishing Mathias back to the shadows. Back to humanity.

"Here you go," Mathilda said, slamming the vials into Zelima's hand. "I hope this magic water is worth it. We almost got killed."

"Mathilda."

"No, Matty. I won't calm down."

Zelima inspected the bottles. She nodded, pleased with their contents. "Haven't you heard magic comes with a price?"

Mathilda wanted to claw that smirk from the witch's face, shredding her flawless skin.

"I'm glad you've returned in one piece. Now it's time to break you into two." The shop owner's smirk stretched. "Just a little bit of humor to lighten the mood."

Mathilda glowered.

119

"Very well. I'll give you a minute to say any last words to one another." Zelima exited the main area of the shop, disappearing into the back room.

"Mathilda—"

"Save it, Matty. For after." Lips sewn together, Mathilda attempted a smile. She didn't know what after would look like, and even though its many possibilities frightened her, Mathilda owed this to Mathias. "I'll see you on the other side."

"It was the only way," Zelima said. "I tried everything. Every spell I could think of." Her voice was hushed, the words quick on her tongue.

"The important thing is it worked. They'll be safe. Both of them. Deanna and I will look after them." The voice was feminine, unfamiliar.

"But one is banished to Penumbra."

"The swamp chose the soul that had lived a fuller life." This voice too sounded feminine and unfamiliar.

Mathias held her breath, listening. "Mathilda."

Mathilda didn't answer.

Mathias couldn't hear Mathilda's thoughts or see what she was seeing. For the first time in her life, Mathias couldn't sense her other half. Bolting upright, she found herself lying on a table in a small room. It must have been the backroom of Lavender's. Zelima was still talking to the other two people, their voices muffled through the wall. Mathias slid her legs off of the table, her feet reaching the wood floor. It was cool and grainy. She shouted at the sight of green muscular legs and slimy webbed feet.

Mathias said Mathilda's name again, but no answer came. Where was she?

Zelima rushed into the room, followed by two women. They shut the door behind them. The shop owner wore the same dress she had when Mathilda and Mathias came into the shop seeking her help. How long ago had that been? There were dark circles under the witch's eyes and lines like small paper cuts surrounding them. Her forehead and chin were also etched with age. Zelima looked fractured, a ball of yarn unwound. Mathias noticed the circular necklace the witch had been wearing was gone.

Zelima noticed Mathias' gaze. "The spell required a lot of magic. I needed to use my amulet, a magical vessel that stalls aging." With one hand she touched the lines by her eye. "You may have noticed I don't look like my usual self. That is what the second vial of swamp water was for. Revitalizing the amulet's anti-aging powers. I'll look thirty years younger the next time you see me.

"Now tell me, how do you feel?" The lines on the witch's face deepened with concern.

Mathias looked at the other two women in the room. They were both young—Mathias thought no more than twenty-five—one woman had tawny eyes, an olive complexion, and wavy dark chocolate hair. She wore black overalls that were frayed at the bottom, licking her upper thighs, and a white and red t-shirt with vertical stripes. The other woman had dark gray hair styled in a banged bob reminiscent of flappers in the 1920s. This woman had green eyes, pale skin, and wore a black tank top and maxi skirt.

Mathias stood. "Where is Mathilda? What did you do to us?" Her eyes darted from woman to woman. "Who are they?"

Zelima reached her hands out in a calming gesture. "Why don't you sit back down, Mathias? We'll get you some water. Rose," she called, her face turned toward the front room.

The door opened. A teenage girl's upper body popped into the opening. She had a kind face with a colony of freckles across each cheek and a long mahogany braid pulled to the right side of her body.

"Yes?"

"Can you get our friend some water please?"

She nodded. "Of course."

Rose returned a moment later with a plastic cup of water.

Zelima thanked the girl and took the water, saying that would be all. Rose nodded and closed the door quietly behind her. The witch handed Mathias the cup. She grabbed it with shaky hands and sucked down the room temperature liquid. The cup empty, Mathias kept it in her hand, squeezing the plastic like a stress ball, each pulse making a small cracking noise. She leaned against the edge of the table, waiting for Zelima to explain what the hell was going on.

"She helps out with the shop a few days a week. Good girl," the witch said.

Mathias huffed, the sound so similar to the one Mathilda made. *Mathilda, where are you?* Mathias searched the crevices of her mind for her other half.

"These are my friends. This is Lilly," Zelima motioned to the young woman in overalls, "and this is Deanna." She motioned to the one in all black. "They are going to help you and Mathilda."

"Where is my sister?" Mathias stood up straight. "I can't sense her." The cup crackled in her hand.

"She is safe."

"Where is she? Why can't I hear her? Why am I the one in control right now?"

Zelima took a step closer to Mathias, who drew her upper body away. "It worked. I was able to separate you. You, my dear, are never going to be locked inside again, shrunken to a voice in your other half's head."

Mathias scowled, her amphibious lips drooping. "What do you mean? Where is she?"

Zelima swallowed, her face stripped of its usual warmth. "To separate you, I had to harness a lot of power. I was able to do it, however, I needed help. Honey Island Swamp is a nexus of powerful magic. It is the intersection of various planes. That of the living, the in-between, and the dead. Its magic has helped me stay youthful for decades." She touched her bare neck. "The only way to keep you both alive was to move one of you to a different plane."

"What are you saying? Where is Mathilda?"

"She now exists on the plane between the living and the dead," Zelima replied.

"It's called Penumbra," Lilly said.

"For how long?" Mathias stumbled on the words.

"For the rest of her life," Lilly said, her tone matter of fact.

"No." Mathias threw the bent cup; it hit the floor with a soft thump. "You have to switch us. Mathilda, she won't survive in a place like that. She needs connection."

"There is no way to reverse it," Zelima said.

"No, no. I don't believe that. You can't do this to me. To us. What am I supposed to do without Mathilda? Where am I supposed to go?" Fat green tears pooled in the creases of Mathias' lips. "It should have been me."

Deanna stepped closer. She gazed into Mathias' eyes and placed one hand on her cheek, the woman's cool flesh soaking up Mathias' tears. "It is hard to accept decisions made by Destiny. Often, people ask, *Why did this happen to me? What is going to happen to a loved one without me?*"

The woman stroked Mathias's cheek. "I believe in Destiny. It drives my life. My every action and decision. I'll admit it doesn't always make sense, but this time it's the perfect divine plan. You've spent your life as a shadow, Mathias. A flicker behind someone else. When you've been in the limelight, you've been a magic trick, a prop. You've never gotten to be you. You, my friend, are destined to be more than someone's echo." Deanna's face lit up when she smiled. "You are destined to be you. Whoever that may be."

Mathias choked back more tears. "No one has touched me since my mother left. People touch Mathilda, but never me."

Deanna nodded, her hand still on Mathias' face.

"I'll never see her again, will I?"

Deanna shook her head. "I'm afraid not."

"Not face to face, at least," Lilly said from behind Deanna.

"There is a way you can see her again," Zelima added. She stood next to Lilly. "If you visit my friend, Isabelle, at Honey Island Swamp she will show you Mathilda. That is if you want to see her of course."

"Of course I do." Mathias' cheeks rose at the thought of her sister, then slackened, sadness crossing her face like a shadow. "I don't even know what I am anymore if I'm not half of Mathilda. If I'm not a Muoro."

"There is a new destiny for you. I can sense it," Deanna said. Her eyes shone, two lanterns in the night.

Mathias' forehead wrinkled, green skin darkening at the creases. She imagined Mathilda making a snarky comment about how Deanna sounded like a fortune teller from Jackson Square. *Step right up. Don't be shy. Pick a card. Any card. No, not that card. Ah, yes. The card says you have a big destiny ahead of you. Oh, yeah?* Mathilda would say to the psychic. *Destiny, my ass.* Mathilda had always hated anything she classified as "woo," being too cynical for that level of spirituality and serenity. Mathias reached within, begging her sister to appear. Listening for her signature snark.

When Mathilda didn't materialize, Mathias asked Deanna, "What *are* you?"

The questions sparked a small smile on the woman's face. "I am a Minister, a Frieda's companion."

"And a Frieda is?"

"One who helps the newly dead find a place of rest." Deanna looked over her shoulder at Lilly.

"Are you...?" Mathias said to the woman in overalls.

She nodded, then shrugged. "It's not as glamorous as it sounds."

Mathias chuckled, the vibrations tickling her vocal cords. She hadn't laughed in a long time. It felt warm, like the sun shining on one's back, an experience Mathias had only ever had briefly. She grinned. "I bet."

Her face folded at a nagging thought. An insect bite itching, aflame. "What about J. Allister? Won't he come looking for me? For Mathilda?"

"He'll come, but he won't find you," Zelima said. "And if he does, he likely won't survive the encounter."

Deanna dropped her hand from Mathias' face, stepping back in line with the other two women. Mathia looked at the three of them—a witch, a Frieda, and a Minister. Magical creatures she never imagined existed or would have believed she would ever be in the same room with. For so long, Mathias had believed only curses existed and that she was the result of one. "What do you mean he won't survive it?" she asked.

"I promised to help you, and I meant it," the witch said. "There's no need for you to be further tangled up with the likes of J. Allister."

Mathias shook her head. Her moonstone eyes gleamed slippery with the beginning of tears. "This is a lot to take in." The women nodded. "Can I see Mathilda? I need to talk to her. I need to make sure she's okay."

"Of course you can," Zelima said. "Deanna and Lilly can take you to see Isabelle today."

"How can I thank you? All of you?"

"By finding your true self. Your destiny," Deanna said.

Lilly snorted. She jerked her thumb toward her Minister. "Can you believe the crap she spouts?"

"It's not crap," Deanna snapped. "I believe it."

Lilly nodded, a grin creeping at the corners of her lips. "I know you do, which makes it even more ridiculous."

"Of course we want you to be happy, Mathias," Zelima added. "To fulfill your destiny. That will make us all sleep well at night. However, there is one more favor you can do for me."

"What is it?"

"Promise me you'll try to live a full life."

Mathias nodded. "I promise," she said, even though she didn't quite believe it.

"Do you know where you'll go, after you visit your sister?"

"I do." Mathias thought of the light breeze drifting along the water, creating soft dimples in its surface. Birds crooning from the live oaks. The alligator's yellow eyes, taking her in. Seeing her as one of them.

"I think I've found my place."

The dock creaked under Mathias' feet.

"I only spend part of the year here, a few months at most," Isabelle said. She was the friend Zelima had told Mathias about; a man-eating siren who lived on Honey Island Swamp and existed on all three planes. It would take some getting used to, but Mathias would come to find Isabelle to be kind and compassionate.

A talented shapeshifter, Isabelle was in one of her many human forms at the moment, pacing back and forth, her plum hair undulating down her back in waves. "You're welcome to stay as long as you like. Over there is Rose's grandfather's cabin. Sweet girl, isn't she? I thought about taking her under my fin, so to speak, but Zelima scooped her up first." She sighed, the exhale nearly a growl. "And on the other side of the swamp is Julia's cabin. She's our resident swamp witch."

The siren's hand lifted to her mouth, in confession. "They're okay as far as neighbors go. We have our issues from time to time. But, overall, it's peaceful here. I like to keep my distance and they do too. We give one another space."

Mathias nodded.

"If you're staying with me, I only ask one thing."

"What?"

"If you see a boat with men coming close, make yourself scarce. There's usually a lot of carnage, and I prefer to dine alone."

Isabelle eyed Mathias before tossing her head back and cackling. It felt very cinematic to Mathias, as though Isabelle were an actress playing a role. Mathias supposed many did just that; the media, ever churning at the wheel of the patriarchy, perpetuated limited categories for queer and femme-bodied people. Isabelle was a literal man-eating siren who delighted in tearing into the flesh of cis-hetero men. She could manipulate her appearance to be anyone her victims' desired, and yet, her true form would be deemed monstrous by most. Mathias knew the shapeshifter was trying to avenge her murder at the hands of an old boyfriend. Why did retribution cast her as a villain instead of the hero of her story?

Mathias rubbed her lips together with a smacking, suctioning sound. "Zelima said you can communicate with those on other planes. She said if I asked you could show me my sister, Mathilda. I know we just met and all, but she's stuck there because of me." Mathias swiped a runaway tear. "I have to make sure she's okay. I have to thank her. I have to set things right, or at least try to." Tears slipped down her cheeks. "Will you help me?"

"Of course." Isabelle offered her hand. "Let's go see your sister."

Mathias took the siren's hand. Isabelle led Mathias to the edge of the dock, their reflections rippling on top of the water's surface. "Think of Mathilda. Conjure her face in your mind. Picture every freckle, scar, or detail that you can. The more specific, the easier I can locate her. And hold tight to my hand until she appears."

Mathias agreed, squeezing Isabelle's hand. She watched as the shapeshifter shut her eyes, eyeballs flitting under closed lids. Mathias expected Isabelle to utter an incantation like Zelima had, but the siren remained silent, her breath even, body relaxed. After several minutes, Isabelle's eyes flickered open. "Look down," she said to Mathias.

Their reflections faded as though rubbed out with an eraser. A tiny water droplet appeared in the center of the now empty surface. It began to stretch, until it was the size of a boulder. "Hello?" a familiar voice said. The circle vibrated, synchronous with the voice.

"Hello?" the voice asked again.

The outline of a face appeared in the water.

Mathias leaned forward. "Mathilda? Is that you?"

Mathilda's face came into hazy focus, the water blending and blurring her face and the world she now resided in. Forever resided in, Mathias reminded herself. Because I wanted to be free. She shook her head. "It's me. Matty."

"I'll give you some privacy," Isabelle said.

Mathias started to thank the siren but she had vanished. "I don't know if I'll ever get used to magic like that."

"Matty?" Mathilda gasped. "It is you. I'm so glad to see you. I woke up here all alone. I've never been alone before, you know?"

"I do."

Mathilda nodded her head. "I guess you do. I was worried you'd never come. But then I told myself Matty would never leave me behind. He'd find a way to bring me back."

Mathias hung her head, guilt overriding Mathilda misgendering Mathias yet again. Her breathing quickened. "I am so, so sorry this happened to you, Mathilda. I came as soon as I could. I talked to Zelima, to Deanna and Lilly, about ways to bring you back." She exhaled. "There is no way to bring you back. I am so sorry. I never wanted this."

Mathilda scoffed. "Of course you did. Little brother got big sister out of the picture. Now you can shine."

This time Mathias knew Mathilda said *brother* to hurt her. "I never wanted this, Mathilda. I would trade with you, if I could."

"Sure you would. Good luck out there, Matty. You have no idea how much I protected you from."

"Mathilda."

She held up her hand. "Leave me alone. I don't want to see you for a while."

Mathias watched Mathilda turn and walk away, her golden hair floating like a cloud in the sky. The portal mirrored Mathias' setting, a softened abstraction of the real thing. Mathias swatted at the water, wanting to erase everything that had led them here.

"Did you mean what you said?" Isabelle asked. The siren materialized without making a sound.

"Excuse me?"

"Would you really trade places with your sister?"

Mathias' head bobbed. "Of course."

"Why? Because you don't believe you deserve to have your own life, out of her shadow?" The siren picked at a stray piece of flesh wedged in her teeth. "Let me give you a little bit of advice. I'm sure Zelima told you I wasn't born this way. Once upon a time I was beautiful, maybe even more beautiful than Mathilda. My beauty came at a high cost, however. Men thought they could do whatever they wanted to me. My cop daddy, my drug dealer boyfriend. I ended up here because of them, you know? It doesn't take much for fetish to become murder.

"Look at me now though, kid. I am vile to look at. I eat men for fun. And I've never felt more beautiful. I had to sever my connection to those men who held me down for so long to be my authentic self."

"Did you…?"

Isabelle grinned, slivers of stretchy gristle caught on her fang. "Who do you think I went after first?"

Mathias realized how similar they were. As a shapeshifter, Isabelle was able to appear as a beautiful maiden or as a towering monster with dagger-like claws and an appetite for male flesh. She was terrifying and tantalizing, which, in many ways, was how Mathias and Mathilda had been. Isabelle understood pain and fragmentation better than most. She had transformed into a powerful creature that could exist on all three planes, and sought revenge on those who had caged her. Death had brought Isabelle to her destiny. Mathias hoped her own loss would be a rebirth like it had been for the Siren of Honey Island Swamp. And maybe it could be a rebirth for her sister too.

After a few months, Honey Island Swamp was home. Mathias stayed on the dock with Isabelle some nights, while others she camped in the grove. Sometimes she had tea with the swamp witch, Julia, a wiry, wild-haired woman with eyes full of lust and sadness. Julia was hungry for companionship, desperately wanting to belong, which Mathias understood better than most.

They had met outside of the swamp witch's cabin, a small, strangely shaped hunk of wood. Julia sat on the steps of the porch and Mathias stood on the dusty earth before her, the swamp at her back. It took Julia the better part of a minute to find her voice when Mathias approached.

Mathias held her hands out in front of her in a gesture of peace. She knew what she looked like, the horror she stirred in people, their screams and cries hurtling from deep in their bellies. The old woman flinched at the sound of Mathias' voice, but her shoulders relaxed when she took Mathias in. "What are you?" she said when she had found her voice.

"I'm still figuring that out," Mathias said. "I was a Muoro. One half of a being. Now I am just my half, a monster."

"A monster in flesh or inside?"

Mathias swallowed. "In flesh."

The old woman nodded. "What are you inside?"

Mathias's forehead wrinkled. "I'm not sure. For so long there were two parts of me and now I'm just—" She sighed. "Trying to figure it out, I guess." The witch nodded again. In a quiet voice, Mathias allowed herself to share a secret with the witch: "I know one thing. I've always known it. I'm non-binary. My other half has never questioned her identity. But me, I question every part of myself. It's not about being female or male or any one gender, it's getting to be a whole person that gets to choose who I am and how I express myself."

Julia smiled. Mathias took a step back, unprepared for such a response. "We are powerless over how or where or what we are born, my green friend, but we can choose to live our lives however we want."

Mathias nodded, her face flushed. "What about you?" she said, changing the subject. "Monster in flesh or inside?"

"Both," the swamp witch said. "But I wasn't always."

"I'd like to hear your story," Mathias said.

"Step right up," Julia said, her voice suddenly taking on that of an announcer. When Mathias didn't move, the swamp witch's face twisted as though she'd just tasted something bitter. "Come on in," she said and waved Mathias into the cabin. The pair shared tea and stories, surfacing at dusk.

Mathias and Julia became fast friends, an understanding of loneliness, neglect, and manipulation between them. They spent much of their time together—fishing, cooking, even singing on the stoop of the cabin, their legs outstretched. Mathias' limbs stretched much longer than the old woman's. Julia would mention this and laugh, but it wasn't biting or cruel. It was a joke, a jab between friends. Mathias shared everything with her—even about her fight with Mathilda.

"You should try again," Julia told her one night. The moon hung milky and full above the still swamp.

Mathias shook her head. "I've tried several times. She hasn't shown since our fight. Mathilda blames me. And for a long time I blamed myself."

How about now?"

"Now I don't want to waste my chance at a new life." Mathias looked at the moon and thought of the Titan goddess Selene. The myth said she fell in love with a mortal, Endymion. The only way they could be together was for him to be placed in an eternal slumber. Zeus granted Endymion this, his lunar lover visiting his dreams. Even though dreams could be sweeter than reality, Mathias knew they could also be a cage. To be without consciousness was to be without choice. For twenty-five years Mathias had felt as though she were in a perpetual state of dreaming, but instead of a passionate love affair with a beautiful goddess, she was a prisoner trying to escape a nightmare. "I don't want to waste this," Mathias told Julia.

Julia spat a wad of saliva at the ground. She turned to Mathias, a wide grin on her withered face. "I think you're starting to get it, my green friend."

It was several weeks before Mathias tried to visit her sister again, the longest the two halves had ever been apart. It wasn't that she didn't miss Mathilda or still feel guilty for what had happened to her sister, but Mathias wanted the chance to try out who she could be out of Mathilda's shadow.

This time Mathilda appeared. "Matty, where have you been?" she asked. "I thought you had forgotten me."

Mathias shook her head. "How could I ever forget you?" She smiled before her face fell. "Look, Mathilda, about the last time we talked—"

Mathilda put up her hand. "Don't worry about it. I was just upset." She squinted. It was always hard to discern reality through the delicate ripples of the swamp water. It was never a perfect reflection of her other half. Mathias looked softer, yet also brighter. And was that clothing? Mathilda had never known Mathias to wear clothing other than during their act. "You look different," she said. "Changed."

"You noticed," Mathias said, giddy. "I wasn't sure if you would."

"Are you wearing a dress?" Mathilda's eyebrow lifted into its signature position.

"Mhm. Isabelle helped me make it."

"It's beautiful," Mathilda said. From what she could see, it was. The dress was a deep shade of blue; Mathilda imagined it to be the same color as the depths of the sea. There was a sheen to it; she imagined it was velvet or a similar fabric. It had cap sleeves that went off Mathias' shoulders, the fabric pulling at his—her—biceps. The dress went to Mathias' knees, revealing muscular calves that Mathilda had always joked were made of steel. "You look beautiful, Matty."

"That's another thing, too. I don't go by Mathias anymore."

"Oh," Mathilda said more as a statement than a question.

"Madeleine. You can still call me Maddy."

"Maddy," Mathilda said, feeling the new letters on her tongue. She had to admit it sounded the same as Matty. "I like it." Her lip quivered. "You seem happy."

"I am. For the first time I get to be me. And I'm not afraid of being laughed at or hunted. I like the swamp, too. Maybe I really am the Monster of Honey Island Swamp after all." Mathias laughed.

Mathilda smirked. "Maybe."

"I miss you, of course."

"You too."

"Tell me, how are things down there?" Madeleine's face was earnest, hopeful that her sister was doing as well as she.

Mathilda looked at her surroundings. Penumbra was cloaked in shadows and gray. It felt like being in an old black and white T.V. show without the beautiful families and clothing and punch lines. It was a strange land. A lonely place where those who had just died journeyed— they reminded her of cattle lining up in a pen, ready to be directed to the barn, or to slaughter. Mathilda did talk to Isabelle when the siren wasn't luring her next meal, and Lilly and Deanna came each night. But they were working, they had their own destiny to attend to.

Mathilda had taken up skipping stones. Some of the swamp creatures joined her. Animals and reptiles could talk in Penumbra. It was startling at first to hear human voices in such beastly creatures, but now if Mathilda closed her eyes, she could almost fool herself that they were real people and she was on the plane of the living once more. She hated it here, without any real purpose. Mathilda was a performer! She belonged in front of the living, showcasing her act. But what act did she have without Maddy? Who was Mathilda if she wasn't a Muoro? And how could she tell any of this to her other half who had spent her life trapped inside? Who had been a spectacle for drunk, rowdy tourists. Mathilda swallowed, pushing a smile onto her face, her cheeks aching with deceit. "I'm doing just fine. I have taken up some new hobbies and I'm working on a new act."

"A new act?" Madeleine asked.

"It's top secret. I've been showing Lilly and Deanna. Maybe one day I'll show you too."

"I'd love that." She paused. "Mathilda, are we going to be okay, you and me?"

Mathilda studied her finger nails before responding. "It's always been you and me, Maddy. And it's always going to be. So, yeah, we're going to be okay."

Madeleine nodded. "Okay, good." She turned her head at the sound of Julia's warbling. "Listen, I have to go. I promised Julia I'd help her with the gators."

"The what?"

"Oh, she's an alligator trainer. Or she was. Or she pretends to be." Madeleine placed her hand to the side of her mouth, to shield her words from everyone but Mathilda. "She's not very good. But I am actually. They think I'm an alligator. And when I talk and walk around on my hindlegs they think I'm some kind of goddess."

Mathilda laughed, her eyes filling with tears. "It was great to see you, Maddy. I'm glad you're doing so well."

"You too. I'll see you soon."

"Okay," Mathilda said. She turned her back to her other half just as tears laid tracks down her cheeks. She knew it would be a while before Madeleine visited again. Mathilda's heart sank to her stomach with the knowledge that one day Maddy might not come at all, leaving Mathilda alone in her cage, a shadow—only half of one whole self.

Conjure

"**C**ome one, come all."

She followed the voice, stopping in front of a red and white striped tent floating in the middle of the swamp. Looked down at her feet, tanned and unlined by age, fish and algae dancing below. She walked on water, young again. The voice called to her a second time, yet now it was familiar. Something slapped the surface of the swamp, bobbing in its blue-green water behind her. She stepped into the tent. Everything went black.

Julia Baudin, known as Crazy Julia or the Swamp Witch, writhed in agony on the dusty ground outside her lopsided cabin. She was a tiny, wrinkled woman with a tangled nest of silver curly hair and medium-brown leathery skin. Twigs and pebbles were stuck in her hair and her long, black caftan was smudged with dirt. Her bare arms were zigzagged with red, swollen lumps. Julia appeared to be in her eighties or nineties. Having spent nearly every day of her life sitting on the stoop of her cabin, the Louisiana sun beating off Honey Island Swamp and onto her skin, had accelerated the witch's aging, or so people said. *How old is she really?* Someone would ask when he heard the story, to which his friend or family member would say, *I don't know. She's been around as long as I can remember.*

The truth was Julia had lived through a handful of lifetimes. She couldn't remember her birthday anymore or how old she was exactly, but she knew she'd seen generations of families come and stay at Honey Island Swamp for summer vacation, filling it with squeals and laughter and the fragrance of hot dogs, hamburgers, corn on the cob, and fresh fruit. It had been over a decade since the families stopped coming. Since then, the swamp had been soundless except for the occasional splash from an alligator's tail or a raccoon scuffle, and in place of the smell of charcoal and meat on the grill and crisp fruit and vegetables, there was a rotten, seething odor. It was as though Death had moved in, taking over the abandoned, dilapidated cabins and campgrounds.

Julia preferred solitude. She had one human neighbor across the swamp, one siren neighbor who spent part of the year on a floating dock in the middle of the swamp, an alligator-looking fellow who shacked up part-time with the siren, and a handful of raccoons and alligators who lived nearby and sometimes hung out on the old woman's land. Julia didn't need all the chatter that surrounded families like dozens of fireflies, lighting up every time someone spoke (which usually meant several were illuminated at once). She definitely didn't need friends, either. Friendship didn't come easily for a mixed-race orphan who had a particular set of gifts, or demons, depending on who you asked. Friendship and family had never come easily for Julia; in fact, they had hardly come at all.

It seemed impossible, but finally the searing pain faded like hunger pangs after getting something to eat. Forgotten, almost like they had never been. Julia crawled out of the protective ball her body had put itself into, and on all fours, made her way to her beloved stoop. There were two wooden steps up to the porch of her cabin; she had always favored the first step and it showed: the pine was cracked and a deeper shade than the rest of the slab of wood.

Julia adjusted her aching bones into comfort on her stoop. She looked out at the swamp and saw an alligator sunning himself on a mis-shapen rock that poked through the water. The reptile's mouth cranked open, his brown, razor-sharp teeth exposed; he tried to cool himself off and she didn't blame him. The swamp was a fiery pit from Hell this afternoon. Julia fanned herself, the skin on her arms flapping with a whoosh, the flesh so loose from the bone it almost seemed unattached.

She inspected her arms, examining the rosy lumps coating the weathered and stretchy skin. Now that the pain was gone, Julia could think straight. And it didn't take much thinking to know who was responsible for her torture and for the remaining chicken pox-like marks. "Zelima," Julia said in a snarl. Her voice was low and sounded like she had gravel stuck in her throat. It was also tinged with a thick twang. She pronounced the woman's name as *Zah-leemur*.

Julia and Zelima went way back. If the wiry, wild-haired woman was seen as a swamp witch, Zelima was a Voodoo one. Both were feared by residents in and outside of the Crescent City as the subject of folklore, reaching mythological status. The two women revelled in their power, in the awe and fear they inspired. Both prided themselves on being above the fickle, petty desire for love and romantic companionship. And while neither woman had given birth, both considered themselves mothers.

Mothers of magic, nature, and beasts.

Zelima Delacroix was born and raised in a Black area of the French Quarter by a family of witches. Magic had germinated from one person in her family to the next, a tree with a thick trunk and strong, intertwined branches. She was born in the early 1950s when racial strife was inescapable, hatred and segregation poisoning the air. But her family had lived in New Orleans for hundreds of years, and their magic was known to all families in the Quarter, not just those in their Black neighborhood. Many called it *Voodoo*, but that was out of ignorance. Folk magic was what Zelima's family called it, or Hoodoo. Even still, their reputation as practitioners of Voodoo, what many believed to be black magic, led to reverence from the habitants of the city. The family then earned respect from their success rate; they never had an unsatisfied customer. Love, money, luck, you name it, they manifested it for you. People from various economic, religious, and racial backgrounds sought out the family for magical help, whether it be nefarious or well-intentioned.

Zelima was raised in a household where magic was as routine as house chores or going to church on Sundays. She was taught to believe her powers were a gift, and that she could do both good and evil with them. Her mother—a glass half full type of person—and her grandmother—a bitter woman broken down by society—each stressed their moral compasses to the young girl, impregnating her with contrasting ideas of salvation in light magic and retribution in using dark. Even with these conflicting ideas, Zelima felt strength and opportunity in her magic. At age eight, she promised herself that no one would ever cause her family or herself harm and get away with it. She never broke that vow, and had been reigning over the French Quarter for innumerable decades. Zelima had crowned herself New Orleans' Queen of Magic and her wrath never let anyone forget it.

Unlike Zelima, Julia had spent years searching for a family of her own. She was born over a century before the Quarter witch, and many miles from New Orleans. Born a bastard—her mother, Dorothée, a slave; her father, Elijah Baudin, the master of a Louisiana plantation—Julia came into the world half-orphaned, after her mother died in childbirth. Elijah showed his adoration for the girl by bringing hand picked flowers and toys he carved out of wood, however, he had to limit his affection for early in the morning and late at night. His wife, Thelma, knew about Elijah's indiscretion and the product of said dalliance, and had no interest in Julia joining the family she had shed blood and years of her life for, so she came up with a plan to rid herself of the girl. She had her own children to think about, two towheaded boys and two redheaded girls. All it took was a business trip, Elijah's beloved pocket watch, and an apple.

The mistress of the plantation told the eight-year-old girl that her father had forgotten his pocket watch, the one his grandfather had given him before he had died. The one Elijah never went anywhere without. Thelma told Julia to take Jax, a seventeen-year-old stable boy, with her. Together, they would go to the small inn her father usually stopped at on his way to New Orleans. Thelma offered the girl a crisp, green apple from the orchard. "Freshly picked," she had said.

Julia and Jax never made it to the inn. The stable boy had been instructed to murder the girl, to carve her heart from her chest, bringing it back to his mistress as an offering. Instead Jax told Julia to run far away. The girl's first experience of wickedness had also shown her kindness, a kindness she would never forget. After that day, Julia never stepped foot on the plantation again, her father forever lost to her. She did, however, visit Thelma one more time, and it wasn't a joyful reunion for the mistress of the plantation.

The young girl, homeless and free from the confines of slavery, wandered to Honey Island Swamp, just outside of New Orleans. There Julia discovered magic and family, and many years later, loneliness. This is where the two conjurors' paths crossed. They knew there was a likeness to them, even some shared experiences, yet there were stark differences that neither witch could ignore, and because of this, Julia and Zelima were enemies.

"Damn right," a voice said in Julia's ear.

The swamp witch swatted at the empty air as though it were a mosquito. Zelima had a way of worming into one's mind. "Go away," she griped. "Haven't you done enough today?"

"Not by half," Zelima purred.

Julia knew better than to look around for the Quarter witch. The old woman was no idiot. Zelima had cast a spell to torture the swamp witch and here she was—at least in voice—to gloat. "Always one for games, huh, Z? You're too liver-bellied to come and face me."

Zelima laughed, the sound shrill and full-bodied, similar to a hyena. A few raccoons who no longer were nocturnal, knowing the pickings were better during daylight, scampered away in fear. "You know my power is great enough that I don't have to come to you to do battle. I warned you, Julia, many years ago. Stay out of the Quarter and my business. But you couldn't help it, could you? Are you really *that* lonely?"

Julia frowned, every ridge on her face deepening. She thought about the dreams she had been having under Zelima's spell. Her body shivered, her ancient bones creaking in their sockets. The magical circus had been at the center of the years she was happiest. Julia knew what she would find if she returned to that dream—the worst day of her life.

Zelima knew Julia had been lonely every day since, reveling in the fresh pain she caused the swamp witch, picking at old scabs that would never heal. Yet the Quarter witch was right. Julia had gone against their agreement, if you could call it that. More like a declaration on Zelima's part. Julia knew she wasn't supposed to help that Charlie fellow, who had been cursed by her enemy, and turned into a blue alligator. But sometimes you had to stir up a little mud, if only to have a little fun. Even though the siren had told her all was forgiven, Julia knew her longtime nemesis better than that. Some fires never quelled. Zelima planned on making Julia pay; the pain and dream had only been the beginning.

"What do you want, Z?" She spat, not caring that it hit the lowest step of her stoop.

"I thought we could talk. Reminisce. For old time's sake."

"Fine." Julia spat again, this time hitting the soft ground in front of her cabin. "You go first."

"No, no. You go." The swamp witch imagined Zelima's arms crossed in front of her, ready to scold a disobedient child. "My story is still unfolding. Yours, on the other hand, is nearly expired."

Julia spat a third time. "Bitch," she said under her breath. She looked out at the swamp, the water rippling, mirroring the trees and sky above.

The golden eyes of several gators hovered above the surface like tiny submarines. Days on the swamp were unhurried.

"Fine," the old woman said after a minute. "I've got nothing better to do."

Julia started at the beginning, or rather, the moment she stood on the precipice of a new life, possibility and love and disappointment finally in her grasp. The plantation, her daddy, Mistress Thelma and her failed murder attempt, it was so far in the past, Julia paid it no more attention than a fly. Everything that happened before led her to Adelaide.

Taking Jax's advice, young Julia ran as fast and as far as she could. Her feet were black from dirt and mud and misshapen with blisters. She was out of food and finding water was a tireless task. That is until she came to the swamp. It wouldn't be known as Honey Island Swamp for another fifty years and wouldn't be a popular vacation spot for one-hundred. There was one cabin on the lake when Julia arrived, yet she didn't notice it.

The mid-afternoon sun on her face, Julia threw her body into the swamp and felt energy return as she moved through the blue-green water. It was the closest thing to rebirth she would ever experience. Julia wasn't a very good swimmer, but she flapped her arms and peddled her legs, managing to keep afloat. The water was cool on her skin and she laughed in exhaustion and relief. Maybe she would be okay after all.

The sound of laughter brought the swamp's singular resident from her cabin. She was a slight woman with brown hair, brown eyes, and heavily freckled pink skin. She wore a corset and petticoat and nothing else.

"Why hello there," the woman said. She spoke with a foreign accent, one unfamiliar to Julia.

Julia froze at the sound of the stranger's voice. The girl thought about swimming away, but her body wouldn't move.

"Didn't mean to scare you, dear. I just don't usually get many visitors during the day."

Julia stared at her, dumbstruck. A white woman had never spoken to Julia in such a nonchalant manner, nor had she ever seen a woman walk around in such a state of undress. She couldn't take her eyes from the woman's freckled chest.

"Can you talk? Or are you one of them silent fellows?" She waved her hand to the side as if to say it was no matter or to swat away a bug. Julia wasn't sure. "I'm Adelaide. A medium and alligator trainer extraordinaire." With a flourish, the woman raised her arms in the air as though she were about to bow.

Julia remained silent and unmoving. Only her feet pumped to keep her body from sinking under the water's surface. The woman named Adelaide seemed to speak in riddles or madness. Julia didn't know what a medium was. She knew what an alligator was, yet she had never seen one before, and she had certainly never heard of alligator trainers.

"Are you hungry? I caught a couple fish earlier." Adelaide pronounced the last word as two syllables: *ear-leer*. She turned and started walking away from Julia. After a few seconds, Adelaide turned back. "Ya coming?"

Julia found herself swimming to the edge of the swamp and pulling herself out of the water. Then her feet followed the mysterious woman to her cabin. The structure was lopsided and made out of slabs of mismatched wood. There was a small porch in front. Inside there was one room with a small straw mattress and quilt, a stove, and a wooden table with two chairs. Standing in the cabin, you could see the outside wilderness through long, horizontal cracks in the wood.

The girl sat in one of the chairs while Adelaide cooked the fish on the stove. The woman offered her dry clothes, yet Julia refused. She watched Adelaide cook, adjusting in her seat every few seconds because of her damp dress. It stuck to her thighs. When the fish was done, Adelaide put a piece in front of Julia. The fish's open, lifeless eye stared at the girl from the glass plate.

"Thank you, ma'am," Julia said in a voice just above a whisper.

"You're welcome. Don't call me ma'am though. Ady or Miss Adelaide is just fine."

"Miss Adelaide," she said, feeling the woman's name on her tongue and the roof of her mouth. "Julia."

"Excuse me, dear? What'd you say?"

"My name is Julia."

"Pleased to meet you, Julia." Adelaide smiled, revealing brilliantly white teeth. She then began to eat the fish before her and Julia followed suit.

When they had both finished their meal, Adelaide said she wanted to show Julia something. She led the girl outside, facing the water. Her hands on her hips, Adelaide grinned ear to ear. "Look around," she said.

Julia did as instructed. She saw the vast swamp and the gnarled, weeping trees encased in Spanish moss and vines. White and gray birds were sprinkled through the trees and several alligators lay in the fading sun, their mouths open, on an island of rocks to the right of them. Julia inhaled sharply at the sight of the large reptiles; they were so close. Too close.

Adelaide said, "Don't worry. They won't bother us."

Julia wrapped her arms around herself, unsure.

"What do you think?" The woman stretched her arms out, open to the sky.

The girl wrinkled her forehead. "It's pretty." Julia wasn't sure what Adelaide was after.

"It may not look like much now, just a big swamp and a little ol' me, but with a little magic it becomes a carnival."

"Magic?"

Adelaide's hands returned to her hips. She turned to face Julia, her eyebrows lifting when she said, "Mhm. Tell me, Julia, do you like magic?"

The girl shook her head. She had heard stories of witches and spells and curses. Of the world beyond this one. That's where Mama was, or so Julia liked to think. But she knew nothing of its truth.

"Have you seen magic before?"

Julia shook her head again.

"Would you like to?"

Julia bit her lower lip.

"Why don't we try a little?"

She nodded her head slowly.

"Close your eyes, okay? When you open them, there will be a circus."

This woman seemed mad, and yet she was kind. Julia didn't sense a threat from Adelaide, but her head was still foggy from the past few days. Julia wasn't sure she could trust her instincts, but she didn't know what else to do. So, she did as she was told and squeezed her eyes shut.

Julia breathed in, filling her stomach and lungs, and then out, releasing the air. She listened for sounds around her; no bugs or beasts. She couldn't even hear Adelaide beside her. The silence was eerie.

Finally, the self-proclaimed medium and alligator trainer told Julia to look. The girl blinked her eyes open, unsure of what she was about to see. Her jaw dropped, a gasp escaping from her throat. A smile spread across Julia's face. The swamp had disappeared, or so it seemed. It was still there, yet it was solid like the floor of a house. Julia found herself stepping off the dirt edge of the swamp and onto the water's surface. Her feet didn't slip or slide; it was as though she were walking on solid earth. It reminded her of a mirror—if she looked down, she saw the water and the creatures that resided inside. Snakes, plants, fish. Julia watched them wiggle and float beneath her as though it were perfectly ordinary.

She heard, "Come one, come all," and lifted her eyes. Ten feet in front of the girl stood a medium-sized tent. It had red and white vertical stripes and a pointed top. The structure illuminated the twilight, casting silhouettes of people or things inside. Julia didn't know who or what waited for her.

"Step on up. You don't want to miss—" came from the tent.

It was the same voice as before. Booming and deep. Male. Julia moved toward the entrance. Afterward she would think about how she should have been more scared, but in the moment, she was enchanted.

At the entrance to the tent, a man in a very tall, black top hat and thin black mustache greeted her. "Step right up," he started. His was the voice she'd heard outside.

Julia looked around the illuminated space. There were three attractions set up: to the left there was a cage with a creature that had the body of a man and the head of an alligator, and to the right there was a man in a black and white striped bathing suit that hung on his body as though he were a coat hanger. He eyed Julia before lifting his arms and floating them behind him, his spine curling as he went, until his hands were on the ground, his body forming a bridge. In the middle of the tent were two cloth partitions that separated the two side attractions from the central one. The front was open, and Julia saw a round glass table with a handful of chairs around it.

141

"That is where I commune with the spirit world," Adelaide said in Julia's ear.

Julia jumped; she hadn't realized the woman was behind her. "How did you—?"

"I'll show you later. Now, however, it's showtime!"

Julia turned to look at Adelaide, but the woman had vanished. The girl saw a line of people at the entrance of the tent talking and gossiping, crowding the entrance, waiting to get in. The man with the mustache and top hat greeted them and collected paper bills and coins from their hands.

"Step on up," he said, "if you dare! Inside that cage is a creature unlike any you've seen before! Half-man, half-beast. Don't step too close or he might rip your hand off." The announcer chuckled as the patrons squealed in delight and terror. "Over here we have a man whose bones bend into unimaginable shapes! He can contort into anything. Really! Folks, don't be shy about asking him to try any shape you can think up. You surely won't be disappointed."

The man in the top hat clasped his hands before his chest. "And last, but certainly not least, our main attraction is the wonderous, mysterious Madame Adelaide. Grab a seat at her table and prepare to witness the unthinkable! The unbelievable! The otherworldly! She will bring you face to face with the spirit world. I guarantee it's unlike anything you've witnessed before!"

Julia looked past the man and saw Adelaide sitting at the glass table in a black dress with a high neckline and a black veil covering her face.

The girl made her way over to the table and sat in an empty chair. She wanted to ask, *What's going on?* and *Where did all these people come from?* But Adelaide shook her head, the veil swooshing, and said, "Later," having read Julia's thoughts.

Within minutes, the other chairs were filled, with additional onlookers huddled around. The announcer pulled a black curtain across the front, closing everyone into that sectioned off space. None of the bright lights peeked in through the partitions; the space was in almost total darkness. Adelaide lit several candles, shadows dancing on the table. Behind the veil, her face was completely shrouded.

Adelaide instructed everyone to take hands. She cleared her throat and began to speak in a strange accent. Later Julia would realize it was a fake European one. "What you're about to witness is no trickery or mockery. I, Madame Adelaide, am a medium. Tonight I am going to bring you to the spirit world. We will reach out to any lost souls nearby.

"Please do not disconnect hands at any point. No matter what you see or hear. No harm will come to any of us."

Adelaide waited a beat before continuing, "I call upon the spirits—the lost souls of this place—trapped in this plane. If you are with us, please offer a sign. Perhaps a flicker of the candle."

Julia looked around at the faces of the people sitting at the table. They stared at the candles before them, in anticipation. Some held their breaths, others panted like tired dogs. Julia held hands with a middle-aged woman with curly hair and an older man with thick mutton chop sideburns. Their gathered palms perspired. The girl's breath was shallow; her heart felt stuck in her gut. Julia wasn't sure she wanted to reach out to a ghost.

"If you are with us, please offer a sign," Adelaide said again.

Julia inhaled. One of the flames quivered. Then another. All of the flames flickered, one after the other, like some kind of strange symphony. Julia screamed. The woman next to her muttered, "Good God." The table rattled, shaking the candles, the flames dancing brilliantly and dangerously close to those sitting around the table. Julia screamed again when a low knocking began. It was continuous and grew in sound each time. The knocking built until it was a rapid thumping in her ears.

Everything went black.

When Julia woke, she sat at the table. The curtain was pulled back, illuminating the space. Adelaide was beside her, the black veil gone. Everything else was gone. The patrons, the mustached man, contortionist, and alligator man. Even the props had disappeared, with the exception of the glass table and its chairs. Julia looked around, in a panic. Her forehead was moist, her cheeks hot.

"Where is everyone?"

"Gone," Adelaide said as though it were common knowledge. Her voice was back to its regular cadence.

Julia's eyebrows knit together. "But how—?"

The woman's eyes sparkled. "A little bit of magic."

Julia shook her head. "Was any of it real? The people? The spirit?"

"Yes, of course."

"Then what—?"

"Wasn't?"

Julia nodded.

Adelaide opened her arms, her palms up. Her elbows rested on the table. "All of this. The tent, the other attractions, the man with the mustache."

"How did you learn to do all of this?"

Adelaide smiled. She clasped her hands against her chest just as the man with the mustache had. "Let's just say this is a very magical swamp. A place of great power and connection to other realms. Much like you, I found the swamp, and a woman found me. She taught me how to use the magic of this place. How to do things like this." Her smile widened. "And now I'd like to teach you, if you'd like."

Julia found herself nodding. Magic was the only word to describe what the girl had seen that night, and she wanted to know how to do it.

For the next century, Adelaide was Julia's mentor. During the first few years, she showed Julia how to write spells, how to use her mind to bend reality and create illusions, and how to commune with the spirit world, known as Penumbra, which fluttered under the swamp, a slow, steady heartbeat. Because of the swamp's connection with the dead, it was the greatest source of power in Louisiana. Adelaide told Julia to think of their connection to the swamp as Ouroboros, the snake that eats its own tail, creating an infinite circle. "We feed on the power the swamp possesses, and it feeds on us in return."

"What does that mean exactly?" Julia asked.

"That we are our strongest right here, hand in hand with the swamp. And we become weaker the further we stray from it."

Julia craned her neck to the side. "So, if we left?"

"We would lose our powers completely, and eventually die. The swamp protects and maintains our vitality."

Julia's eyebrows furrowed. "Our what?"

Adelaide crossed her arms in front of her. "You'll see soon enough, dear."

It wasn't until Julia turned eighteen that she understood what Adelaide had meant all those years before. Julia woke one morning to Adelaide kneeling beside her. There was only one bed in the cabin, but the women made it work, learning to sleep on their sides and to not stretch out throughout the night.

"Get up," Adelaide said, the remnants of a smile on her face like an afterthought or leftover crumbs. "Today I'm going to show you how to stave off the effects of aging and prolong life."

Julia jumped out of bed. For years, she had wondered how her mentor stayed so youthful; Adelaide was frozen, unchanged by time, while Julia continued to age, perky little rosebuds blooming on her chest, fine, dark hair sprouting on her legs and armpits; even her hair seemed to be expanding, her curls reaching new heights. Her curls had grown so high they now cascaded down her back instead of skyrocketing into the air. Julia had to admit this was an improvement, however, she was tired of her ever-morphing body. She wanted to be like Adelaide. Timeless. Ageless. And she desperately wanted to harness more magic; the fingers in her bones ached with the expected elation of additional power.

The women stood at the swamp's edge, Julia in a white cotton shift and Adelaide in her usual ensemble—corset and petticoat and nothing else. Adelaide instructed Julia to walk in until only her head remained above the surface. Adelaide walked in up to her waist, her petticoat ballooning around her. She stuck her hands into the clear water. "When I say *her*, you say *I*," she instructed before beginning. Adelaide cleared her throat. "Earth, Penumbra, Netherworld, I call upon your magic that courses through this water. Come together, three sacred entities, and combine your magic into the water surrounding this woman. Encircle her with your power, binding her youth, her magic, her lifespan, with this body of water. In return, she will be your servant, promising to never abandon the swamp unless she's ready to succumb, leaving Earth for Penumbra and the Underworld."

As Julia repeated after Adelaide, she felt a tingle climbing up her leg. The sensation spread, feeling more like a tentacle or arm; Julia imagined a great water beast latching onto her, climbing up her body, consuming her whole. Yet it didn't frighten her. The tingles were warm and inviting. Soothing, even. Years later, Julia would liken it to the moment where her body found ecstasy during climax. The rapture of the tingling, of being enveloped in its heat, made her feel alive in a way she hadn't before.

They finished the spell as the sensation reached Julia's head, tickling her curls. A haze settled over her; she slipped in and out of consciousness, a pale pink glow connecting one realm to the next. She awoke floating in Adelaide's outstretched arms.

"How do you feel?"

The water was electric on her skin. Julia grinned. "I feel...alive."

Adelaide smiled. "We are not immortals," she assured Julia. "But the swamp is a powerful entity, connected to the living, the dead, and the in-between. We will both die one day, but we will live our lives in the in-between for a long, long time."

Julia's breath scraped against her chest. "How old are you?"

Adelaide's cheeks flushed a pale pink. "I stopped counting about five decades ago. You'll quit counting someday too."

The hint of a grin took root on Julia's face. She couldn't help but feel the flicker of joy when she recalled those days. Zelima cleared her throat, pushing the old woman to continue her story.

"Didn't your momma teach you patience, Zelima Delacroix?"

It was always dangerous to bring up Marie, Zelima's mother. Julia felt the air around her thicken as her surroundings paused. The sun-bathing gator frozen with its jaw cranked open. The raccoon tussled indefinitely. Flies hovering mid air. Julia sighed. "Oh, c'mon, Z. I didn't mean nothing by it."

The Quarter witch cleared her throat again. "We're almost to the good part. What happened next, Julia?"

Julia adjusted the flesh around her sit bones. "Over the next few decades, we resurrected the circus night after night." The fly flitted around her. The raccoons kicked up dust as they scuffled. The alligator slipped into the water to cool down. Julia gulped air. "It didn't take long for people to buy the open plots of land around the swamp, building year-round cabins and small vacation homes. Somewhere along the way it started being called Honey Island Swamp, even though there's no island." She shrugged. "The name stuck.

"For a while, Adelaide and I were called the Two Witches, a name that housed both fear and adoration. We had an agreement with our neighbors—they didn't ask about the circus or why we didn't age. The unexplainable was no stranger to New Orleans and its country dwellers. Besides, the circus was fun and exciting."

"It's a shame that it all came to end on the day of the great storm, huh?" Zelima interjected, her tone smug.

Julia grumbled a curse under her breath.

"I was just a little girl, only eight years old," Zelima said. "That storm was the beginning of the end for both of us, J, wasn't it?"

Julia nodded, a grainy memory of Zelima coming back to her. She remembered the girl's large brown eyes and little black braids. Zelima had played with wax dolls while her mother and aunts conjured the storm that took everything Julia cared about.

"Remember, I didn't start the feud. I was just a child."

"No, you didn't, but you preserved it. That devilry is in your blood."

Zelima scoffed. "Always so theatrical, Julia. You forget the blood on your own hands."

Julia swatted away tears. If only she could forget.

It happened fast, like a chilling breeze in the middle of the night that turns your bones to ice and makes you shiver, pulling the blanket tighter around your shoulders and chin. Adelaide cooked fish and created the circus out of thin air.

A week later Julia rocked Adelaide's lifeless body in her arms.

Julia woke to find herself alone in the cabin. This wasn't unusual; Adelaide was an early riser. At dawn, she'd go fishing, train her alligator compatriots, or commune with the spirits. The witch said the only way to start the day was in the swamp, whether it be on a boat in the middle of it or sitting on the cusp of it, her feet pressed into the muddy shallows, as she spoke to the most recent soul to enter the spirit world.

Julia went outside in her shift, her feet stopping when they met earth. Death crawled along her skin, stealing her breath. Resembling a sleeping princess, Adelaide floated on her back, eyes closed, hands resting on her stomach.

Adelaide was gone.

Julia crumbled where she stood. Hands digging into the moist earth, she clenched and unclenched them, feeling the soft sand and splintered grass rub against her palms. She stayed there, her hands deep in the ground, until Adelaide's body drifted over. Having found its keeper, the witch's body needed no rope or dock to keep it in place. Julia looked up from the ground as a flash of white slid toward her. Adelaide's corset and petticoat. Her eyes scanned her chest, arms, stomach, legs, and feet for bruises, scrapes, blood—wounds of any kind. There were none. Julia studied Adelaide's face. It really looked as though she were sleeping, her face soft and serene.

It was obvious: Adelaide's death had not been natural, but magical.

Julia didn't let herself think about who or what had caused this nightmare. Instead, she pulled Adelaide's body from the water, marveling at how such a grandiose person could be so small. "I'll see you soon," Julia promised as she rocked the body in her arms.

Julia placed her mentor on the ground beside her. Then she leaned forward, her fingers devouring the earth, and let out a howl. Ice swept the surface of Honey Island Swamp. As soon as it had spread, a black tent popped up, its three points frosted. From inside, the man with the mustache and tall top hat could be heard saying, "Step right up. Don't be shy! Today will be a magnificently spectacular, unusual show!"

Julia knew the neighbors would start pouring into the tent, which is precisely what she wanted. She pulled her hands from the dirt. Stood and walked to the cabin, the slime of gravel, sand, and mud past her wrists. Entered the house she had shared for over a century with Adelaide and closed the door behind her. She didn't reemerge until the black tent was full.

Julia stood at the edge of the swamp, beside Adelaide's corpse, in the black high-neck dress and veil Madame Adelaide had worn. She wrapped the body in a bedsheet from the cabin and sprinkled rosemary, thyme, and lavender over the cocoon for protection, peace, and purification. Only Adelaide's face was visible. Julia looked at it one more time, trying to memorize every freckle, line, angle, and curve. Then she started across the glacial swamp surface to the tent.

The crowd went silent when Julia entered. They knew what that outfit meant: a séance. Madame Adelaide's communication with the dead was the most popular attraction at the circus. The patrons didn't realize it was Julia under the veil; in fact, she had been conducting the séances for months now per Adelaide's request. Julia cleared her throat and began to speak in the dialect Adelaide had always used. "Welcome. Tonight, there is only one attraction—a séance. But it will not be like any you've witnessed before. Tonight, we will not sit at a table and light candles, asking for a sign. Tonight, we will meet the spirit world. Ladies and gentlemen, I'm gonna die tonight, and I'm taking y'all with me."

The crowd muttered and whispered to themselves. Was this some kind of act? Had Madame Adelaide gone mad? Should they leave?

"No one is leaving," Julia said. She lifted her hands into the air, the appendages curled like a beast, ready to dig its claws into its prey. "Earth, Penumbra, Netherworld, I call upon your magic that courses through the water below us. In the name of Adelaide, I bring thee a great sacrifice. Let the water swallow everyone in this earthly plane, let our bodies and souls nourish and replenish your magic. We are, as ever, your humble servants. Take us in your waves of fury and retribution, cleanse our sins, and send our souls to the underworld."

The ground trembled. A strong wind hissed and flicked against the tent. Cracks as loud as thunder sounded from below. The crowd screamed and cried as the ice broke beneath them. Some were pulled into the water by cerulean tentacles, others by prehistoric alligators. Some jumped from one jagged slab of ice to the next, in a desperate survival attempt. It was no use; there would be no survivors.

Julia's knees bent to steady her body on the quaking, splintering ground. A low laugh started in her gut and traveled through her throat, spewing from her mouth like lava. Fat tears streamed down her face. In between fits of laughter, she said, "I'm gonna die tonight, and I'm taking y'all with me."

A series of large waves grew outside the tent, and closed on top of it, a Venus fly trap snapping shut. The tent and everyone inside it vanished. All of the structures surrounding the swamp—the homes and vegetation—were gone as well. Adelaide's body had been swallowed by the storm, but the lopsided cabin survived, mostly. Bowed wood dangled like lifeless limbs. The remaining ice melted, the waves shrank, and the blue-green water became still once again. Julia's laughter continued, seemingly endless, an echo against the silent wasteland that had just hours before been the home of two-hundred people.

Julia woke in a dark, wooden box, her throat full and on fire. Her chin was wet, her tongue and lips chapped. She must have been coughing in her sleep, trying to rid her lungs, throat, and nose of swamp water. Pounding her hand against her chest, Julia took long, deep inhales. A slight wheeze floated from her mouth. She swallowed, breathing in through her nose, and exhaled through her mouth, creating a deeper whistling sound. She tilted her head to each side to release the water and pressure that had welled up.

Julia took one more deep breath and closed her eyes, preparing herself for the afterlife. She was ready to be with Adelaide again. Julia pushed on the wooden top of the box—it was slimy from being saturated in swamp water—and it opened above her head, bringing light onto her face. She squinted at the brightness and shoved the top toward her feet, flooding her body in sunlight. Pressed herself up to a sitting position, her breathing still laborious. She hadn't expected such human vulnerabilities in the afterlife. A shriek escaped Julia's mouth. What she saw wasn't the afterlife at all.

She was at Honey Island Swamp. It remained intact—though everything else had been destroyed in the deadly storm Julia's spell had given birth to. She saw no snakes or alligators or raccoons. Heard no birds or insects. There was no grass or trees or flowers—the earth surrounding the swamp was soaked a deep brown.

Julia sat in a wooden coffin floating in the water. Hundreds of identical coffins surrounded her, dotting the swamp. They bobbed so slightly that at first glance Julia thought it was a trick of the eye. The coffins hadn't been a part of her plan, but there was something poetic and somber about them. A mass gravesite on a swamp.

Julia was very much alive and on the plane of the living. The witch's spell had gone horribly wrong—she had miscalculated in her grief—her lifeforce was bound to the swamp, her powers emboldened by its water; therefore, she could not be killed while within its borders. Julia cursed herself for being so foolish to believe she could join Adelaide that way.

Her thoughts shifted to the coffins, but she didn't need to check them; she knew they held the dead. Her eyes scanned the boxes, trying to count them, trying to remember the faces of the people inside of the tent, their unique qualities, yet they were all faceless. Her memory of them was singular. Her magic had murdered these innocent people and had destroyed the community that had been built around the swamp over several decades. A community Adelaide adored. Why had Julia done this? Adelaide was still dead and Julia was alive. Now she would know what true loneliness was.

Julia sprang to her feet, the coffin rocking back and forth, forward and backward. Adelaide. Julia needed to find the coffin that held her body. She needed to give Adelaide a proper burial and put her to rest. After, she could leave Honey Island Swamp for good, her body and magic withering until she no longer existed on the plane of the living. Then Julia could be with Adelaide, her only family, again.

Her tongue weaved a spell to reveal her heart's desire. A coffin on the opposite end of the swamp wiggled back and forth, a dog wagging its tail when its master came home. Julia dove into the water. Upon reaching the coffin, she yanked the top off. She choked on the smell that flooded her nostrils. Salty, damp, rotten flesh spewed from the open lid. The immersion of the body in briny water and the humid climate had quickened decomposition. Adelaide's once petite figure was swollen, as though she had gorged herself to the seams or been stung by an entire beehive. Her once pink, sometimes reddened, freckled skin was ghoulish in hue. Flies circled the body, ready to feed and harvest their larvae on Adelaide's corpse.

Julia swatted the flies away. "You can't have her," she said, knowing she was powerless to stave off the process of decomposition. Julia took one side of the soggy, splintered wooden coffin in her hands and started to push it toward the shoreline.

This proved more challenging than Julia had anticipated; her hands kept losing their grip on the box. Several times, the coffin slipped from her grasp and began to float away. She managed to push the box against the shore and up onto the muddy ground. Used it to pull herself from the water. Forcing the coffin inland, her knees gelled in dark brown slime as they slid in the slick earth. The box melted into the ground, and Julia let her lower half sink with it.

For a moment, she rested her head on her arms on the edge of the coffin. Closing her eyes, she tried to remember her last conversation with Adelaide. It came to her in flashes and blurs, more dreamlike than a palpable, physical moment from only a day ago. Had it only been a day? Julia couldn't be sure of anything anymore. She remembered Adelaide had asked Julia to stand in for her that evening. This had become almost a nightly routine. For weeks, maybe even a month, Adelaide had asked Julia to play her role at the circus. "Think of it this way: you're the understudy, I'm the lead, and tonight you get to star in the show," Adelaide had said each night she asked this favor. She never offered an explanation, and Julia never asked for one. She had no reason to question her mentor.

One morsel of memory stuck out to Julia. They stood in the cabin after dinner. Adelaide had already requested that Julia perform the séance that night. Julia changed into the black dress with the high-neckline Madame Adelaide donned. Adelaide stood in her everyday attire and said, "Do you know how proud of you I am?"

Julia nodded and smiled.

Adelaide took Julia's face in her palms—they were soft and giving, pliable to Julia's cheekbones and flesh—and said, "Always dreamed of having a daughter to share my magic with. You stumbling into the swamp was the best surprise of my life."

Julia could see three distortions of her face reflected in Adealide's glassy eyes. Her mentor's face widened into a smile. Julia remained stoic. The two women looked at each other in silence for several minutes. Then Adelaide said, "You better get ready. I'll see you later, dear." At that, she turned and walked out of the cabin, the door swinging several times before settling.

That was the last time Julia had seen Adelaide alive.

Julia's eyes fluttered open, her cheeks and hands greasy with sweat and tears, to the sound of footsteps slopping and dragging in the mud. She lifted her head and saw four women and a little girl standing in a line about ten feet before her. Each woman had midnight hair twisted into braids that were assembled on top of her head in a turban of various patterns and colors. They all wore black fitted dresses to their calves. They had light brown eyes and skin a shade darker than Julia's. The women resembled one another so closely it was as if invisible mirrors were stationed around, reflecting the image of one woman instead of four. The girl resembled the women, however, her features were softer and she wore her braids down to her slender waist. She was in a blue jumper, a flash of color in a sea of darkness. Julia could smell the magic on them like perfume. It wafted from the hair on their arms, the lines of their faces, their hair. It was the first coven she had ever seen.

One woman fell to her knees crying, a squishing sound as her skin met the muck. Two grabbed for each other in the way only twins would. One woman surveyed the mass gravesite and Julia with her arms crossed before her. The girl's chin was turned downward, her eyes squeezed shut, as though she wished herself to be somewhere, anywhere else.

The woman with her arms crossed took a step forward. Her turban was striped black and white. She wore large, hollow gold hoops and a thick brass necklace around her thin, elegant neck. She spoke in a voice as soft as butter swept onto hot, fresh biscuits. "Are you the witch who caused the storm that killed these innocents?"

Julia swallowed. "I am," she said, her voice low, resembling humming.

"My sister, Daya," she gestured to the crying woman, "has the power of vision. She saw the deadly storm in a dream. We didn't know if you were still alive."

"I wish I wasn't."

The woman studied Julia's face for a moment. "I'm sorry for your loss. Your mother?" She motioned to the coffin Julia clutched.

Julia swallowed a moan. "Closest thing I ever had."

The woman nodded. "You are a very powerful young woman." Her voice was steady, her demeanor serene.

"I'm not as young as I look," Julia said, her nostrils flaring.

"Neither am I." The woman tapped a circular amulet peeking from the top of her dress. Julia hadn't noticed the talisman before. She squinted, trying to make out the symbol etched into the top part of it.

"I'm Marie. This is my sister, Daya, my cousins, Lucille and Cecile, and my daughter, Zelima."

Julia's eyes lifted to meet Marie's. "Your coven."

Marie nodded, the stripes in her turban creating an optical illusion. "Part of it, yes."

"What are you going to do with me?"

Julia's question seemed to surprise Marie. Her forehead puckered before smoothing. "I don't take it lightly having to do this to another witch. A sister of magic." Her voice was chunkier than before, once soft butter solidifying in the refrigerator.

"I'm ready to die."

Marie nodded. "I know you are."

Julia stood. She tilted her head. Her mouth opened, showing square, pale yellow teeth. "What are you going to do with me?"

"What we have to do. To make sure you don't do anything like this again."

"You should kill me," she begged. "I can't hurt anyone if I'm dead."

"You and I both know I cannot kill you. Not when you are so deeply rooted in this swamp." Marie sighed and shook her head. "I don't want to kill a sister witch." She seemed almost maternal toward Julia even though the swamp witch was more than half a century older than the Quarter witch.

Julia scratched her head, her mountain of curls shaking. "If you won't kill me and you won't leave me the power to do this again—"

"My coven is going to bind you to this place."

Julia's lower lip trembled. "But if you do that I'll never die."

Marie nodded. "Not for a very long time."

"But I could just do it again. Lure people here with a spectacle. Then annihilate them."

"The rest of my coven is preparing a spell on the outskirts of the land. No human will be lured to a spectacle on the swamp ever again. Only those with a magical destiny will be able to enter this land." Marie crossed her arms in front of her chest. The sunlight shone on them, highlighting the lean muscles in her biceps. "You will live the rest of your life alone."

Julia's legs began to shake, her knees knocking together.

"Powerful, brimming with magic, but unable to use it for anything other than to entertain yourself and the gators. You will never be able to hurt a human again."

Julia's legs collapsed, driving her body to the ground with a thump. "You can't," she sobbed. "I won't let you do this to me." Marie stepped back in line with her family. The four women and the little girl watched Julia. They clasped hands.

"It's already done," the Quarter witch said.

Then Marie and her coven spoke in unison: "We call upon Earth, Penumbra, and Netherworld. Lend us your power coursing through this water. Bind this witch to this land, keep her from harming man. We promise this witch no harm; we simply want her disarmed. Let her live her days in solitude, we beg of you in earnest servitude."

A shimmering pink shield appeared between the Quarter witches and Julia. Julia could see the women through it, yet when she tried to move toward them she couldn't. Her body was frozen, stuck in a crumbled position on the ground. Her eyes—the only part of her mobile—followed the sparkles, watching them swallow the swamp and its surrounding land. A magical force field. A witch's prison.

Tears slid down Julia's face in streams, but she couldn't swat them away. She closed her eyes and thought of a spell in her head. She waited, but nothing happened. The spell was supposed to cast down any enemy of the swamp witch; she had been hoping it would take them all down. Even the child.

The four women and the little girl stepped backward, their fingers interlocked, eyes focused on Julia. Marie said, "Your powers won't work while the spell is in progress. Once we are gone and the spell is finished, your magic will return. Then you will be able to bury your mother in peace."

"Tell me what you did to her."

Marie paused. The other women and the girl halted as well, their gaze shifting from Julia to their leader. "You confuse me for an enemy," Marie said. "Think of the spell you cast, the great storm you erected."

The women resumed their walking, now almost to the tree line. The oaks, monstrous in height and thickness, with Spanish moss and vines dripping from their limbs. The shimmering ended at that border. Julia saw Marie's lips twitch into a frown then back to neutral. "I am sorry to have to do this to you," she said. "But you gave us no choice."

Julia cursed them in her head, promising she'd seek revenge for what the coven had done to her and what she was certain they had done to Adelaide. The Two Witches couldn't die as long as they were connected to Honey Island. The swamp had saved Julia, and it should have saved Adelaide. Now the sole Swamp Witch, Julia committed the faces of Marie's coven to memory. Focused on the little girl, Zelima. She was the leader's daughter, her one weakness. Julia would wound Marie by getting to her child.

The women disappeared into the trees. The sky no longer glistened with sparkles and pale color. The spell was complete. Julia's jaw dropped open. She bent her neck side to side, a loud crack sounding with each motion. She could move again. She stretched her limbs out, the muscles groaning in gratitude. Then she leapt to her feet and ran full speed at the tree line shouting a spell. Her body slammed against the invisible wall, knocking her onto her back. The forcefield was intact; she was caged.

Julia's face contorted. She walked back to the edge of the swamp to Adelaide's body. Kneeling in the mud by the coffin, she said, "What am I supposed to do without you?"

She reached inside and took Adelaide's clasped hands in hers. They made a squishing sound. Julia grimaced at the noise. She turned and looked at the swamp behind her and the hundreds of bobbing coffins. With her free hand, Julia waved them away. They disappeared, the swamp empty once again. She turned back to Adelaide, placed her arm on the wooden edge of the coffin, and rested her cheek there. Julia began to speak, telling Adelaide everything she could think of ever wanting to say.

Hollow clapping echoed around Julia. A gray heron took off across the swamp, spooked. "Your ability to transform into the victim is impressive. Did you hear yourself?" Zelima sneered. "You planned to kill an innocent child in the name of misplaced revenge." She swallowed, the swishing of saliva audible. "You weren't able to kill me, yet you still managed to destroy my family. I lost my mother and then you took my Aunt Daya with your false visions. Tell me, Julia, how can you be the victim when you're a murderer?"

Julia licked her dry, cracked lips. To an extent, the Quarter witch was right. Ten years after the coven trapped Julia, cursing her with eternal loneliness, she had led Daya to the swamp with phony prophecies. The witch gifted with foresight failed to predict her own drowning. Julia bound Daya to the swamp, then crafted a storm, wave after wave flooding the woman's lungs until she drifted to the bottom of Honey Island, bait for fish and gator. Julia hadn't known Daya's sister, Marie, had died from breast cancer three weeks before. How could she? The whole point of her sentence was isolation. Julia had acted based on the information she'd had.

Zelima, then eighteen, became the new leader of the coven. She remembered Julia well; in fact, she had given her the nickname Crazy Julia, spreading tales of hauntings and peril to those who ventured to the swamp—some were true, others fiction. Zelima always had a flair for storytelling.

Of course, both witches knew what happened next. Zelima came to Honey Island Swamp following her aunt's murder. As soon as Julia saw her, Julia knew the young witch and why she had come in place of her mother. Zelima wore a long black dress with her mother's thick brass necklace and large gold hoops. Her mirror image. Unlike Marie, however, Zelima did not wear a turban. Instead, her braids sashayed freely around her hips, dozens of tiny snakes dancing. As elegant as her mother, but hardened.

Zelima's full lips parted, revealing snow-white teeth. "Julia," she said, her voice silky smooth. "Julia, Julia. What am I going to do with you?"

The swamp witch sat on the stoop of the lopsided cabin she had rebuilt to look just as it had before the storm—a sprinkle of magic accomplished a lot. She picked her teeth with a long, thin reed, threading it through with both hands before wiggling it, catching the remnants of fish, her daily breakfast. She narrowed her eyes at the Quarter witch, her captor, and continued cleaning.

"Don't you have anything to say to me? An apology perhaps?"

Julia spat a piece of fish meat on the ground in front of her. Then she fit the reed in between two new teeth.

"I don't take it lightly doing this to another witch." Zelima's words conveyed sincerity, yet her face told another story—it was angular and apathetic.

Julia stopped wiggling the plant. She left it stuck in her teeth, a flimsy, wavering line hanging from her mouth. "You sound just like your mother. I'm surprised she didn't come herself."

Zelima's face twitched before returning to stone. "My mother is dead."

Julia beamed. "I know. It's a shame not all witches possess the power of immortality."

The young witch laughed and shook her head, her braids lapping at her thighs and buttocks. "You are not immortal, Julia. Don't think anyone has forgotten how you ended up here. How insignificant your longevity has been."

"I assume you're here about the other witch. What was her name again? Die-a?"

Zelima's smile melted into a scowl, her eyes slits of golden brown. "All these years and you still think my coven killed your mother. How many lifetimes has Honey Island Swamp granted you, Julia?" A faint horizontal line crossed Zelima's forehead. "No one from my coven harmed her. Not my mother. Not my aunts and cousins. For Adelaide to die, she must have left the swamp until her magic became weakened. Until she became mortal. It was her will to die."

"But I found her in the swamp." Her heart echoed in her ears, a frantic beat.

"Maybe she used her last bit of magic to return to you."

Julia's mouth closed, the reed poking out. She closed her eyes, remembering Adelaide's body drifting in the swamp, how serene she had appeared.

"We could have been kin, Julia," Zelima said softly. "You shaped me into an enemy. Contrary to what you believe, I don't enjoy using my magic this way." Zelima crossed her arms in front of her chest just as her mother used to. She cleared her throat, raising her voice. "For your latest crime, you will receive a new punishment. The Quarter is mine. This—" She glanced over her shoulder at the swamp. "Is yours. You will not interfere with my coven, my people, or the Quarter. You are to have no relationship of any kind with any magical or human creature."

Julia opened her eyes and snorted, trying to sound unthreatened. The retort was nasally, unconvincing. She knew Zelima saw right through her, saw the depths of her pain.

"You do not want to go after anyone else, Julia. I am not as good-natured as my mother. I see you for exactly what you are, and I will not hesitate to—"

Julia crossed her arms, mimicking the Quarter witch. "To what? What could you possibly do to me?"

"I'll strip you of the one thing you want. A reunion with Adelaide. If you test me, I will keep you alive for eternity, alone, without your mother." Zelima's hands dropped to her hips. "I understand you perfectly, Julia. I hope that now you understand me."

Zelima turned and walked away, not waiting for a response. The snakes in her hair bounced and hissed with each step. Julia watched Zelima go, her fists flexing until her knuckles were bloodless.

Julia's body jerked, sending her head between her legs. White, hot pain scorched her limbs. "Not again," she groaned. Her head pounded, her throat tight. "Damn you to Hell, Zelima."

"No, dear J, damn you," Zelima said, her voice fading to a whisper. "I told you, the Quarter is mine. This reminiscing was fun, I suppose. I'm glad we could do it one last time."

Julia expected her body to throw itself onto the dusty ground, twisting from the stabbing pain. But her limbs didn't prickle, no new red lumps popped up on her skin. Her mind spasmed, a hard drive overheating and crashing. She knew she was still sitting on the stoop—the moist, splintered wood poked her bottom—yet her hands reached out in front of her feeling wet, pliable wood. She coughed, her chest constricted. Water dribbled down her chin. Her eyes were open yet without sight. Julia inhaled the scent of soggy heat, salt, and soured meat. She knew where she was, where the Quarter witch's enchantment had banished her. Julia pushed against the wood, praying this time would be different than the last. This conjure could be undone. But the lid wouldn't budge, sealed. She went to scream, her parched throat only releasing a pathetic wheeze. It was just as before—Julia was alive, Adelaide was gone, and hundreds of coffins lined the swamp.

Julia Baudin, known as Crazy Julia or the Swamp Witch, formed the name of her torturer with her tongue. White stars twinkled in the darkness as she choked, unable to unleash a curse on her nemesis. Alone, she coughed up swamp water, entombed in a wooden box of her own making.

J. Allister's Shop of Horrors

An old brass bell clanged. A pair of small feet pitter-pattered on the scuffed wooden floor. The little girl darted in, a flash of brown hair, flushed cheeks, and worn clothing. She threw a series of coins—pennies, nickels, dimes, and two quarters—onto the wooden desk that served as a register and ticket booth. She ripped the white paper ticket from the old man's withered hand and ran toward the door. She yelled, "Thanks, Mister," over her shoulder.

She heard the old man muttering to himself. Pictured him pulling out his ratty, yellowed handkerchief from his shirt's chest pocket to wipe off the money before handling it himself. Imagined him calling her a filthy rodent under his breath. This wasn't a fantastical thought; he'd called her something similar before. And much worse.

She twisted the glass knob for the entrance, leaving oily finger-prints behind. No doubt the old man, a Mr. J. Allister, would wipe those off when he was done cleaning the change and the desk's surface. He couldn't stand the filth. The girl knew this but didn't care. She could see evil resided in him. She was no idiot; she knew when to fear someone. Living on the street quickly teaches you who you can and cannot trust. The girl didn't trust Mr. J. Allister, however, she couldn't stay away from his shop of oddities and antiques, from his museum of the bizarre.

Her name was Jessi, and this was her thirtieth visit to the museum in the old man's shop. She came every afternoon she could afford—her rule was eat first, then play. She begged for spare change from tourists, locals, and street artists around Jackson Square and along Bourbon Street so she could buy a beignet or lemonade; whatever was left went toward visiting the museum. It was Jessi's favorite place in the entire world—or at least what little she'd seen of it—and she found it funny that her favorite place was also the scariest. The Bell Man said it wasn't ha-ha funny, but ironic. "Sure," she replied, even though she didn't know what ironic meant.

Jessi was nine years old. She knew this because the Bell Man told her so. He knew many things, most of them about life and death. She wasn't worried about that second part because the Bell Man told her he didn't see her dying for a very long time and he was almost never wrong about these kinds of things. It wasn't fair of the girl to say her friend was wrong; sometimes Destiny stepped in and changed the future. Sometimes you were supposed to live for forty more years, and whoop, Destiny changed its mind, and tomorrow you'd die from a heart attack. Life's a bastard, the Bell Man always said. He then shrugged, as he always did, to communicate that he had nothing else to add.

That was fine with Jessi. Life was a bastard. When you didn't have a climate-controlled house to go home to after playing in the sweltering Louisiana heat all day or a delicious home-cooked meal that consisted of more than fried dough doused in powdered sugar. She did alright though. The Bell Man kept her company at night at Armstrong Park—watching over her while she slept—and during the day she took care of herself, hustling tourists on the humid, bustling streets of the French Quarter. Jessi thought she was a natural street performer like that lady that turned into the Honey Island Swamp Monster, though tourists didn't ooh and ahh about her dancing or juggling the way they did over the monster lady. The Bell Man said fame wasn't everything, and that Jessi should strive to be better than a fraud. "That woman is not what she appears to be," he told her but refused to explain further.

Come to think of it, Jessi hadn't seen the monster-shifting lady in a while, but that wasn't something to worry about. Street performers came and went. It was "the nature of the beast, pun intended," she said to the Bell Man. His ghoulish blue-white face twitched almost imperceptibly, which meant he was amused by her joke. He was the girl's only friend. She didn't mind; he was the best friend a girl like her could have. There was one thing his friendship couldn't give her though, one thing she wanted more than anything, and that was a doll.

Many little girls love to play with dolls. Barbies, American Girl Dolls—porcelain, plastic, cloth—it doesn't matter. You can play dress up and make-believe with them. Take them on playdates, to school, to family dinners. Hold them in your arms while you sleep. Jessi was desperate for one, which would have probably been surprising to most who saw her around the city. She didn't look like a girly girl, certainly not one who wanted to braid a doll's Saran or Kanekalon hair and dress her up in a variety of outfits.

Jessi was tough, literally, her sunburnt skin taut, hardened around its edges. She wore shorts and a t-shirt, never dresses. Her hair was wild, unmanaged. She cursed when the Bell Man wasn't around to scold her for such foul, unladylike language. She ran around Jackson Square Park like a monkey, her fingers in her armpits as she hopped around, swinging from the bars of the iron fence enclosing the park. She stood on the base of the bronze statue of Andrew Jackson and swallowed bugs and other items for money. The Bell Man said that wasn't an appropriate way to honor the general who helped win the Battle of New Orleans.

Jessi shrugged. "It just looks like a dude on a horse."

The Bell Man shrugged in response, dropping the matter.

What the people who stopped to watch Jessi perform her various talents didn't see was that her t-shirt and shorts were the only clothing she had besides a white sweatshirt—now brownish in color—that said *laissez le bon temps rouler* in large neon purple letters. She hid it behind a dumpster, a large rock on top of it, outside of a barbecue joint on hotter days. Jessi had never had the option to wear a dress or a skirt or even bows in her hair. She never had the chance to see if she was girly or more tomboy or neither. She had seen all different types of kids in New Orleans, yet none of them seemed to be like she was. None of them made sense to her. Seeing girls—and sometimes boys—with dolls was one thing that did make sense to her though. Jessi wanted one to play make-believe with and to hold close to her chest at night. She wanted what she called a forever friend.

But she couldn't go into just any store and buy a doll. Jessi had lost count of the number of times she had been eyed nervously by shopkeepers along Royal Street while she looked around, their words clipped and sharp as they said, "Please don't touch the merchandise." It always surprised her how a word like please could sound so harsh and accusatory. Sometimes the shopkeepers even chased Jessi out of the store, shouting after her, "Thief!" or "Rodent!" The girl quickly learned that they saw her as dirty and untrustworthy simply because she was homeless. The shops along Royal Street were for the wealthy tourists too inebriated to realize half of the shops in the stretch sold identical merchandise.

Three months ago, however, Jessi stumbled upon a different kind of storefront, one tucked away from busy streets like Bourbon and Royal. One devoid of tourists, panhandlers, and discarded mardi gras beads. Jazz echoed down the block, fading the further she went. The quiet and stillness were unfamiliar to the girl. She rolled off the unease crawling along her spine. On the wall of the building was a portrait of a bearded woman. The woman wore a tall collar with a brooch in the middle. A thick black beard tickled the pin. Tapped beside it, a flyer said, "Love the bizarre? Come to J. Allister's Oddities & Antiques to behold a collection of the weird, the scary, the wacky. $5.00 entry."

The words did little for Jessi, mostly because she read at a first-grade level. The advertisement seemed crowded to the little girl, trying to be fancier than it was, however, one thing piqued her interest. Below the words was a black and white photograph of a doll. It was poor-quality— grainy and not completely in focus—but the doll's face was perfectly clear to Jessi. Like she had seen it before. The doll had a pale face with high, curved eyebrows. Eyes large and wide—pupils nearly exploding— with thick eyelashes. Lips, a heart without the pointed bottom. Cheeks rounded with painted circles. The doll had lopsided dark bangs and wore the expression of someone who was paralyzed by fear.

A few people stopped to look at the flyer while Jessi was there. She scowled as they said, "That doll looks possessed," or "Why would I want to see a creepy doll when I could see a bearded woman? Where's that exhibit?"

Jessi curled her arms, bringing her fingers to her armpits. She bared her teeth and began to make monkey sounds until the people hurried away. She shook her head. She thought the doll looked beautiful and lonely, like she needed a friend.

And Jessi planned to be just that.

To visit Mr. Allister's museum, she needed $5.00. Every now and then a stranger would take pity on the skinny girl with greasy, limp strands of brown hair and yellowed skin—no doubt a sign of malnourishment—wearing a t-shirt and jean shorts pockmarked with holes, dirt, and age, and give her $5.00. Sometimes even ten. Usually, however, she was ignored. Seen as a pest. As garbage. Most days she was lucky to end up with a dollar or two. And that was hardly enough for a bag of potato chips, let alone entry into the museum to see her beloved doll.

She had wanted to name the doll as soon as she had seen the photo on the flyer, but Jessi told herself to wait until she met her. The Bell Man always said patience was a virtue, and even though the girl didn't know what *virtue* meant, she thought it sounded similar to *virgin*, which she knew to be a good thing.

It had taken two weeks—an eternity for the young girl—to save up the money to enter the museum and meet her doll. Her heart pounding, she rushed inside. When Jessi saw Mr. J. Allister's store she thought she must be in the wrong place. The shop was dark, the air dusty, filled with little specks, and cloaked in shadows. Only a few dim lamps lit the space. Shabby, moth-eaten oriental rugs went wall to wall, so it was impossible to see the floor beneath them. Chairs, benches, desks, and end tables were scattered around the room. Old paintings, some with gilded frames, featured portraits of white men and women and plantations—an ode to the ways things used to be—lined the off-white walls. That's how Mr. Allister had explained them to the girl, a twisted smile on his face when he ogled them. She'd come up to him, her finger crusted with grime, and pointed at a painting of a woman with a hairdo so big it could hold a toy ship or birdcage and said, "What's up with the old, dead white lady?"

The old man immediately disliked Jessi. He wore his hatred for her on his face as effortlessly as the Bell Man wore his black bowler hat. Even before she asked that question about the big-haired lady, the girl could see the shop owner disapproved of her, and she didn't care.

From the moment Jessi saw Mr. Allister, she knew he was bad news. The Bell Man always said you shouldn't judge a book by its cover unless it's a rotten cover and then you drop it and run. Mr. J. Allister was rotten to the core; Jessi could see that just by looking at him. He was a wicked-looking man—his back hunched so much that the girl and he were eye to eye—with waxy black hair streaked white and silver. The little thin hair he had was yanked across his head and glued into place as though he'd plucked strings from a violin. His eyes were nearly black and beady like a rat. His nose was large, birdlike, and his olive skin was ashy, dusted like everything else in the shop. His face wore various dashes and crevices, and Jessi wondered if bugs ever landed in there in an attempt to find a cozy place to rest. His lips were pale pink, nearly white, and so thin they almost seemed like a continuation of skin. The old man wore a withered tuxedo, stained and marked with holes.

He reminded Jessi of a villain. She could see in his eyes how much he longed for power. She knew some people were born powerful, magical, while others followed behind, playing pretend. This man was the latter, but that didn't mean he wasn't dangerous. She imagined him as the devil's butler, and she was smart enough to know not to mess with the Devil or any of his servants.

"Are you going to buy anything or just insult the artwork?" he had said to her. His voice was low and husky. Jessi wondered if he had a cold or something lodged in his throat. She fought the urge to ask.

"Where's the doll? The one on the flyer." She pulled the crinkled flyer from the back pocket of her shorts.

The old man eyed the girl. His face flexed in discontent. "That'll be $5.00."

Jessi nodded. Her fingers dug into her front pockets. With care, she pulled out two sweaty dollar bills, six quarters, ten dimes, seven nickels, and fifteen pennies, setting them onto the counter. She met the man's gaze, waiting for him to give her permission to enter.

Mr. Allister studied the change, his face contorted in disgust. He picked up a pencil that had been lying on the counter and pushed the change around with the eraser end. He frowned and cleared his throat. "The glass doorknob behind you. Close it once you enter. Don't," he said, "touch the glass. Or anything else for the matter."

She turned away from him, walking toward the door with the glass knob. Pausing, she craned her neck to read the word scrawled in faded white ink. It started with an *m*, but she couldn't sound it out. Later, the Bell Man would tell her it said *Museum*. She clasped the knob and twisted. The door creaked open. She stepped inside and closed it behind her, following the old man's instructions.

The museum differed from the rest of the shop. It was well lit with fluorescent panels on the beige ceiling; there was no space for shadows to hide here. The museum was nothing more than a room—about double the size of the antique shop. Rows of floor-to-ceiling glass cases were erect. Light poured through them, demanding visitors' eyes to look at their items. Inside these glass cases, dozens of items were displayed. Disembodied eyeballs of all shapes, sizes, and colors that seemed to follow you as you walked by them; an entire case dedicated to marionettes—human-looking ones, animals, dragons and other beasts—made from wood, cloth, string, and wires; a section of deformed skeletons, belonging to someone who had had a hunchback, one with six toes and fingers, and adult conjoined twins. There was even a case filled with human body parts—brains and hearts and giant cysts. These things were strange and frightening, sure, yet none of them would distract Jessi from the object she desired.

She walked past the eyeballs, the puppets, skeletons, and body parts, only flirting a glance in their direction as she searched for the case filled with dolls. She found two such displays, side by side, in the last row of cases. Jessi scanned the plastic, glass, porcelain, and cloth faces. She was surprised to find two puppets—a male and female matching pair—in the case on the left, unsure why they were with the dolls instead of the other puppets.

She bounced with excitement when she recognized the doll from the photo. It was even more beautiful in person. Her eyes were painted a deep blue and her hair was dark brown. Staring at the doll through the glass, studying her, Jessi had the feeling she was being looked at or watched. She studied the doll's eyes; something flickered behind them. She was sure of it.

Jessi looked from one case to the next, scanning all the dolls' faces. They appeared almost lifelike; she half expected them to stand up and begin to move about. The girl shook her head. Quit scaring yourself. She turned back to the doll from the flyer. Reached her hand toward the glass.

"What's your name?" she said out loud. In her head, she began to think up names. Greta? Delphine? Emily? Marie?

"The doll's names are written on the signs on the glass. If you can read, of course," the old man said and snickered to himself.

Jessi felt her cheeks redden. She kept her eyes focused on the doll, her back to Mr. Allister.

"Don't touch the glass." He stressed each word.

Jessi lowered her hand, her fingers balled in a fist. "Got it, mister." What she wanted to say was, *Beat it, mister*, but that wasn't very polite and the last thing she wanted was to get kicked out.

"I'm watching you, girl," the old man said.

She shot him a glance over her shoulder. He narrowed his eyes at her before turning around and exiting the room. The door creaked closed.

That was when she heard it.

A whisper.

"Josette."

Jessi braced herself to fight or run. She surveyed the room. No one was there.

"My name is Josette," the voice said. "Can you hear me?" This time it spoke louder, revealing itself to be a woman's soft and melodious voice.

"Hello?" Jessi said. She breathed heavily.

"Hello. Over here," the voice said.

Jessi followed the sound of the voice, her hand over her mouth. She gulped air through her nose. The sound seemed to be coming from the doll. Jessi leaned closer to the glass, thinking she might be able to find a wire or recording device. She had known that old man was evil. Toying with a young girl like that was just plain mean though and she planned to tell him that. With profanity.

"Hello. Can you hear me?" the voice said again.

Jessi crossed her arms in front of her chest. "Very funny, old man. Let's see how funny you think this is when I give you a meatball sandwich."

"What the hell is a meatball sandwich?"

"A meatball sandwich is…wait a minute. I'm not telling you. You'll feel it soon enough."

"I'm afraid I don't feel anything. Not physically anyway. That's a basic principle of being an inanimate object. A doll made of porcelain and cloth and stuffing. I'm like a damn pillow. I feel nothing, I can't move on my own. I'm not supposed to talk—I have no teeth or a tongue—but," the voice exhaled deeply, "here we are."

"This is some kind of trick. Dolls don't talk. Well, fancy ones do sometimes," Jessi said, "but not like this." Her forehead and temples perspired.

"It's no trick. I wish it was. Look as hard as you want. Look around the entire room. You'll find no wires, no speakers. This is me, baby. Josette."

The girl did as Josette suggested. She searched the museum for wires, speakers, and recording devices. She found nothing. Jessi came back to the case after several minutes, her face flushed.

"Let me guess, you found nothing?"

Jessi shook her head. "Nothing."

"That's because I'm telling the truth."

"Does he know?" She thrust her thumb backward.

Josette laughed. It was eerie to hear the maniacal sound come from the doll's sealed mouth. "Know, honey? Who do you think did this to me?"

"He made you a talking doll?"

"God, no. He turned me into a doll."

Her eyes popped in wonder. "What were you before?"

"A magical being only known in fairy tales." Jessi asked what kind. "An Aahna."

"What the hell is that?" Jessi's eyes grew large. They darted around the room as the girl waited to be scolded. But no reprimand came. The Bell Man always said to never curse in front of company. Josette seemed like company to Jessi. She swallowed and said, "Heck," correcting herself.

"An Aahna is a magical being that can give life temporarily to inanimate objects."

Temporarily made Jessi think of *tempura* and she fought the urge to giggle. A few weeks ago, the Bell Man had said, "Life as we know it is temporary," and then he explained what the word meant. Jessi didn't know *inanimate* though. She tried to sound it out, but only *inanimal* came out of her mouth. She blushed.

"Inanimate. Rocks, toys. That sort of thing," Josette said. "Things that aren't alive."

Jessi understood what she meant. Her eyes grew wide. "Dolls?"

"You betcha."

"But if you can only turn toys tempura-ir-ily into being alive, then you're going to go back to being yourself soon. Right?"

"I wish. The old bastard used dark magic to twist mine. I don't have any powers in this body, but even if I did, I wouldn't know where to begin. My magic gives life; it doesn't take it."

Jessi felt her cheeks spike with heat like when she had a fever. Her eyes stung. She squeezed them shut, feeling moisture roll onto her eyelashes. The door creaked open. Jessi blinked her eyes open, ignoring the building tears. She turned around to see the old man standing in the doorway, his face pinched.

"The museum's closed for the day."

"But I—" Her cheeks were on fire now.

"Closed," he said in a way that made it clear she couldn't negotiate. "Remember, don't touch anything on your way out but the doorknob." Then, as if remembering himself, he said, "Have a good day. Come again."

Jessi knew he didn't mean those remarks; they were just phrases shopkeepers were programmed to say to seem polite. He was phony-po-lite and she didn't like that. She frowned but nodded. Then she turned back to face Josette. She didn't want to leave her here. With him. She could feel the old man watching her.

"I'll be back," she promised.

She turned back to face Mr. J. Allister and walked out of the museum, past the old man, and out of the store without a glance or a thank you. Phony-polite people didn't deserve respect.

"Hi, Josette," she said. "Hi, Darla. Hi, Colleen. Hi, Benjamin. Hi, Christophe."

She greeted each of her friends. They said hi to her in unison. Even after months of visiting the museum and talking to them, Jessi couldn't get used to hearing the dolls and puppets talk while their faces remained set, stationary and blank. It was creepy. Sometimes she imagined picking the lock to the puppet case and playing puppeteer. Jessi could manipulate Christophe and Darla's mouths to open as they talked. The little girl was good at picking locks, but her friends told her the cases were enchanted with dark magic.

"And, no offense, but we don't want to be treated like puppets," Darla said. "Right, Christophe?" She said to a male puppet. He agreed. "Sorry, Jessi."

Jessi didn't only want to open the cases to play with her friends, she also wanted to free them. It wasn't fair for them to be locked in cages like animals at Audubon Zoo. The girl had come up with dozens of possible ways to get her new friends out, most of which involved some grand escape. They thanked her for her dedication, for caring so much, but told her it was hopeless. Even if she could get them out of the cases, they were magically bound to the old man.

"Think of it as a magical tattoo," Josette said. "Except it's not just body art. It's a way to tail us. Because of it, we're tethered to him for eternity." They told her the only way they knew to break it was death, and none of them were ready for that.

Darla, Christophe, Colleen, and Benjamin were like Josette. Each a magical being, almost all of which belonged to a human body. Each trapped by Mr. J. Allister. It had taken several weeks for all of them to talk to Jessi; they were wary of her, having never met anyone else who could hear them.

Colleen, a blond-haired china doll with brown eyes filled with dread, would curse anyone who owned her, or so a piece of paper on the glass to the right of her said. She told Jessi that it felt like they were ghosts. Haunting the shop, this earthly plane, utterly invisible. She didn't know how long she had been trapped like this. Neither did the others.

"What were you before?" Jessi asked.

"A witch," she said. "Curses were my specialty. If someone even looked at me the wrong way, I'd place a hex on them. Baldness. A loveless marriage. Impotence."

"Impo-what?" Jessi said.

"Colleen," Josette interjected, her tone scolding.

"She's going to learn about it at some point."

"She doesn't need to today. Benjamin, why don't you tell the girl your story?"

One by one, each told his or her story. Benjamin was a large doll whose body was made of cloth, his face glass, resembling marble. He had small black eyes, a pointed nose, and two white fangs that hung over his bottom lip. Specks of red had been painted on the pointed teeth. In real life, as in doll form, Benjamin had been a vampire.

"The old man wasn't very creative with that one," he said.

"Vampires are real?" Jessi's mouth hung open.

"Yes."

"Does that mean Frankenstein and werewolves are real too?"

He sighed.

"At least she didn't ask if you really drink blood," Christophe said.

"Answer that next." Jessi beamed at the vampire, doing her best to charm him.

"I've seen a werewolf or two in my time."

"Which has been really long. He's really, really old," Josette quipped.

He cleared his throat. "As I was saying, werewolves exist, but it's unlikely you'll see one around these parts. They prefer the swamp." His voice echoed disgust. "That is, of course, unless Mr. Allister gets his grimy mitts on one of them." He sounded excited at the prospect of a werewolf being trapped.

"And Frankenstein?" Jessi said.

"Just a story." The girl then asked about the blood. Benjamin sighed again. "Yes, I drank human blood to survive."

"Holy shit." Her eyebrows shot upward near her hairline.

Josette, Colleen, Christophe, and Darla laughed at her reaction.

Darla and Christophe shared next. Their wooden faces remained blank as they spoke. Bouncy red curls exploded from the top of Darla's head. Christophe had shiny black hair styled to the side with a slight wave in the front. They wore matching his and her outfits—Darla, a black and white checkered dress with white lace accents, and Christophe, black slacks with a black and white checkered button-down, black bowtie, and black jacket. They both wore black dress shoes. Their eyes were large as though they were eternally surprised, and their lips were parted softly as though they were about to speak. At their elbows were joints, meant to give a lifelike bend when they were moved by their manipulator. Strings hung from the top of their hands, their feet, and the back of their necks.

Unlike the others, the pair of puppets had been created, not born. Yet they had been sentient, able to talk and move on their own free will from the beginning of their existence. The pair had always thought it was good fun to play tricks with their manipulator, a man named Orwell. Before heading to bed, he'd place them on a shelf in his office, and when he came back in the morning he'd find them splayed in front of the door or sometimes on the other side of it, their legs and arms cactused at the joints in the hallway.

Jessi laughed at that part of the story. "But what's changed for you? What did the old man take from you?" She didn't get it. They had always been puppets; what was so bad about it now?

"We lost our free will. We can't move anymore," Darla said. "We're stuck in a cage."

As she thought about what it must feel like to be stuck, frozen in place, Jessi moved her mouth around as though she were swishing water. "Sorry. That sucks."

"Yes, it does," Christophe said.

"At least you're together." The Bell Man always said to look at the bright side of things.

"That's something," the puppets said in unison.

It had taken Jessi a while to understand why the old man was trapping these magical beings.

"Collecting," Josette answered. "He says we're part of his collection."

"A collection of what?"

"Magic."

"Why would someone want that?"

"Power. What else?" Josette said.

Jessi asked how a hunchbacked old man could trap these magical beings. A vampire, a witch. Josette and the others remained quiet. All they would tell her was that he was a lot stronger than he looked. And to never, ever let him touch her.

"Why not?"

"Just don't get near him, okay?" Josette pleaded; it reminded Jessi of her own voice when she begged for food from cheap or dismissive people.

"Okay," she said. "I won't."

She asked the Bell Man about Mr. Allister. Afterall, her friend knew many things. They sat side by side on a step leading to a bridge that overlooked a fountain in Armstrong Park. The park was nearly empty, save for a few teenagers getting high and several homeless folks. Jessi and the Bell Man were alone though, tucked behind the wall of the bridge, their conversation protected by the spitting of the fountain below. The Bell Man nodded, his lips thin and tightly knit together.

"He's evil, huh?"

The Bell Man nodded. His lips parted. "Don't get too close to him, Jessi. You don't want him to see your light."

She turned her body to face him. "My light? What light?"

"Have you ever thought it odd that only you can hear the dolls and puppets?"

The girl's forehead wrinkled. "No," she said. She could feel the word *but* warm and heavy on her tongue, ready to come out. She let it go, let the word fall back into her throat, and closed her mouth.

"What if I buy them? Everyone has a price."

The Bell Man nodded. "That might work."

Jessi rested her head on his shoulder, a few bells clanging as she adjusted herself. The pair sat in silence as the sun set.

"I've been thinking about how I'm going to break you out," Jessi said to her friends.

There was a collective sigh from the dolls and puppets. After a long silence, Josette said, "What's your plan?"

"I'm going to ask to purchase you. All of you."

Now the group laughed, a series of awkward chuckles, throaty and wheezing, nervous, high-pitched giggling, and deep cackling that made Jessi shiver.

"Oh, honey," Josette said.

"That'll never work," Darla said.

"Never," Christophe said.

"Ever," Colleen said.

Benjamin remained silent, his face stoic and feral at the same time. His silence communicated his agreement with his fellow dolls and puppets.

"Everyone has a price. Everyone wants something," Jessi said, confident, certain she could buy out the old man who dabbled in the dark arts and trapped magical beings, displaying them, forcing them to be surrounded by life yet never able to experience it for themselves again.

"I'll get him to make a deal," she said, to reassure herself more than anything.

"Should you tell her or should I?" Colleen said.

Josette cleared her throat. Through what sounded like clenched teeth, she said, "Jessi, honey, that's so kind of you. Really, we appreciate it so much, but I don't know if you've thought this through."

Jessi tilted her head to the side. "What do you mean? You're my friends, he's a bad man, I want to save you. And I will!"

"But Jessi you're forgetting something. You have no money. You can barely even feed yourself."

"Or wash yourself," Colleen added.

Jessi swallowed. Her face grew hot. Suddenly, it felt as though ten eyes were regarding her, judging her. For a moment she felt as though she were the one trapped behind glass, on display. She could see through the clear surface how greasy and lifeless her hair looked. How thin her face was. She wiped the back of her hand over a streak of dirt on her cheek. Maybe her friends were right. What could she offer a powerful man like J. Allister for the prized pieces of his collection?

Jessi began to shake her head, her big plan slipping away, nothing more than a fool's dream. She looked at each of her friends then back at her own reflection in the glass. The girl's eyes flickered, blazing with ideas and hope. She smirked, nodded her head, and said to herself as much as her friends, "I'll make him an offer he can't refuse. And I'll do anything to make it happen."

For three months, Jessi worked to raise the funds. She performed a one-man show of sorts where she embodied a variety of kooky characters, she sang, danced, juggled, anything she could think of to draw a crowd in. She wasn't very good at singing—her voice sounded like tourists crunching forgotten Mardi Gras beads under their feet, or so a little boy told her one afternoon—and her dancing was sloppy and spastic. But it worked well enough, and she stole the rest she needed, pickpocketing bills and change here and there, lifting entire wallets out of backpacks and back pockets.

In all her years on the street, she had tried not to steal. The Bell Man told her it wasn't very noble behavior. She didn't exactly know what that word meant, but it sounded fancy and she wanted to align herself with what fancy people did.

On a Thursday afternoon, Jessi strolled into Mr. Allister's shop with the money gripped tightly in her hand. She rolled her shoulders, trying to seem relaxed. At the register, the man read an old leather-bound book. She waited. He continued reading his book, ignoring the little girl. She cleared her throat. When the old man finally looked up, his gaze was full of venom. Jessi blushed.

"I don't mean to bother you, mister, but I have a proposition for you," she said. She had been practicing the word *proposition* for weeks. Josette said it made her sound smarter and more serious.

The old man's face twisted into a sinister smile. The girl reminded herself not to get too close to him; she didn't want to get scorched by the Devil's butler. "A proposition?" He mulled the word over, his tongue rubbing against his teeth.

Jessi nodded. "Yes, sir. Mr. Allister," she said, correcting herself. Josette had also suggested calling the man by his name.

"I'm listening." His eyes narrowed.

She swallowed. "As you know, I've been coming to your museum for months now."

"Mhm." He nodded as he spoke.

"I love the dolls and puppets you have in there. I've never seen anything like them."

"I can't imagine you have."

Jessi told herself to ignore his blatant dig. She didn't need him to like her or respect her, just to take her money. "That's why I'm prepared to offer you $300 for them." This was another sentence that she had practiced.

Mr. Allister's eyebrows threaded together, making one long line of peppered black. "For what?"

"For Jo—" she remembered herself. "For three dolls and two puppets. I can show you which ones I mean. That's sixty bucks a pop."

The old man slapped the desk with his hand and his neck jiggled, laughter erupting from his throat.

"You don't believe me? Here," Jessi said and slammed the cash on the wooden surface. The bills were crumbled and gray from her sweaty palms.

This made Mr. Allister laugh even harder. He now resembled a hyena, his tongue and teeth visible as he chuckled.

Jessi placed her hands on her hips. She gave the man a nasty look, her lips pulled back like a dog growling, preparing to tell him off. The doorbell bellowed behind the girl, distracting her from her rage. Her lips curled into a smile. Jessi watched Mr. Allister take in the man entering the shop. The shopkeeper's eyes bulged, the red veins swimming around his irises like little snakes. His mouth snapped shut, the faint echo of his laughter remaining in his throat. She watched Mr. Allister struggle to quiet the cackle; it reminded Jessi of having to sneeze when you're playing hide and seek, trying to keep it in, but are unable to.

The man was tall with an average build. His skin was ghostly pale, translucent, with an icy blue sheen to it. He looked as though he had just climbed out of freezing water. His eyes were black pits. His nose was average like his build. For lips, two thin blue lines set in a perpetual frown. Slight creases extended from each side of his lips from the downturned expression. He appeared middle-aged or older, but his face bore no lines or signs of wear. He donned a black suit with a white dress shirt and a long skinny black tie. On top of his head was a black bowler hat. On every available surface of his clothing hung tiny bells. They were not ringing. Not at the moment, anyway.

The Bell Man.

He strode toward Jessi and Mr. J. Allister, pausing beside the girl. He nodded to her, a glimmer in his eye.

She grinned. "Mr. Allister," she said, "have you met my friend?"

The Bell Man bowed to the old man. Mr. Allister shrank from them, trembling.

"Originally, Mr. Jerome Allister and I weren't supposed to meet for quite a while, but things changed. Destiny changed." The Bell Man spoke carefully, his words pointed. His lip twitched to the right, pushing up his cheek. "I believe my friend has given you a proposition." The old man remained silent. He blinked rapidly. "A simple nod will suffice, Mr. Allister."

The old man nodded, reminding Jessi of a bobblehead.

"Very well. I assume from your reaction, you don't want to sell your dolls or puppets for monetary value." He smirked, air audible from his nostrils. "A nod will suffice again, Mr. Allister."

The old man shook his head.

"I'm sure we can come to some sort of agreement, don't you? Perhaps a trade? You and I know how valuable one of the items in your collection is. There are plenty of others here. You and I can both sense that."

Jessi frowned. What did he mean by *sense*? Was the Bell Man suggesting one magical being for another? She didn't want to save her friends only to trap someone else. She remained quiet; she trusted the Bell Man.

"A trade," Mr. J. Allister said, his voice hoarse and shaky. "I might agree to a trade."

The Bell Man nodded.

"The girl can choose one of the five she wants in return for a new item of equal or greater—" He paused, his eyes landing on Jessi. "Importance."

The Bell Man nodded again. "That sounds reasonable."

"Good," Mr. Allister said. "My collection is extremely valuable." The words hung in his throat.

"I'm aware."

The old man's face flushed. His shoulders relaxed. "I actually have an item in mind," he said. He looked at Jessi again. "Can we talk openly in front of the girl?"

The Bell Man met Jessi's gaze. His eyes said *trust me*. "Why don't you go in and see your friends, Jessi? Choose the one you'll take tomorrow." His phrasing wasn't accidental. It was a hint; her friend intended to make a deal with the old man today and find a way to double cross him in the future. He was going to save them all.

Jessi and the Bell Man walked out of J. Allister's Oddities & Antiques hand in hand.

"I don't like that man," she said. "He acts like I'm stupid. Maybe he doesn't like girls. Maybe he's a seck-ist."

"You mean sexist." The Bell Man enunciated the *x*. "Why do you think that?"

"Because he wouldn't talk to you in front of me. And he kept giving me weird looks."

The Bell Man smiled. "That is because he was scared."

"Of me?" Her chest swelled with pride.

Her friend wheezed, his version of laughter. "No." She asked who then. "The man is scared of me. Mr. Allister is used to threatening and frightening magical beings. Then trapping them. And he's very good at it." The Bell Man's face creased. "He doesn't see your light though. He's unaware you have magic in you. He thinks you're just a girl. And that's a good thing. We don't want him to figure it out."

Jessi's face wrinkled in confusion. I'm magical? She remembered a conversation she'd had with the Bell Man a few months ago. "Is that why I can hear the dolls and puppets?"

"Yes."

"So, the old man just thinks I want some dolls to play with?"

"Yes."

"And if he finds out that I've got magic he might try to trap me like others?"

"He'll certainly try."

"How come he doesn't try to trap you?"

"Because I don't exist solely on this plane. His powers cannot trap me."

"That's why he's afraid of you."

"Yes."

She twisted her mouth. "But what exactly are you?"

"Some call me the Seer of Death."

She raised an eyebrow. "What am I then?"

"A Seer of Life."

She liked that answer. "That's pretty cool," she said and began to swing their intertwined hands.

"Yes, it is," the Bell Man said.

They stood at the entrance of a themed playground in City Park, below a pink and yellow sign that read *Storyland*. It was evening, the sunset bathing the sky in soft twilight. The park was closed; neither Jessi nor the Bell Man had ever let that stand in their way. The sign above them was supposed to be a vibrant medieval banner, the sides of it around yellow poles. A small red flag hung on the top left corner of one pole and a blue one on the top right. To the left, Humpty Dumpty sat on a brick wall. To the right, Little Bo Peep and her sheep. Behind them, live oaks dripped in lush strands of Spanish moss. A black fence, surrounded by low bushes and plants, enclosed Captain Hooks' pirate ship, a red, yellow, and blue ship for children to run around on, pretending to be pirates or Peter Pan and the Lost Boys.

The whole thing seemed silly to Jessi. Mostly because she didn't know who these characters were. The Bell Man tried to explain the tales, but she dismissed them. "Why would I care about a made-up story about an egg that kept falling off a wall and a lady who lost her sheep when witches and werewolves and vampires are real? And I know them!"

The Bell Man nodded. "Fair point." He gestured with his arm to the park in front of them. "This is where the old man said he'd chased her to."

Jessi's head tilted to the right. "Her? The voodoo doll is a girl?"

"It appears that way."

She perked up, her chest pushed forward. "What's her name?"

He shrugged. "I don't know. She might not have one."

Jessi planted her hands on her hips. "But everyone has a name."

"I don't." The Bell Man said this calmly, conveying a disinterest in his lack of name.

"You have a title though. The Bell Man." As Jessi said this, she brought her hands in front of her, thumbs touching, before moving them away from one another in a sweeping motion. This was a motion she'd incorporated into her one-man show. It added a little extra.

The Bell Man nearly chuckled, a dry sound escaping his lips. "That's not so much a title as a description. I am, after all, covered in bells. And I am a man. Sort of."

"Does that mean I'm only sort of a girl?"

He nodded several times before replying, "You could say that."

Jessi was about to press her friend for more information about what exactly she was when he said, "Over there. Under the tree." He pointed with one pale, slender finger. "Do you see her?"

At first, she saw nothing but nearly black bark. She kept looking, however, and saw a tiny burlap sack against one of the tree's revealed roots. "I think so. Should we go over to her?"

"You should go over to her. You know the kind of reaction I typically receive."

She nodded. Anytime someone saw the Bell Man straight on, he reacted like Mr. Allister had. Some ran, some shrank into themselves, some even screamed. Because of this, the Bell Man usually only came out at night, leaving Jessi to tend to herself during the day. She knew he was always watching though; she could feel his gaze on the back of her neck, tickling the fine baby hairs. Jessi never understood what other people saw that she couldn't. Sure, he had a peculiar look with his pale skin and collection of bells. But he looked no stranger than many of the people she saw every day around the French Quarter. One guy, for instance, dressed up as a neon-colored cat monster. The Bell Man wasn't nearly as frightening as that thing.

When Jessi saw her friend, she felt at home. After all, the Bell Man was the closest thing she had to a family. No one had stayed with her as long as he had. She even thought his face appeared kind sometimes—like when he smirked or almost laughed.

Jessi walked over to the voodoo doll and kneeled. Above them, the live oak stretched its monstrous limbs, the Spanish moss on the branches offering brief solace from the heat. The doll had no mouth, nose, or ears, but she did have black eyes made from buttons. Its head was round and she had two arms and two legs streaked with dirt. There was a tear in her side and moss trailed from it like internal organs.

"Hello," Jessi said, her voice low and soft.

The voodoo doll didn't respond.

"I'm not here to hurt you," she said. "My name's Jessi. What's yours?"

"Me," the doll said in a meek voice.

"Me?"

"Me," she repeated.

Jessi smiled. She liked that.

"Wait. You can hear me?"

"Of course I can."

"No one's ever heard me before," her voice sad. "I've always been invisible."

181

"Well, I hear you and see you," Jessi said. "And it's very nice to meet you."

She put her hand out for the voodoo doll to shake. She felt Me's hand on the tip of her middle and ring fingers. It was no heavier than a leaf blown from a tree. Her hand was made of wax and had an oily quality to it.

"Do you know the scary man?" Her voice trembled.

Jessi frowned. "I do."

"Are you here to save me from him or take me to him?"

Jessi swallowed the phlegm lodged in her throat. She didn't want to tell Me that she was going to trade her for her friend. But could she lie to her? Pretend she was going to save the voodoo doll? Jessi looked back over her shoulder at the Bell Man. He was still standing below the sign for Storyland. Only his chin was clear in the evening night; the rest cloaked by the brim of his hat. He nodded at her, and she nodded in response. "I'm here to save you," she said. "You never have to see that scary man again."

Jessi scooped the voodoo doll and carried her over to the Bell Man. She knew he would understand why she couldn't turn over Me to the old man, she knew he would help her. But how were they going to save Josette and the rest of Jessi's friends?

They headed toward Armstrong Park, a several mile-walk from City Park, where they usually rested at the end of the night. Jessi held onto the sleeve of the Bell Man's jacket with one hand and clutched Me against her chest with the other. They followed the sidewalks, strolling in shadows except for the occasional streetlight bathing them momentarily in light. Jessi marveled how in the dark she and the Bell Man looked the same, their skin gray, their bodies moving masses.

The doll too was gray. Me clung to Jessi, and asked her questions most of the walk. She had started with, "Who is that man?"

"You mean him?" Jessi said and pointed to the Bell Man. The voodoo doll said yes. "That's my friend, the Bell Man."

"He's scary looking like the scary man."

Jessi glanced at the Bell Man to see his reaction to Me's comment. His gaze remained forward, his face stoic. "He's the best man I know," she answered.

"How many men do you know?"

"Not many. Not well, at least."

"He looks like Death."

"That's not a nice thing to say, Me."

Again, Jessi looked to her friend to see his reaction. His face didn't flinch. However, his eyes did shift to meet hers. "What's she saying about me?" he asked.

"You can't hear her?"

The Bell Man shook his head. "I'm a Seer of Death, remember? I can only see when someone is going to die or already dead. You," he said, "see where there's life."

"So, my doll and puppet friends…you won't be able to hear them either?"

"No," he answered. "Not unless Death approaches them."

"He talks funny," Me chimed in.

"Hush," Jessi said to her. She craned her neck to study the Bell Man. How different their purposes were, yet also connected. There was no life without death, after all, just like you couldn't have a beignet without powdered sugar. Jessi smiled. She liked the idea of being linked to her best friend.

Jessi and the Bell Man sat on the wooden steps leading to a bridge in Armstrong Park. The nearby lanterns cast shadows through the handrails that lined them. Me was in Jessi's lap, her head against the girl's belly. The voodoo doll snored softly. "Can voodoo dolls dream?" Jessi asked the Bell Man.

"I don't know."

Jessi's lip quivered, the start of a frown.

The Bell Man eyed her. "But I don't see why not."

Her cheeks rose into a grin. Then her forehead wrinkled, her smile vanishing. "What are we going to do? How are we going to get out Josette without giving him Me?"

"Let's think about it for some time."

"Okay. Let's think on it." Jessi leaned her head against the Bell Man's arm. Think, think, think. Her eyes began to flicker, closing a second longer each time.

When she woke the sun had begun to rise, casting away the darkness like a spell. The sky was both orange and gray, a combination the girl loved. It reminded her of the Bell Man and herself. He was night, the gray clinging to the sky, and she was day, vibrant and promising light. Jessi sat up, raised her arms above her head, and stretched. She looked down at Me, who was still asleep against her stomach. Then looked to the Bell Man, who was staring ahead at the sky.

"I fell asleep," she said.

"Yes," he said.

"I didn't come up with any ideas." Her voice was heavy, weighted with guilt and fear. What were they going to do?

He glanced down at her. "I did."

"You did?" Jessi exhaled with a huff, her lungs pulsing, unaware she'd been holding her breath. "What is it?"

"It's simple, really. We promised him a trade and we'll stand by our word."

"We will?"

"A magical being for a magical being. That was the deal."

Jessi didn't understand.

"We will trade him a magical being, however, it won't be this one."

"I don't get it. Who will we trade instead?"

"He wants this voodoo doll."

"Me," Jessi said, feeling the need to use the doll's name, making her alive and more than an object.

"He wants Me. I pressed him about why he wants this particular voodoo doll. He finally told me it was because of who made her."

"Who?"

"A powerful Quarter witch who took something from him. Me won't be just another item in his collection. Her purpose is revenge."

"He told you all that?"

The Bell Man shrugged, the bells rattling in their cages. "I have methods to get people to talk."

Her face cracked into a grin. "I'm sure you do. What are we going to give him instead of Me?"

"Another voodoo doll."

The girl shook her head so fiercely the tendrils of her oily hair lashed at the Bell Man's jacket sleeve, creating a whipping sound. "We can't trap another doll. These beings are alive. Conscientious."

"You mean conscious. Aware."

"Yeah. That." Her face flashed red.

"I don't know any other voodoo dolls that are conscious. Do you?" The hint of a smile pressed into the Bell Man's cheek.

"No, I don't," Jessi said.

She was beginning to get it.

Jessi and the Bell Man stood outside of Lavender's, the Quarter witch's shop. The girl's hand gripping her friend's jacket sleeve so hard her knuckles were white with red splotches. Me was in a safe spot, hidden with Jessi's sweatshirt behind the dumpster. They would get her after; Me had promised not to go anywhere. The doll continued to make comments about the Bell Man. Said she didn't trust him. That he gave her the willies. Jessi told Me she couldn't keep talking about her best friend that way. That they were all going to be friends—Jessi, the Bell Man, Me, Josette, and the rest of the dolls and puppets at Mr. Allister's shop.

The Bell Man told Jessi he would wait outside. "Before you go in," he said. "I'm going to cloak your light. Just in case."

As they walked to Lavender's, Jessi had asked, "How do you hide my light?" He had only ever told her he shielded it; she had never seen him do it.

The Bell Man was silent for several moments. He looked down at his chest, where his beating heart would have been if he had one. Here, a small hook attached to his black tie. Hanging from it was a brown bell with little smudges on its brass surface. He lifted it, holding it in front of him so that Jessi could get a good look. The bell was skinny compared to the hundreds of others on his clothing. It reminded her of someone or something that she couldn't quite place. The Bell Man reached inside the bell. Jessi watched his wrist flinch, then still. His hand remained inside.

She tongued her upper lip. "You hold the bell to hide my light?"

"I hold the clapper to keep your light hidden."

"So, all of these bells…?"

"Each represents a person or being, yes."

"All alive?"

His lips pressed together, forming a thin line. "For now," he said. "Go on it. I'll be out here."

Jessi knew not to push her friend for too many answers. He never gave more than he was willing.

Inside the shop, she found a voodoo doll that resembled Me; which wasn't difficult as several of the dolls could have been Me's twin. There were four of them altogether. Jessi couldn't remember the word for five twins; she knew it started with a q. She said hello to all of them to see if any would talk back. None did. The girl working the shop—a teenage girl with dark brown hair twisted into a braid down her back—smiled at Jessi when she heard her greet the dolls. Jessi knew she probably looked crazy, but she didn't care. She needed to know. Jessi felt a pang of guilt at her relief that these dolls weren't like Me. They were just wax dolls with herbs and moss inside. Not alive. Or conscious.

Outside, she showed the Bell Man the doll. He put Jessi's bell back over his heart and it chimed cheerily back in its rightful place. "This should work," he told her. "There's just one more thing we should do before we bring it to Mr. Allister."

"What?"

"See how fresh the doll is? The wax is pale and stiff. It looks brand new like we just bought it."

Jessi shrugged. "Well, we did just buy it."

"True, but we don't want Mr. Allister to know that." She asked what they should do. "We need to make it look a little more worn. A little more real."

Jessi nodded. "I know how to do that."

She led them around the corner to the alley where the magic shop collected trash and recycling. Jessi peeled back the lid of the can and pulled out various pieces of trash—to-go cups, rotting fruit, crumpled tissues blackened with soot and brittle herbs. She upended the cups, letting the last bits of coffee and tea drip onto the doll. She smeared a banana peel against the belly of the voodoo doll. She rubbed the remnants of soot of herbs onto the doll's arms and legs.

Jessi clicked the lid back into place. She turned to the Bell Man, the dirtied voodoo doll extended, a prized offering. "Whatcha think?"

He nodded, the bells on his hat jingling. "It looks good."

They made their way to J. Allister's Oddities & Antiques. Knuckles white, Jessi held the doll to her chest, her other hand gripping the Bell Man's jacket sleeve. They passed the bustle of Bourbon Street, green, purple, and gold mardi gras beads swinging from drunken hands, a cacophony of shouting and thumping music, the stink of humid bodies, spilled beer, and urine. Jessi eyed her friend, studying how his face flexed in disgust. "Unconceivable," she said, her voice low, her lips puckered.

"Inconceivable," he corrected. The corners of his mouth lifted.

They turned down a narrow street lined with houses and hotels. Colorful flowers spilled over the railings of the building's balconies. Gas lanterns flickered yellow in the sunlight. It always amazed Jessi how in the city one turn could transport you to another world. She wondered how magical it must be to live in houses like these. Jessi knew it was something she'd never have, but she didn't have to tell her imagination that.

She chose a three-story house with two balconies and the largest floral arrangements. Pink, purple, and orange flowers shined from their baskets. On the second level balcony was a wicker couch with cotton candy pink and white striped cushions and white pillows with giant green leaves. Jessi pictured herself sitting on the couch, Me, Josette, and the rest of them beside her. The Bell Man stood behind the couch, preferring the shadows to the sun. There was a table in front of the couch filled with steaming bowls of food. Fried chicken, mac n cheese, jambalaya, fresh cornbread. Jessi and her friends would never sleep at Armstrong Park again. They would never be dirty or hungry or lonely. They would be together forever.

She could almost taste the salty crunch of the first bite of fried chicken.

"This trick will work once," the Bell Man said.

Jessi scowled. They were outside of Mr. Allister's shop, beneath the small wooden sign swinging over the entrance. The chicken vanished, her mouth empty and wanting. "What?"

"This trick will work once."

She shook her head. Jessi didn't know what the Bell Man was saying. Really, she didn't want to hear it. She knew the deal had been for one of the magical beings. She had hoped there would be a way to save all of her friends. "But what about your powers? Can't you threaten him with death? You scared him pretty bad before."

"Badly," he corrected. "I see death, like, like smelling rain before a storm. I do not control when it comes; that is Destiny's power alone."

"So, we have to leave the rest of them there?"

He nodded.

"I won't be able to come back to visit, will I?"

He shook his head. "You won't ever see them again. It's too dangerous. Jerome Allister could figure it out. You out." For a moment he was silent. "I can silence your bell, dimming your light, as I have every time you've entered the store, but it doesn't ensure the old man isn't clever enough to figure you out. Even the fact that he knows you are important to me leaves you vulnerable to his dark desires."

"I understand." And she did. But it felt as though pieces of her were breaking off, like she was imploding. She didn't want to leave the rest of her friends—Colleen, Darla, Christophe, and Benjamin— behind. How could Jessi leave them with him? Trapped with no one to talk to but each other. She knew they'd accept it better than she could. That deep down they never really believed she'd be able to get them out. They loved her for trying. "Thank you," Jessi said after a beat, "for helping me. For coming up with this idea."

The Bell Man replied, "What are friends for?"

Jessi beamed.

Mr. Allister's shop was dark and dusty as ever. The old man stood behind the register in his faded, moth-eaten suit, his face obscured by shadows. Jessi imagined the Devil's face emerging, a snake baring its fangs ready to bite.

"It pleases me that you've returned so quickly," he said.

Jessi gripped the Bell Man's arm tighter.

"We made a deal,," the Bell Man said, his voice monotone.

"You have it?"

"Her," Jessi said before she could stop herself. She felt the Bell Man's arm stiffen under her. She flushed, hoping this slip wouldn't be their undoing.

"Yes, yes. Her," Mr. J. Allister said, annoyed but unfazed by the girl's knowledge of the voodoo doll. "Let's have her then." He emphasized the word *her*, a perverted smile on his withered face.

Jessi and the Bell Man walked closer to the shop owner. Jessi's hand shook, jingling the bells on that jacket sleeve. "Why don't you go in and pick your doll?" the Bell Man said to her. "Mr. Allister and I will complete our transaction. Out here."

"Why don't you go in and pick your doll?" the Bell Man said to her. "Mr. Allister and I will complete our transaction. Out here."

Jessi nodded; he was giving her time to say goodbye.

Once inside the museum, she pressed the door shut, the vintage hinges whistling. She stood by the closed entrance for a moment, taking in the rows of clear cases and the bizarre items within their glass borders. The room was bathed in light, and she closed her eyes, pretending it was sunlight warming her goose-pimpled flesh. Her eyes fluttered open and she made her way to the two cases that held her friends. She stood in between them, the puppet case on her left and the dolls on her right. Her hands twisted in front of her, the skin on the sides of her fingers sweating.

"Hi, guys," Jessi said.

They said hello.

A smile crept onto the girl's face. "It's good to see you all."

She studied their faces and wondered how long they would be forced to live in these bodies, unable to smile or frown or move their limbs. Her chin dropped to her chest. Sobs poured from her open mouth, a guttural sound similar to a goose honking for its lost kin. Jessi wished her friends would throw their arms around her. But, of course, they couldn't.

"What's wrong?" Josette said.

Jessi brought her hands to her face, crying harder. The skin of her palms grew soggy.

Her friends remained silent while she cried. Then Colleen said, "It's okay, honey. We know you did your best."

The rest chimed in, agreeing they were grateful she had tried to free them.

Jessi lifted her head and looked at her friends. She sniffled before speaking, wiping the back of her hand against the bottom of her nose. Her hand glistened with snot and tears. "You knew I couldn't save you all?"

"We knew you'd try," Colleen said.

"And we appreciate it," Christophe said.

"Yeah," Darla said.

Benjamin sighed, which Jessi took as his agreement.

"You've given us a sliver of life we never thought we'd have again," Josette said. "For that, we'll always be grateful."

Jessi's stomach flipped. "My friend—my other friend, I call him the Bell Man—he and I made a deal with Mr. Allister. I get to take one of you. Josette," she said.

She hoped her other friends wouldn't hate her for this. But Josette was the girl's first and dearest friend at the museum. She was what brought the little girl there in the first place. She could never abandon her.

"The old man thinks we're making a trade—one of you for another one like you—but I couldn't do it. Not to another magical being." She sighed. "But I won't be able to come back. Not ever." The words tumbled out: "I hope you'll forgive me. I wanted to save all of you, I wanted us to all be together. I'm so sorry." She looked at the ground.

"There is nothing to be sorry for. You did something no one else has been able to do," Colleen said.

"Thank you," Christophe and Darla said in unison.

"Thank you for trying," Benjamin said.

"Protect yourself from him, Jessi," Colleen added. "Don't ever let him see your light."

Jessi opened her mouth, ready to promise her friend she'd do her best. Before she could speak, however, she heard Mr. Allister enter. "Ready?" the old man demanded.

The girl said yes, gulping back the howl building in her throat. It wasn't safe for the old man to see how much these dolls and puppets meant to her. Not for them or for her. Jessi turned to face the glass case on the right. "I want this one." She pointed to Josette.

The old man eyed her, the many lines and crevices of his face deepening. He hobbled over, a ring full of golden keys jangling in his hand. He unlocked the cabinet and took out Josette. Jessi snatched the doll from his wrinkled hand and drew Josette to her chest, giving the old man her meanest expression.

"That's it then," the Bell Man said. "Come on, Jessi. Let's go."

The air was still and heavy. The girl's heart rapped in her chest. She hurried toward her best friend, her legs soft at the knees, ready to take off. When she reached the Bell Man, she took his hand in hers. It engulfed her small hand, hiding all but the very tips of her fingers from view. Jessi worked to slow her breath. They had fooled the old man so far, and the plan was almost done. They just needed to get away undetected.

The Bell Man nodded at Mr. J. Allister.

The old man bowed his head. "It was a pleasure doing business with you."

Once they were outside, Jessi curled into the Bell Man, sobbing for the friends left behind. He held her until she was able to walk. Josette remained in her arms, repeating *it's okay* in a sing-song voice to soothe the girl.

Jessi didn't stop crying until she had both Josette and Me in her arms. Sniffling, she asked, "What do we do now?"

"We go somewhere new," The Bell Man said. "There is a place outside of the city where magical beings are safe from prying eyes and evil sorcerers." His face twitched, an almost smile. "Somewhere new would be good for a while."

"I agree," Me said.

"Me too," Josette said.

Already, the dolls were friends.

Jessi hugged the dolls to her chest and slipped her fingers into the Bell Man's. "Somewhere new sounds nice."

The little girl walked with her three friends away from the Quarter and J. Allister's Oddities & Antiques. The bells on her best friend's jacket, pants, and hats clanged with each step, a symphony of life and death and shrill clanging.

When the Bell Man Tolls

The man in the black suit, bowler hat, and bells is the rapid pang in your chest when you wake in the middle of the night from a bad dream, your skin pasted in heat and beads of sweat. His pale blue-white skin that is just faintly translucent shines in your dreams like the moon. Slick and smooth and untouchable. The hundreds of bells attached to his clothing mock your vitality, your hopes for the future, and coax you into the darkness. They jingle and clang as he walks, a funeral procession of brass. This man, this creature or being or monster, is the Bogeyman you've been warned about. But he doesn't just take naughty children, oh no, he's much more inclusive than that. He collects lives, the souls of humans and other beings. In the end he takes us all. He is the grim reaper knocking on your door, taking you to Honey Island Swamp for passage to another plane after Death. If you're lucky, it's a final resting place of peace. If you're not, well, good luck.

The Bell Man usually only slinks from shadows when the moon is high and the world is cloaked in mist and shades of gray and black. For if you gaze upon his face you'll shriek and shrink in horror. You'll see not one face, but dozens, their skin loose around the eye sockets, hollowed at the cheeks, icy blue in pallor. Their mouths stretched wide in agony and fear like Munch's "The Scream." You will know who he is then, and you cannot escape that knowledge. The knowledge that the grim reaper exists. If it is not your time, if he is not coming for you yet, the Bell Man will shake his head to tell you so. To tell you to relax, breathe, and go on living your life.

While you still can.

If it is your time, a single bell will ring, calling to you, announcing your doomed fate and the arrival of Death.

If you dare to seek him out, to sneak a peek, you can find the Bell Man at night with a companion in Armstrong Park. A little girl, aged nine. He loves her, yet this isn't why he keeps her near. His softness toward her is an inconvenience. An unexpected turn of events. Of emotions he didn't even think he was capable of possessing. She is his truest friend, his family, and his annihilation. Her light can undo his darkness, his shadowy existence, as easily as one flicks on a light switch. Yet the girl doesn't know what it means to be what she is or that they are destined to be enemies. That it is her destiny to destroy him.

If you are brave enough or stupid enough to look for the Bell Man and his companion and find them together in the park late at night, you'll see the girl's limp, mousy brown hair pressed against his jacket sleeve, the one patch of cloth without a bell. Her eyelids gently closed, her breathing raspy as she dreams against her closest friend. She imagines all the things they'll do together—adventures and precious moments—and smiles at such a future for them.

Childhood is a time of optimism and hope, of seeing things in vibrant colors instead of black and white and good and evil. This girl is without a home, and so she seeks comfort in this shadow of a man, unable or unwilling to see the danger he presents or the malignancy that lurks inside him. She hopes their time together will be endless.

The Bell Man too finds himself hoping, even though the very core of his being fights against such a foolish feeling. He hopes that the girl won't discover her destiny, that she won't undo him. He hopes that maybe, just maybe, they can continue as they have been for years, him protecting her from harm by both humans and magical beings, and her, in turn, unknowingly protecting him from destruction. After all, what does the grim reaper fear most?

His own death.

You, my dear tourist, should not forget your fragile mortality, and the ticking clock that goes with it. Don't let your curiosity get the better of you. If the man finds you lurking, if he takes you as a threat to his companion, Destiny may not be able to save you. The Bell Man has friends that lurk in the darkness, ready to snatch and devour until there is no trace left of you. Creatures like the loup-garou, who wait in the twilight, licking their fangs, tasting your sweet flesh in their mouths.

Tourists, after all, are the city's catnip.

Acknowledgements

This book consumed me. During the Summer of 2018, these characters were more real to me than anything or anyone else. Muoros and Ministers and Friedas were living, breathing beings. Penumbra was a place I could map. For months, I spoke in jumbled sentences, spewing riddles, that only made sense to me. Like the circus on Honey Island Swamp, I was enchanted. My husband, Alex, can attest to this.

So, first, I want to thank him for supporting this project even when he didn't understand it. Even when he thought I was losing touch with reality (especially then). Alex listened to me for hours while I obsessed over one line or a single plot point. He created a gorgeous book cover that perfectly encapsulates the vibe of this book. I hope it's the beginning of many creative collaborations between us. Thank you, honey. I love you.

I would be remiss if I didn't thank my dear friend, Nick Gregorio (who is now my pressmate. Woo!). He read this book and liked it so much he offered to pitch it to the lovely folks at Maudlin House. This book would not be here if it weren't for his support. Nick is a kind human and an excellent writer I really admire.

Thank you to Andrew Katz, Brenna Dinon, Charlie J. Eskew, Joanna C. Valente, Lindsay Lusby, and Nicholas Perilli for your notes on this book. Your feedback greatly shaped this collection as your friendship has shaped me.

I'm grateful to the journals that published stories from this collection. An earlier version of "The Avenger of Evil" was published by Sage Cigarettes Magazine and the kind folks over there also nominated it for Best of the Net. An earlier, condensed version of "J. Allister's Shop of Horrors" was published by Maudlin House.

A big thanks to the folks at Maudlin House for liking and publishing this weird book of mine. I honestly didn't know if it was too weird to be published, and Maudlin House is the perfect home for it. Thank you for believing in this story.

To my readers, thank you for picking up this book. I hope you've found *Creole Conjure* to be strange and endearing, as well as a little bit horrifying. I hope you've fallen in love with New Orleans, just as I have.

The stories in this collection draw inspiration from a variety of fairy tales, myths, folklore, pop culture, and places I love. Both "Alligator Blues" and "The Monster of Honey Island Swamp" are re-imaginings of "Beauty and the Beast." "Lady Mariticide" reinvents "Bluebeard," while exploring my fascination with female serial killers. "To Break the Curse, Kiss the Siren" is a mixture of "The Little Mermaid" and the Rusalka from Scandinavian folklore. I find myself drawn to siren stories, of mermaid-like she-beasts that were once human and now thirst for vengeance. "Penumbra" stems from my personal ideas about the afterlife and planes of existence. Lilly and Deanna stem from my love of Greek mythology, the two women akin to Demeter and Hekate journeying to the underworld together in search of Persephone.

The two pivotal characters in "Conjure" are based on real-life people. Zelima Delacroix is supposed to bear resemblance to Marie Laveau the First and Second. This mysterious and powerful mother-daughter duo is often reduced to one person that becomes more legend than human. I named Zelima's mother, Marie, in honor of them, and hope that I have created a resilient and compelling character. It was also important for me to write a New Orleans witch and woman of color that did not practice Voodoo. Voodoo is an Afro-Haitian religion that has been appropriated and sensationalized for hundreds of years and is often wrongly tied to devil worship and "black" magic.

Julia Baudin is based on Julia Brown, a woman whose legendary wrath caused a hurricane in 1915 that wiped out the community living around Manchac Swamp, about twenty-five miles outside of New Orleans. I first learned about Julia on a swamp tour in May 2015 and knew I needed to write a story about this woman. Manchac Swamp is, in my opinion, the most peaceful place in the world and was the inspiration for this fictional rendering of Honey Island Swamp, which is also a real swamp in Louisiana.

I should mention that the Honey Island Swamp Monster, also known as the Cajun Sasquatch, is very much a part of Louisiana folklore. I used accounts of this figure, as well as the Creature From the Black Lagoon, for the depiction found here.

"J. Allister's Antiques & Oddities" is modeled after my favorite antique shop in Philadelphia, Anastacia's Antiques. I have been afraid of sentient dolls and puppets since watching *The Twilight Zone* episodes "The Dummy" and "Living Doll." With this story, I had the opportunity to lean into the uncanny, magical energy of antique shops and lifelike puppets and subvert the narrative, making the dolls innocent instead of sinister creatures. The Bell Man is meant to be a blend of the Grim Reaper and the Bogeyman, a figure parents and babysitters tell children stories about to scare them into behaving. The irony, of course, is that the Bell Man's best friend is a child, Jessi, who manages to see the world and all its ugliness while never ceasing to marvel at its beauty. A lesson for us all.

Christina Rosso-Schneider lives and writes in South Philadelphia with her rescue pup, Atticus Finch, and bearded husband, Alex, where they run an independent bookstore and event space called A Novel Idea on Passyunk. She received an MFA in Creative Writing and MA in English from Arcadia University in 2016. Her debut chapbook, SHE IS A BEAST (APEP Publications), was released in May 2020. CREOLE CONJURE, her first full-length collection, is forthcoming from Maudlin House. Her fiction and nonfiction work centers around gender, sexuality, and fairy tales, and has been nominated for Best of the Net, Best Small Fictions, and the Pushcart Prize. When she isn't writing or working at the bookstore, she leads various writing and occult-based workshops.

CPSIA information can be obtained
at www.ICGtesting.com
Printed in the USA
LVHW090539161021
700500LV00002B/89